I know not how long I slept but, opening my eyes, I found myself regarding an idyll which any painter would have been pleased to depict: Mrs van den Heuff had slipped into the pool, where, her hair streaming out about her, she was now floating upon her back.

Her figure, unclothed, was quite beautiful. Her breasts were perfectly round, no doubt made firm by the coolness of the water; her body, long and slim, was uniformly brown (suggesting that the sun was no stranger to her beauty); her arms and legs handsomely formed, the latter tapered, the trimness of her ankles and calves gradually thickening to thighs plump but strong, between which a muff of yellow accentuated a dark fissure infinitely tempting . . .

Also available from Headline

Eros in the Country
Eros in Town
Eros on the Grand Tour
Eros in the New World

Eros in the Far East

**Further Adventures of a Lady
and Gentleman of Leisure**

Anonymous

HEADLINE

First published in 1990
by HEADLINE BOOK PUBLISHING PLC

10 9 8 7 6 5 4 3 2 1

ISBN 0 7472 3449 3

Typeset in 10/12¼ pt English Times
by Colset Private Limited, Singapore

Printed and bound in Great Britain by
Collins, Glasgow

HEADLINE BOOK PUBLISHING PLC
Headline House
79 Great Titchfield Street
London W1P 7FN

**For the convenience of the reader
we here record a note of
IMPORTANT PERSONS APPEARING IN
THE NARRATIVE
in the order of their appearance**

Andrew Archer Esq, our hero.
Lady Phyllida Walkett, a neglected wife.
Lady Frances Chichley, a lady of fashion.
A rustic couple.
A footman.
Lieutenant Robert Hooke, first officer of the *Proper Pride*.
Mrs Sophia Nelham, our heroine.
The Misses Kate and Vivienne Pondersend (two minxes in Mr Hooke's narrative).
Mrs Edward Pondersend, their mother.
Edward Lockyear, Esq, a gentleman.
Sir Douglas Sperries, another.
Lady Frances Sperries, his wife.
Mr Fountain, a magistrate.
Mr Hedgeley, a ship-owner.
Mr Richard Midgely, an artist.
Mr St John Thripp, a surveyor.
Miss Emmeline Grant (an acquaintance of Mr Hooke's).
Mopsa, a Capetown bob-tail.
Kenny, a Hottentot, servant to Mr Archer.
Mrs van den Heuff.
Mr van den Heuff, a violent gold-miner.
Dr Stephen Nadge, a ship's surgeon.
Kinau, Queen of Hawaii.

Sir Wormsley Gillard, Governor of Ceylon.

Lady Gillard, his wife.

Lieut. the Hon. Denys Potter, his nephew.

Miss Jane Petty, Lieut. Potter's affianced.

A Kandian whore.

Thakombau, a Fijian.

Tui Nayou, King of Fiji.

Mrs Fitzpatrick (?), a lady of Pusilava.

A number of Fijian citizens.

The Tui Rara, a Fijian courtier.

A number of Caffres.

Miss Jane Knowles, a young woman *en travestie*.

Captain George Retallack, an officer of artillery, at Singapore.

Captain Wendsley Dale, another.

Lieut.-Col. Jamie Ferguson, Officer Commanding the garrison at Malacca.

Loi, a Siamese.

His Majesty the King of Siam.

His officers.

Tiu-Hon, a Siamese lady.

Lamqua, a Chinese pirate chief.

His crew.

Chapter One

The Adventures of Andy

The Lady Phyllida Walkett summoning her footman and having me thrown bodily, and in a state of nature, from her bedroom was the occasion of my considering whether my time was being profitably spent.

Those readers who have been so kind as to express their pleasure in my former accounts of my various adventures in and out of town, will recall the strenuous activities consequent upon my embarking on a voyage to the New World, and will not be surprised to hear that upon my return to London with my dear friend Mrs Sophie Nelham (who I had happily been able to rescue from an unfortunate embarrassment attendant upon the rescue of two black slaves from the southern States of America) I determined to lead a quiet life.

But those same readers will be equally sanguine at the news that my determination lasted no more than a few months. The truth was that I had too little to do. My friend and boyhood companion, Sir Franklin Franklyn, of Alcovary in the county of Hertfordshire, had during my absence performed a great service for me. Hearing of a venture to mine for platinum in the Ural mountains of Russia, he committed all the capital which had been the result of a joint business venture between us to the matter.

This might have been a recipe for disaster, had not my friend been a shrewd businessman (something he inherited from his father, whose fortune had been made by the meticulous operation of a house of pleasure in the west end of London). A student of history, he knew that great supplies of mineral deposits had been known for a thousand years to exist in that area of the mountains around Narodnaya – and so was not only able to advise his fellow speculators to invest (against the instincts of many city men), but was actually able to direct explorers to an area where indeed platinum in enormous supplies was discovered – but also iron, manganese, nickel and copper.

Within a year, it was clear that we would both by this operation be provided with an income more than sufficient to keep us in luxury for the rest of our lives. Frank's reaction was to retire to Alcovary with the wife he had just married, and to devote his time and energy to country pursuits. Mine, on discovering my happiness, was to buy myself a small but commodious house near Regent's Park, and to live happily among the citizens of the world's finest metropolis.

I was not, myself, married, nor did I intend to emulate my friend's example. I had as yet found no woman with whom it would be congenial to me to live on intimate terms – though many with whom intimacy was a pleasure on a more temporary basis; and my experience from a tender age was that upon the latter terms, a large number of ladies of all ages and temperaments could be persuaded to share my company and to assist in the expression of those passions with which my readers will, if they are honest, be familiar.

My only problem was that I had become accustomed to variety, and that to be frank, once conquered, a lady, however delightful, somewhat lost her charms. The sight of a charming woman was enough to tempt me to pursue her; the chase was invigorating and the capture inspiriting; and having bedded such a beauty, it was not my wish to cast her aside, for almost always – since physical beauty was not my only criterion – she was not only pretty, but witty, so that it was a pleasure to remain on terms of conversation, to take tea with her, accompany her on walks in the Park, and so on. The problem was – and I cannot but be honest – that such ladies were no longer content with such innocent pastimes once they had tasted more lascivious pleasures; and I was only too conscious that the lips that sipped from the teacup preferred another source of pleasure, and the hands that so delicately toyed with a pet dog ached for a more substantial plaything. I was happy (what man would not be?) to be the source of admiration; but unfortunately, where the edge of my own devotion had been dulled, though the spirit was willing, the flesh sometimes failed to provide the mechanical means to pleasure.

This was the case with Lady Phyllida. I had been introduced to her at a summer party given by my friend Lady Chichley in the gardens of her fine house by the river Thames near Greenwich. It was an afternoon in August, so warm as almost to be called hot – so much so, indeed, that our hostess had invited the gentlemen of the company to remove their coats, and shirt-sleeves were the order of the day; indeed, but for the greenness of the lawns, kept watered by an army of gardeners, we might have been in Rome or Athens, the trees framing a distant prospect of the vast dome of King Charles's palace at Greenwich together with a glimpse of Mr Inigo Jones's house built at the same place for Queen Anne.

I was leaning against the trunk of a lime tree looking out over the river when Lady Chichley came up, leading by the hand a young lady who seemed to be perhaps fifteen years of age – and whom she introduced to me as Lady Phyllida Walkett. The infant shyly curtsied to me, revealing as she did so that the charmingly cut lawn dress she wore concealed a figure more mature than might have been expected by the casual observer.

'There, my dear,' said Lady Chichley, pointing to a bank which rose towards a little rose-garden not far away, 'is a vantage point from which you can watch all the traffic of the river. I have a word to say to Mr Archer, so . . .'

The girl gave her a grave look from large, brimming brown eyes, and turned to make her way to the bank, where presently she sat, tucking her skirts modestly about her person as she did so.

'Andy,' said Lady Chichley (and I should say that we were on terms of informality, consequent upon a service I and my friend Sophie had been able to do for my lady and Viscount Chichley) – 'Andy, I wish you would keep Lady Phyllida amused for a while. Her husband is really the most boring creature upon earth, and is at present reducing Chichley to tears with an exposition of the liberal constitution recently introduced in Baden, and the possibility of the establishment in England of such a Diet of Chambers as is now to be set up there.'

'Her husband!' I remarked. 'Not . . .'

'Yes, indeed,' my friend said. 'Lord Walkett of Brierley.'

'But he is of an age to be her grandfather!'

'Great-grandfather,' said Lacy Chichley. 'At the least. The poor girl is in the extremity of frustration. Her father married her off to Walkett for the sake of connection with the aristocracy; though why he should have wanted her, I have no notion – to my certain knowledge he has been unable to consummate the act since 1794, when an affair with my cousin Sarah Pauncely ended in consequence of that same inability. So . . .'

Lady Chichley at this point lowered her right eyelid in

what the vulgar might have termed a wink.

I bowed.

'She is – of an age?' I asked.

'You need have no concern on that score,' said Lady Chichley. 'Nor on any other. What Lady Phyllida needs is a man, and soon, or she is very likely to turn mad.'

As I walked towards the bank upon which the young person gracefully reclined, I found it difficult to credit my friend's last remark – for Lady Phyllida was the very picture of modest virgin beauty; yet no-one was more keenly aware than myself of the ferment of emotions which can boil beneath the placid exterior of the female form.

Conversation with the lady was not easy. I opened to her several subjects, upon none of which – even the play, which can usually be relied upon to interest the ladies – was she eager to discourse; and finally, I rose to my feet with the suggestion that, the day being hot, we should stroll for a while in the shade of the trees closer to the river's edge, where a pleasant coolness would be more appropriate to pleasure.

She took my arm, and I seemed to feel the slightest quiver in her hand as it met the warmth of my side – for a thin silk shirt was the only garment I wore upon my upper person. However, she remained distant as we walked along a path which wound between the trees. This led, finally, to a low wall which bounded the Chichleys' estate, beyond which was a low common strand from which came the sound of cries and splashing.

Leaning upon the wall and looking out, we saw a crowd of boys and girls of all ages from infants to young people who looked no younger than Lady Phyllida herself, some entirely unclothed, some covered merely by their shirts or by cotton skirts and trousers which, being wet, emphasised rather than concealed their forms.

Such a sight, entirely free from self-consciousness, could not but be charming; and I confess that I was happy to lean upon the wall for a while and regard it – my interest being perforce fixed upon those older girls whose forms would elsewhere be less susceptible of observation, for their pleasure at the coolness of the waters encouraged them to ignore the decencies, freely exposing to the sight breasts which, while tender, were fully expressive of feminine charm; they even, from time to time, offered a glimpse of firm thighs and full bottoms – to which the boys of the group, more aware than they of the advantage offered by the occasion, could not from time to time resist the opportunity of offering a friendly smack, which in turn called forth a shriek of protest (more pretended than real) at the familiarity, and provoked a chase through the flying drops of water which flew into the air like an upward rain.

Enjoying the sight as I did, I was for a while oblivious of my companion – but when I caught at last a glimpse of her face, found it to my surprise suffused with a deep blush – though her interest was such that she could not take her eyes from the scene; from which I inferred that the sight of unclad human beings – even of the very young – was new to her.

Without any comment, I once more offered her my arm; which she took, this time, somewhat more warmly – it seemed even pressing the back of her hand to my breast.

We followed the low wall until it curved inland and the strand upon the other side gave way to the green of a field, and finally of a spinney, where again we fell into cool shadow. In a moment, as we walked in silence, I became aware of a series of low cries from the other side of the wall. From their nature, I immediately inferred their cause; but Lady Phyllida clearly did not, for she lifted her finger to her lips, listened for a moment, then said: ' 'Tis a creature in pain! We must release it . . .' and stepped forward to look over the wall.

I followed, and together we leaned over. There, beneath us, we saw what I had expected: a boy and girl of perhaps seventeen, their clothes lying carelessly upon one side of a small patch of grass, were engaged in just such a pleasure as a warm summer's afternoon invited. Fortunately (for humankind is not in general pleased to be observed at such moments of intimacy) the girl was kneeling upon all fours with her head turned somewhat away from us, presenting to her lover – and incidentally to us – an alluring rear, the twin, pear-shaped haunches not yet thickened by the years, and supported by thighs so fine that any sculptor would have wished to immortalise them. Her arms were folded under her breasts, which were buried in them as she pressed her head almost into the springy turf, so eager was she to offer her lover access to that spot upon which his attention was most keenly fixed.

He was himself of that age when nature first awakens a vigorous longing to satisfy new desires, his body balanced between boyhood and manhood, the twin globes of his arse (also presented to our view) as tight, smooth and hairless as an egg. The cries of the girl were (of course) the result of the movements of his hips, which with a fine rhythm were thrusting into her an instrument the sight of which we were denied, but which from those cries was evidently sufficiently sturdy to give entire satisfaction.

The interest of the sight was such that I was for the moment unconscious that, being somewhat behind Lady Phyllida, I was now pressing my lower body against her own, and that a certain portion of my anatomy, aroused by the scene, could not but betray its presence and state; my instinct was to press forward even more warmly, which I did, and was interested to feel no shrinking – indeed, rather a returning motion (though once more I saw a blush rising upon her neck, to which, now, I found it impossible not to press a kiss).

Feeling her wriggle, and fearing she wished to be released from embarrassment (and having no wish to offend) I drew back somewhat – but turning about, she now flung her arms about my neck and fixed her lips to mine in a kiss which was warm, yet clearly inexperienced, those lips remaining firmly closed until, with what tenderness I could, I slid my tongue between them, whereupon with an eagerness that warmed me, they immediately opened, only to close once more, embracing my tongue in that most delightful warm and sucking motion, offering a cave of delights which (I could not but hope) might mirror that other cavern of pleasure below.

The grave innocence of the lady's former demeanour was now no more: the sight she had seen had broken the bonds of that propriety which had held back what floods of desire! – for seemingly oblivious of the fact that we were in a public place, she thrust her body against mine, and with inexperienced hands began to caress me, pulling the shirt from my trousers, and clawing with her fingers at my back, which she soon rendered devoid of clothing.

Taking her by the shoulders, I pushed her as gently as possible away from me – only in order that I should be able further to loosen my clothing; but I fear she believed I was rejecting her, for in order the more to impress her eagerness, she laid hands upon her dress and with one movement rent it at the bosom so that it fell to her waist, her panting white bosom rosy with eagerness, the buds knotted into firm advertisements of desire; and almost without pause, she bent to step out of the dress, and turning, knelt at my feet in just such a pose as the girl we had observed!

I need not pretend that I was long in stripping as bare as she; but realising that it was only inexperience that suggested to her that the position in which we had observed our young lovers was the only one permitted by convention, I gently turned her so that she faced me and I was able to pay her breasts the compliment of a kiss. She was too eager, however, for such niceties; and though entirely green in amorous matters, was sufficiently inspired by passion to throw her legs apart so that I fell between them, my engorged prick almost finding its own way to that part of her body which most strongly ached for contact with it.

It took all my experience to reserve my own pleasure from immediate expression, for there is no aphrodisiac so strong as another's desire, and Lady Phyllida's passion was almost insupportable. However, by dint of concentrating my mind on other matters, I was able to retain command of the situation for some minutes, until with a cry of agonised pleasure which sent the birds wheeling in fright from the trees above us, the lady clenched her hands upon my arse, the nails deeply scoring it, and the pain immediately resulting in the breaking of my own dam.

The next thing I knew was the sound of laughter from above, and a young voice exclaiming that I would not be able to sit comfortably for a week! Glancing up, I saw the amused faces of the two lovers whose amours we had observed, and who had now returned the compliment. I feared that Lady Phyllida would be uncomfortable at such an audience; but her happiness was so new and so complete that she merely smiled – and even the revelation, upon my rising, that her pleasure must have been mingled with pain (for clearly I had taken her virginity) was not sufficient to upset her – though the young couple, observing the signs, fell silent and moved away, with that tact which is not always an attribute of the lower orders.

The occasion had been so pleasant that I confess to anticipating further enjoyment, and indeed the young lady being avid for experience, and willing to be taught the most lascivious tricks to be commanded by an experienced mistress, it was no pain to me to call upon her while her husband was at the House of Lords, and to instruct her as best I might.

But at last, my problem arose; for within a month, I began to lag behind her in eagerness. Her person was delightful, but her conversation ineffably tedious – indeed, she had none. In short, the afternoon came when, having promised to attend her, I reluctantly mounted the staircase to find her awaiting me between the silk sheets of Lord Walkett's bed – but found myself entirely unable to arouse that interest which would enable me to satisfy her. Nor could any of those tricks which she now displayed – lubricious poses, nor the attentions of fingers or tongue – rouse me. The passion which her unfamiliarity and eagerness had aroused was dead; and nothing could replace it.

It was at this point that she rang for the footman, and ordered my expulsion. The gentleman in question being extremely strong, I was unable to resist; and found myself cast out of the front door, entirely unclad, into a street mercifully devoid of pedestrians (it being that time of the afternoon when few ladies and gentlemen took the air).

I hid for a while in a doorway, considering my situation. Then I heard a window open, and in a moment my clothes flew through the air – hurled by the footman, whose upper body, I observed, was now devoid of clothing

– from which I took it that Lady Phyllida had not been long in replacing her lover (or, perhaps, had done so earlier – for it is true that there had recently been as much as four days between my visits). I quickly dressed, and made my way home.

My state of mind at this time was therefore such that the prospect of some new amusement of an unromantic nature was welcome to me; and as it chanced, I was in a coffee house near the Haymarket on the very day following the incident I have described, when at the next table I heard a gentleman speaking to another of a voyage to the Far East.

'We shall not stay long in the south of Africa,' he said; 'for it is to Ceylon that my chief envoy is directed – then to the island of Siam, whence we return with freight. I need not say that the prospect of a view of all these places cannot but be attractive to any man of spirit, and I shall certainly keep the journal you suggest, on the prospect of its being published should it be deemed of sufficient interest.'

On the elder gentleman rising and taking his leave, I lost no time in introducing myself to the younger – a man of much my own age, who on my making it clear that my interest was not that of one seeking employment, was happy to inform me that the voyage of which he had spoken was to be undertaken by the *Proper Pride*, leaving Gravesend only five days hence for Cape Town, a voyage of some three months' duration. On my enquiring, the stranger, Mr Hooke, who proved to be the First Lieutenant of the vessel, told me that a passage was available – and on my enquiring whether any ladies were among the passengers, assured me that such was not the case, the single cabin which alone was available being still untaken.

The fact converted my sudden interest into a decision,

and I made immediately for the office in the city whither Mr Hooke directed me. There, in exchange for a bankers' draft, I received a written promise of carriage from London to Siam and back – and then returned to Regent's Park, whence I sent written notes of my intention to my two closest friends, Frank and his half-sister Mrs Sophie Nelham, and set about the task of having sufficient belongings packed into the single trunk the company, whose ship was already overstocked with goods, would permit me.

A message from Frank arrived within two days, followed a day later by the dear chap himself, who, knowing my predilection for travel, was surprised less by my departure than by its suddenness. On my confessing that a part of my reason was escape from the ladies, he was yet more astounded, regarding me as an inveterate lover of the sex; and I believe was incapable of understanding even when I had explained my feelings. Nevertheless, he wished me well, and made me promise to make notes of the minutest adventure I should have, in order that on my return he should have a full account of them.

From Sophie, I heard nothing – even to the moment I went aboard, at Gravesend. That she had been on a small exploration of her own to the Lake District, I was aware; and could only suppose that my letter had not reached her. I was sad – such were the bonds between us – that I could not bid her farewell; but she no less than Frank would relish the fact that I had gone in search of new experiences, rather than be sad at it.

We left Gravesend at eight o'clock in the morning, with a fair wind and fine weather, and in the evening came to anchor in Margate roads, to await the return of the tide. Early the next morning, I awoke to feel the motion of the vessel already aswell, and went upon deck to find that the anchor had just been raised, and we were under way. On our port bow, another vessel of similar size to our own was also slowly moving towards the sea – and upon deck I saw two ladies looking keenly towards us. One – surely . . .?

I seized a glass from a surprised officer and directed it towards the other vessel – to recognise indeed the figure of Sophie, who at the same moment, through a glass of her own, recognised my own features! With what eagerness we signalled our surprised affection, can be imagined; but it was fruitless to think of closer contact, for within a short time both vessels were round the South Foreland, with a fair breeze at north-west, and the shores both of England and France soon clearly visible as we passed between Dover and Calais.

On my enquiring, when he had leisure, of Mr Hooke, I heard that the vessel on which my dear friend had been seen was the *Flower of Kent* – and from a conversation with her mate, with whom he was acquainted, he had learned that she was bound for the West Indies. So we travelled in opposite directions – and would no doubt meet again only when we both returned to England. The reason why Sophie should be on such a voyage could not be guessed by me, who however did not wonder at it, knowing her to be as inveterate an adventurer as myself.

We finally lost sight of the *Flower of Kent* late in the afternoon of the next day, as, having passed Start Point, we made into the open sea with a harsh wind at our back which blew sufficiently hard to send occasional waves clear upon our deck. I stood for a time looking with a kind of delighted fear at the foaming surface of the troubled ocean, until the motion of the vessel sent me below in a sudden bout of sickness. I assured myself, even when feeling at my least happy, that this should not last long; and indeed, after only a few hours, I recovered, and was able – as the wind dropped and our progress became less violent – happily to return on deck and engage in conversation with Mr Hooke, or Robert, as he invited me to call him.

In time, the motive for my voyage was broached, as it was bound to be; and on my tentatively offering some explanation of it (which was, that I had been too much with the ladies of my family, and felt inclined for a period away from them) he entirely caught my drift, and confessed that while he found the sex agreeable, he agreed that some time in exclusively masculine company sharpened those appreciative faculties which otherwise might have dulled the edge of affection.

'But then,' he said, 'I was introduced to amorous pleasures at a peculiarly early age, and found in my very first encounter that while enough is as good as a feast, a superfluity can provoke indigestion.'

How was that? I enquired. Whereupon he told me, as we sat upon deck, amused by the sight of a school of porpoises swiftly playing about the ship, the following story:

I was sent to sea (he said) at an early age, and by thirteen counted myself an experienced seaman, and found myself midshipman on a naval vessel sailing to station in the Mediterranean. Though it was not normal for civilian persons to be conveyed, there came on board as we sailed a gentleman, his wife and two daughters, sailing to Alexandria, where he had been appointed consul. Mr Edward Pondersend was a man of advanced years (or so it seemed to me – he was perhaps forty and five) whose wife was somewhat younger than himself, and in my eyes the acme of matronly beauty: statuesque in aspect and with the kind of dignified charm which made her instantly the queen of my heart. Her daughters were one of sixteen, one of eighteen. Katherine, the youngest, was a playful creature who was immediately my friend; the elder, Vivienne, seemed more the princess – at the same time distant and courteous, but far from unfriendly.

You will understand that I was by now a man in physique if not in experience. My body had shown itself for some time expressive of desire – yet I scarcely knew for what, since there were no boys of my own age on board, and I could not bring myself to enquire of my elders what should be done with that part which suddenly provoked me by a sudden vertical posturing, accompanied by a kind of dull ache which only occasional nocturnal incidents (equally inexplicable to me) relieved.

For a while, the presence of Kate took my mind from this troublesome matter. A tomboy by inclination, she begged of me a pair of old trousers, scandalizing her mother by donning them, and with short hair and undeveloped bosom appearing no less a boy than myself! At first, rebuked for being unladylike, she was firmly replaced in skirts; but upon her capering in the lower rigging, the glances of the crew made it clear that those were no safe garb for a girl so adventurous, and she was permitted to resume my breeches!

I was happy to show my familiarity with the vessel by explaining everything about her, during those afternoons when – set on our course through calm seas, with a warm wind behind us – I was at leisure; at other times we had less freedom to converse, since I was still a pupil, and had to work at my astrolabe and compass. My time of rising was 5.30 – no distress on warm mornings, when the sun was already up. My first action was to make my way to that quarter of the deck where a tarpaulin, spread, permitted the hauling up of sea-water and its use for washing.

On one particular morning, I had awakened to find my recalcitrant lower limb in a state of rigidity so determined that it seemed unlikely it would ever resume dimensions sufficiently modest to be crammed into my clothing. Hastily wrapping a towel around my waist (my determined yard trapped between it and my belly) I hastened to the deck, and hauled in a bucket of water – which was insufficiently cool, the sea having been warmed by months of sun, to have an immediate shrinking effect. I was reduced to scooping double handfuls of water from the bucket, and dowsing this lower limb, in the hope of reducing it; when, looking up, I found Miss Kate within a few feet from me, her round eyes fixed upon that which she had never before seen.

She solicitously enquired whether I had been injured, and approached nearer, the better to examine this strange phenomenon. No, I hastily assured her. My own feelings were mixed: while I was obscurely excited by her presence, I instinctively knew that anyone observing me in that condition and in clear view of a young woman, would find the situation reprehensible. The very knowledge resulted in an immediate diminution in size – which itself astonished young Kate, who showed no signs of turning away; and wrapping the towel hastily about me, I made my excuses and returned below.

When we met that afternoon, it was with something of a subdued air that she enquired after my health; and it took a little while before she believed my assurances that all was well with me – and after some hesitation asked whether what she had seen was not the product of some sickness, perhaps associated with the heat? No, I assured her; my situation was entirely comfortable – indeed, the condition in which she had observed me that morning was a temporary one.

But was not such a sudden growth painful? she asked – confessing that once in every month she herself became acutely uncomfortable in just that region where she had observed what she called 'the thing'.

She clearly did not understand my explanation – which indeed could only be cursory, for I did not comprehend the phenomenon myself; and finally asked whether I would not permit her to observe that part of my body at more leisure, a favour which she would return by allowing me the same privilege.

Nothing appealed to me more strongly, for I was curious to know in what the difference between the sexes consisted, other than those of softer voices and, in Kate's sister and mother, mysterious swellings of the upper body.

Once more, I instinctively knew that our behaviour would be considered reprehensible by adults, and was careful that we should not be seen as we returned to my cabin – which was little more than a cupboard, so that in unclothing ourselves (which we immediately did) it was impossible to prevent an occasional contact between our bodies, which was strangely exciting to me – so much so that my yard was once more firmly at stand when the removal of my trousers exhibited it.

Kate immediately fell to her knees, and not content to look, in a moment began to examine with her fingers not only the chief object of her interest, but the pendant spheres beneath, lifting and gently squeezing them – then returning to the chief object, moving the skin upon its surface with a soft exclamation – and bringing from my own lips an involuntary moan of pleasure which in an instant became a sharp cry almost of pain, for the soft touch of her fingers resulted in the sudden explosion of feeling which liberally drenched her neck and shoulders with a liquid as plentiful as it was expressive of delight.

My horror at the event was soon allayed, for she appeared less perplexed than pleased at the experience, in an obscure womanly instinct being conscious of the compliment; and reaching for a cloth, wiped herself, then dabbed away the drops still pendant from a tool which had already somewhat shrunk – though not to insignificance, for as you will remember, at that age we are no sooner in the descendant than we begin to recover – which was certainly the case as, taking my turn, I raised her to her feet and took my turn at innocent exploration.

What was revealed to me will be no mystery to you, Mr Archer (my friend continued); though you may perhaps have somewhat forgotten the keen interest quickened by a first apprehension of it. The young grotto which I now saw was feathered by a delicate mist of down, while the shaft of light which fell across it from the small porthole which was the only source of illumination revealed lips of the most tender pink, between which was an inviting darkness.

I looked up at Kate – whose face was all pleasure, which quickened as I gently laid my hand upon the treasure below. Her breast rose and fell as her breath quickened, where two slight mounts, each tipped by a rosy point, presented themselves to my delighted view – and which, as I immediately apprehended, were the infants (as 'twere) of those larger mounds possessed by the older ladies.

We knew not the proper use of what we had; and if, with an instinctive movement, Kate pressed herself towards me, inviting my hand to a sort of caressing motion, it would be idle to pretend that she in any way experienced a pleasure as keen as my own; and disappointment, though without rancour, resulted in her too soon clothing herself and returning upon deck – whereat I, needing no other lesson and once more burning, counterfeited the movements of her hand with my own, with a resulting release which pleased me (and enabled me in subsequent voyages, unaccompanied by the female sex, to quieten my febrile longings).

You may think that the end of my story: but it is only the beginning, though I shall be brief – for that cloud beginning to lower in the east seems to promise a storm. I had not reckoned on Kate confiding in her sister (though now I should be more cautious); on the following morning I was astonished – Kate being a slugabed – to be once more disturbed at my ablutions by her sudden appearance; and no less surprised when, approaching me without the slightest hesitation, she expressed disappointment that I was not (as she put it) manned for action – the experiences of the day before perhaps being responsible for my awakening, for once, unaroused.

Laying her finger upon her lip, she then led me without ado to the cabin she shared with Vivienne – where the latter was abed but awake, and greeted me with a smile. The towel which as usual girded my loins was removed without my protest – and what was my pleasure when Miss Vivienne followed the example of her sister, and was soon as unclothed as myself.

It is obvious to me now that the elder minx was experienced – through what circumstance I cannot say. Having assured herself by a glance of my sturdiness – which indeed was sufficiently exhibited – she at once laid herself on her bunk, threw her legs apart, and before I could more than glimpse the heaven offered, positively lifted me between them and with an accommodating wriggle succeeded in engaging me for the first time in a proper embrace. After that, I needed little further tuition, and though unconscious of the refinements of pleasure, was able to satisfy both sisters – for though the sudden new pleasure set me off long before Vivienne was ready, Kate secured the benefit, the pain of a first encounter being easily outdone by the concomitant pleasure; while an impatient Vivienne, upon my showing myself ready with reasonable speed for a third encounter, positively shrieked with joy – so that I feared I had injured her, and was about to enquire as to her state when the door of the cabin opened, and Mrs Pondersend entered, who hearing her elder daughter's cry, had feared some accident.

You will believe that I was in a state of fear – as were the girls; not every mother discovering her daughters in the closest proximity with a naked midshipman would be so sanguine as merely to raise an eyebrow and retire.

Upon this, we dressed; both Kate and I apprehensive in the extreme – but Vivienne, to our surprise, showing no such distress, and simply advising us to await developments. I, by now, had another fear, attendant upon my being forty minutes late on deck for my instruction by the mate, a man of impatient nature who, on seeing me, addressed me for some minutes in language which became only a little milder at the approach of Mrs Pondersend – who to my astonishment, informed Mr MacLally that I had been engaged upon a task for her, and should be forgiven. He reluctantly ceased his raging, and released me; on which Mrs Pondersend bade me, that afternoon, to come to her cabin, where indeed she had a task which would not, she hoped, be beyond my strength.

What this was, you will already apprehend; nor will it surprise you to hear that it was Mrs Pondersend who, deprived of a normal relationship with her husband in consequence of that gentleman's age and infirmity, taught me early some tricks which astonished me – and which I was not slow to pass on to her daughters.

My newfound accomplishments were sorely tried for the rest of the voyage, my attentions being demanded in the morning by one or other – or both – daughters, and in the afternoon by their mother! Ten days of this went far to convince me that in love, as in everything else, moderation is not only to be commended but should be positively courted if the appetite is not to become jaded. And since that time I have been careful to husband my resources, and certainly have never again been caught in the situation – no doubt coveted by those who have never encountered it – of serving three women at the same time!

Robert concluded his story just as several large raindrops began to fall; and I was left to draw the moral as I lay, clutching the edge of my bunk, in a tossing cabin while the sudden storm blew itself out above, below and around the vessel.

Chapter Two

Sophie's Story

Although I am never long satisfied, as my friends will confirm, with a life devoid of excitements of one kind or another, from time to time it is necessary for me as for all humankind to rest and enjoy a slower pattern of life; and so it was that in the early summer of the year of which I write, I was making a brief tour of the Lakelands of England, and at the time at which this narrative commences was staying in a small but sufficiently commodious inn in the village of Kirkland, overlooked by the mountains which lie between the lakes of Loweswater and Ennerdale.

One morning, I took my hired horse – a steed excellent more for those sturdy qualities which enabled it to be at ease with the hills of the area than for its fleetness of foot – and rode the two miles or so to the neighbouring village of Ennerdale Bridge, then turning to the left, on for another mile, when (as I had been instructed) a lane on my right led down to the shores of Ennerdale Water itself.

This, the quietest of the English lakes, is a most enchanting place, and my first glimpse of it under a full sun, its waters undisturbed by more than the slightest ripple, promised me a day of the most pleasant recreation.

I engaged with the landlord of the Anglers' Inn to leave my horse in his paddock, and walking past a handsome manor house to the water's edge, turned to the south-east and continued along the bank, my path interrupted only by the occasional spinney or by a shallow stream, easily forded.

I was stepping through one such stream, my shoes in my hand and my skirts tucked up, when I was conscious of being watched, and glancing up caught the eye of a fine man of middle age, clad in breeches and shirt only, and similarly bare-foot, who was lounging upon the bank of the rivulet near a bush which had at first concealed him from my sight. To his nod of greeting I returned the slightest curtsy, and having myself for the moment walked far enough in the heat of the day, asked his permission to sit by him while I recovered my breath.

We fell into conversation, and on my revealing that 'twas my first visit to the district, he congratulated me on discovering it, for it was (he said) one of the most beautiful yet rarely apprehended areas of Great Britain. I expressed my agreement, and remarked on the expanse of water before us – which though not great (the lake is perhaps two and one half miles long only, and less than one mile across at any place) was extremely fine.

'And viewed from the lake itself,' my new acquaintance remarked, 'the Pillar and the Steeple and other landmarks are much more so. But perhaps you will permit me? – I have command of a small craft in which I should be delighted to row you the length of the water.'

Indeed, not far from us I saw a little skiff equipped with oars; and the man seeming respectable, and appealing to me by an openness and lack of self-consciousness which seemed to mirror my own, I agreed – whereupon without more ado he led me to the boat and handed me in, himself taking the oars and propelling us across the surface of the lake.

After only twenty strokes, I saw that the linen of his shirt, where it fell beneath his arms, was already wet with

perspiration, and without his appeal remarked that he
should not hesitate for my sake to remove it – which he
did not hesitate to do, revealing (as I confess I had antici-
pated) a deep chest, deep shoulders and a skin brown
enough to suggest that the sun had already fallen freely
upon it.

I will not disguise the fact that the next fifteen or
twenty minutes were pleasant enough, the gentle motion
of the boat, the rhythm of the rowing, and the play of
sun on the muscles of the rower being equally appealing.
But the sun was hot, and I was not surprised when my
guide lay upon his oars for a moment, his breath coming
somewhat short.

'Perhaps,' he said, laying the oars along the side of the
boat, 'I may rest a moment and introduce myself. My
name is Edward Lockyear; I am a guest at the manor
house which you may have seen on your approach to the
Water – the guest of Sir Douglas and Lady Sperries, to
whom perhaps I might have the pleasure of introducing
you a little later? If there is one drawback to this place, it
is the lack of civilised company, for having exhausted the
conversation of the local parson, there is no nearer con-
troversialist than the poet Mr Wordsworth, who is not
for all callers.'

I returned the compliment by allowing him to know
my name; after which, both somewhat affected by the
heat, we were for a time silent – when Mr Lockyear
remarked that the water was tempting to the swimmer.

'Then why should we not try it?' I asked.

At first, surprise was his response.

Did I swim? he then asked.

I had learned some years ago, I said, as the result of an
accident during which I had nearly been drowned on the
upsetting of a boat while embarking ship at
Brighthelmstone (an incident which will be recalled by

readers of my account of my Grand Tour, as published by the amiable and ambitious firm of Messrs Headline, of Great Titchfield Street in the city).

But (he remarked) . . .

Ah, I replied, it was ever my opinion that the proper clothing for swimming was the skin, and if he had no objection – and seeing that he had none, but performing the elementary courtesy of turning my back, I lifted my single garment over my head and in a moment, in an action of which my swimming tutor would have been proud, launched myself over the side of the little craft and with only the merest scattering of drops, penetrated the cool depths of the water.

As my head broke the surface and I shook the water from my eyes, I saw the figure of my companion dive from the prow of the boat, with less grace (I flattered myself) than I.

We swam together, comfortable as two swans, his lack of grace compensated by an admirable power; what I lacked in power, I do believe was countered by a certain elegance. In a while, cooled but somewhat exhausted, I lay upon my back and floated – not unconscious, I must admit, that my breasts, breaking the waters momentarily, their peaks drawn into knots by the coolness, and the length of my thighs, ever slender and well-formed, were being admired by Mr Lockyear; who then himself floated upon his back, whereupon I could not but observe that his observation of my person had had the result that his manly part defied the cold, and while by no means rigid, displayed that somewhat swollen aspect which I took to signal his approbation of my own form.

'Allow me to be of assistance, Mrs Nelham,' he said as we approached the boat; and swimming behind me, took me by the waist and by dint of a vigorous kicking and lifting, aided me to grasp the side of the boat – then grasping it by one hand and placing the other beneath my fundament, positively lifting me aboard before himself emerging from the water, drops running down his sides and chest, and flooding down belly and thighs – to which my eyes could not but be attracted, since he lowered himself to the thwart immediately above me.

'You will inform me if I take too great a liberty, ma'am,' he said, 'but may I take it that you would not be averse to relieving me of those sentiments aroused by the outstanding beauty of your person?'

The force of those sentiments was now perfectly clear, for as the sun dried his body, that part of it which the coolness of the water had restrained now took on the proud appurtenance of simple lust, rising handsomely between his thighs.

I took it as a compliment that he should apprehend my feelings so correctly, and that he should not take the insulting course of pretending to be otherwise than excited by my unclothed state; and for answer stretched out my hand and gently grasping the symbol of that excitement, drew him to the bottom of the boat and embraced him; whereat, in a very few moments, the small craft was rocking with a motion entirely comprehensible to anyone who might have observed it from shore.

I will not pretend that the unprotected wooden boards were comfortable; yet I have been served in more opprobrious circumstances, and Mr Lockyear was enough of a gentleman to spread his forearms over one seat and place his ankles over another, and thus supported was able entirely to relieve me of his weight, the only contact between us being that distended instrument which now pierced me, moving in a delightful rhythm exacerbated by the rocking of our craft – our pleasure increased by the ease with which, disembarrassed of the necessity to be embraced at length, we were able to observe those motions of our persons which in no long time brought me to a delighted repletion, and shortly afterwards (as was signalled by the force with which the liquid of life spent itself, as he courteously ensured it should, upon my belly) enabled his own.

The exercise had brought us to a new pitch of physical heat, which only another bath reduced; after which he could not restrain a look of equal admiration – but denied himself the pleasure of following it, by remarking that while entirely inspiriting, the exercise lacked comfort; and giving it out that 'twould be no difficulty in my being accommodated that night – and so many subsequent nights – by Sir Douglas and Lady Sperries, whereupon our entertainment (should I agree) could be accomplished in the luxury which my beauty invited.

His gentlemanlike manners, together with an admiration of his person which I need not rehearse at length, encouraged me to accede; whereon, pulling his breeches on with difficulty over a still damp person, he set about rowing the boat back to the north of the lake, while I dried my body as best I might with my dress, before resuming it, sadly crumpled.

We reached the manor house just as a carriage bearing Sir Douglas and Lady Sperries drove up to the front door, and as they descended, Mr Lockyear introduced me. Lady Sperries, a pleasant, fresh-faced girl of about my own age (as I should guess) greeted me kindly; Sir Douglas was less accommodating. He was a dry, dark-faced man, rough and inelegant, who gave me the barest salutation, and only grunted when Mr Lockyear proposed that he might offer me hospitality for the night. Lady Sperries – or Frances, as she soon insisted I should call her – was more than welcoming, however, carrying me off immediately to her rooms, and on learning that I had brought no luggage with me being kind enough to offer me clothes of her own. She then showed me to a room just down the corridor from hers, and instructed her servants to bring me water and towels; so that when I descended to dinner, an hour later, I was freshly bathed and groomed, my hair tidied, and in a dress which I might have chosen for myself. Mr Lockyear, I apprehended by a look in his eye as he rose to greet me from his place on a chaise-longue at Frances' side, was not displeased at my metamorphosis. Sir Douglas, when he entered, scarcely seemed to notice me, paying more attention to his wife – but not the attention to be hoped by a spouse: rather the jealous glances of someone entirely resentful, wishing every remark made to be made to him; and when Mr Lockyear went to take his place at dinner between myself and our hostess, he called out 'Ned, sit by me, won't yer?' – at which Mr Lockyear ungraciously relinquished his place.

After dinner, we retired to a pleasant but undistinguished drawing-room, where Frances played upon the piano, and Sir Douglas seemed entirely pleased that it should be I who turned the pages for her rather than Mr Lockyear. It was still early when he rose and invited us all to retire; which politeness forced us to accede to, following him up the great staircase and bidding each other goodnight along the single corridor, in which Frances's room was at the far end, her husband's next it, then Mr Lockyear's, and finally my own. Sir Douglas lit his wife to her door and waited to see it closed before gruffly bidding us goodnight and almost slamming his door behind him.

'The man is uncouth!' said Mr Lockyear, 'and positively a monster! Failing to pay his wife the courtesy of attending her, he is fixed in the idea that every other man wishes to do so!' – adding, in a soft voice, 'Wait upon me when you will, madam; your chamber is a single one – I have a bed large enough to accommodate all our pleasures!' And taking my hand, he planted a kiss upon its palm, and bowed me into my room – which, as he had said, was a tiny one which, though entirely satisfactory in the way of courtesy to an unexpected guest, had a bed which cannot have been more than three foot wide, and thus scarcely great enough for the comfort of one person, let alone of two – however immovably they might have spent the night (which was not our intention).

Frances had offered me a night-gown, but I had refused it, saying – which was true – that I did not agree with the modern notion of dressing for bed; but concerned not to damage her evening gown by an excess of joy in the greeting to be bestowed upon me by Mr Lockyear, I slipped out of it and drew my own soiled dress about me before slipping out into the silent corridor. As I made my way to the next door, I thought I heard the creak of a board further along the passage – and paused; but nothing further stirring, continued until I felt beneath my hand the knob of the door, and turning it, slipped within.

There, a single candle was set on the dressing-table, and its light fell on a fine four-posted bed the clothes of which had been piled upon the floor, so that what remained was merely a cushioned stage on which was already stretched the unclad body of my lover, who no sooner saw me enter than he rose to embrace me, and in a moment had almost torn my poor dress from me in his eagerness.

We spent some time in mutual exploration – of the eye no less than of the hands; for the strangeness of our situation in the afternoon had made leisurely examination unwise, lest we should be observed by some peasant upon the bank. Now, however, we were able to feast our eyes at leisure, and both were pleased with what we saw.

Mr Lockyear turned me about and about, instructed me to walk and to recline, stretch my body and to relax it, and every moment seemed to be additionally delighted; and I must confess that at that time, in those admirable years between unripe youth and the middle age, my person was generally admired – my breasts being full but not drooping, the nipples turned slightly outwards, and the lower surface of the globes more acutely rounded than the upper, so that they appeared pert and willing; my belly small and round, my thighs slender but sufficiently strong to represent perfectly balanced columns supporting hips broad but not stout; my arms and hands graceful and feminine, my feet small and well-formed, and between my thighs a muff of moss concealing that instrument which, giving quite sufficient pleasure to myself, could offer the stronger sex embraces which proved almost too delicious for the inexperienced, while offering the true man generous reward.

As for my lover, he was in every respect a proper example of his sex; his strength and the extent of his manhood I had already observed and experienced, while the proportions of his figure in relaxation could now be seen to be markedly fine. If there was a fault, 'twas in the slight distension of his waist, which seemed to speak of too great an enjoyment of his victuals, for though seeing my glance he drew in his belly, there was a certain thickness which could not be denied. Yet 'tis a venial fault, and after all the food which thickens the waist often contributes a vigour and energy which outweighs any slight lack of perfection in the figure.

Having viewed each other extensively, we lay side by side the better to confirm by touch the beauties discovered by our eyes; and I soon found that Mr Lockyear was a lover of some experience. To teach a young man the art is delightful, but often trying – since innocence is often partnered by a febrile excitement which prompts too sudden an end to pleasure. I had not for a moment thought Mr Lockyear a virgin – yet had wondered whether he was too much the countryman to be capable of other than a swift encounter. I soon discovered such was not the case, for rather than throwing himself immediately upon me he began that careful wooing which discovers the true adept – complimenting with his tongue the delicate whorls of my ears, then tracing the outline of my jaw; tasting the swell of my lower lip and sucking gently upon my tongue; paying the most delicate attention to each nipple, till they swelled almost to a painful apprehension of pleasure; and finally, having gently parted the portals of my lower lips with his fingers, exploring the outskirts, then the ramparts, then the very inmost secret room of love.

I was by now almost aflood with pleasure, yet was determined to show that I too knew something of the game, and turning him upon his back, began my own tribute, no less apprehensive of the prickled texture of his cheeks than of the springy, curled hairs about each pap; no less of the strong muscles of his thighs than of the tower which lay between them, whose strength seemed adamantine, yet the velvet covering of whose core was sensitive to the gentlest touch of lips or fingers.

At length, all preliminaries must cease, and together by a single instinct we prepared ourselves for the final pleasure – myself turning upon my back to offer the plainest and most simple target – for whatever interesting postures may be tried, for the first leisured embrace I commend the most common as being at once relaxed and inspiriting, the lady, by throwing herself fully open to her lover, showing her approbation of his admiration; the man, by piercing her in so purposeful a posture, displaying that admiration so clearly that there can be no question of his love.

Our playing had so enchanted me that I was liberally bedewed – indeed, so much so that I scarcely felt his approach. However, as his engine pierced me, I was able by a contraction of the muscles to embrace it and apprehend its purposefulness – at the same time showing him my pleasure; yet something more was needed, and in a moment I threw up my legs, resting their calves upon his shoulders, so that his member could sheath itself to the very hilt – and indeed, my own protective muff met the coarser hairs which decorated its base, so completely were we embraced.

Even in the dim light of the single candle, I could see, as he began the motion of love, that his teeth were biting into his lower lip – presumably because he feared to reach his apogee too soon; but giving myself up entirely to pleasure, I allowed my emotions to mount, and in but a few moments a star-burst of my own contented me – and reaching down, I grasped his bollocks and by the gentle but firm application of my nails brought about his own completion.

He gave a cry, raising himself upon his arms – one on each side of my shoulders – and at the same time it seemed that our world positively exploded with pleasure. In a moment, I felt a flood of liquid upon my breast, as though saliva had flooded from his mouth – then, entirely enervated, he fell heavily upon me.

It was a moment before I was conscious of anything unusual – before I saw, over his shoulder, not a single candle, but two – and in the light of the second, the red face of Sir Douglas Sperries, bloated with fury, and seeming to be surrounded by a haze of fog. In a moment, I smelt powder; and was at the same time aware of the utter stillness of the body which lay upon my own. With a horrified grunt, and a great effort, I threw it off – and saw, as Mr Lockyear fell upon his side, that a torrent of blood had gushed from his mouth.

My horror was only equalled by that of Sir Douglas Sperries.

'Madam!' he cried, then turned as a figure appeared behind him – that of his wife. In a moment, he had turned the gun upon himself, placed the muzzle between his lips, and discharged the second barrel.

It took some time, as will be apprehended, for myself and Lady Frances to recover our senses. With the help of brandy, however, I was able to come at the reason for the astonishing scene in which I had played a part.

Frances had married Sir Douglas – or rather been married to him, in consequence of an agreement between him and her bankrupt father – when she was merely sixteen. After one article of commerce between them, which deflowered her, he had left her entirely alone, his temperament being cold. Yet regarding her as a complete possession, his jealousy had become inordinate, every man who stayed in the house regarded as a possible lover.

She would clearly have had it so, for she was by no means without feeling; yet only once or twice had she fallen, and never – she assured me – with Mr Lockyear, who had come to the house to survey it for some extension Sir Douglas planned. He had indeed admired her, but his attentions had from the first been made impossible from the watch which her husband had kept upon them. Yet the suspicion was impossible to allay, and it was doubtless (she said) the conviction that their guest was swiving his hostess that had led Sir Douglas to Lockyear's room – on which, seeing our coupling figures – he had assumed I was her, and had dispatched Lockyear with a single shot in the back, the second killing himself when he discovered his mistake.

Our decision was a speedy one: leaving the bodies where they were, we first ensured that every trace of blood was removed from my own body, then, having dressed myself in the gown which Frances had loaned me, I joined her in rousing the servants – who slept in a separate cottage next to the house, and had heard nothing. One of them rode for the nearest magistrate, who next day arrived from Cockermouth.

I was somewhat apprehensive, not only for my reputation (though certain that Lady Frances would not divulge my part in the incident) but for my hostess's. However, Mr Fountain upon the spot concluded misadventure – Sir Douglas' mania of possessiveness being well-known. If he suspected that one or other of us was involved, he said nothing. I was able to assure him that I had seen no sign of any commerce between Lady Frances and Mr Lockyear, and that to my knowledge her ladyship was nowhere near his room when I, hearing the shots, came to it (which I could swear with an easy conscience).

Sympathising with our fearful experience, the magistrate took his leave, and I supervised the removal of the bodies, making arrangements for Sir Douglas's burial in the family vault in Croasdale, where he lies now beneath the epitaph,

> *Pause, traveller, and in your heart reflect*
> *Upon the fate of those who may suspect,*
> *Without due cause, their loved one's honesty.*
> *One such lies here; be you not one like he.*

– a verse which I composed myself for the occasion. Mr Lockyear's body was returned to his home in Keswick; he proved unmarried and with no living relatives, so that only I mourned him, as being a man of considerable attributes besides those known to his colleagues and friends.

Frances made a swift recovery from the shock, the pleasure of being relieved from the pressure of living with an unloving (or too loving) husband equalled by the news that his estate, now her own, was considerable. Invoking the necessity of a change of air, I invited her to travel with me to London, and to stay with me there – which she accepted, and it was with pleasure that I intended to introduce her to the *beau monde* – a process started by my inviting ourselves to dine with my friend Mr Hedgeley, a ship-owner to whose son I had been of some assistance in the matter of a trial for 'crim. con.' (or criminal connection) with a lady of easy virtue and dishonest predilections, who, her temperament being known to me, I was able to send packing without too great expense.

It was at dinner that Mr Hedgeley, in the way of conversation, revealed that one of his ships, the *Flower of Kent*, had been commissioned by the Admiralty to set forth on the first stage of a voyage round the globe, with instructions to survey certain insufficiently unknown islands and inlets in the Pacific, among them the Sandwich Islands, Fiji, Hawaii and Malaysia.

My interest was immediately aroused, and I enquired whether passengers were to be carried.

None, said my friend – though there was a double cabin now unoccupied, in consequence of one of two artists commissioned to accompany the expedition crying off – 'and at the last moment,' he said, 'for she sails on Wednesday next.'

In two days!

'I can be ready by then,' I instantly said.

My friend laughed.

' 'Tis no trip for ladies!' he said – which only made

me the more determined, and on getting from him the terms upon which the vacant cabin could be mine, secured it!

Frances had remained silent during this time – but then asked whether she could not accompany me?

'Another madcap!' exclaimed Mr Hedgeley – but the matter was now out of his hands, his having reluctantly consented to my taking the cabin. Nevertheless, I did my best to dissuade my new friend, explaining that the various adventures of my life – with which my regular readers will be sufficiently acquainted – in places as far apart as Greece and the Mississippi – had prepared me for discomfort and danger, whereas she . . .

'Have always craved both,' she said, 'but without the possibility of either, as it seemed, until now!'

Taking leave of our host, we discussed the matter as we were carried home, and long into the night; but I was unable to dissuade her, and finally capitulated. And, after all, I was pleased to do so, for she was an amiable and spirited young woman, and two women, on a ship entirely crewed by men, were undoubtedly safer than one (if, indeed, safety were to be one's aim).

The haste in which our preparations were made can be guessed at; but we were ready – and woke one morning in the cramped conditions of our cabin, aboard the *Flower of Kent* at Gravesend, with the motion of the ship sufficient to indicate that we were under way. We hastened upon deck to bid farewell to England, when I saw that another vessel, not far from us, was moving in the same direction. On her deck stood a figure observing us through a glass, and who suddenly began to wave his arms in a distracted manner.

Thinking 'twas only in friendship, I waved back; but his gestures becoming more wild, borrowed a glass from an officer, and to my amazement descried the features of my friend Mr Andrew Archer, who I call indeed brother (though no relative of mine, we have been more than friends since we were striplings).

I could have no commerce with him, for both ships were making now for open sea. Our officers opined that she was bound for Africa, probably to make harbour at Cape Town – being a commercial vessel laden with various supplies for the settlers there. For what purpose Andy could be on board, I could not surmise; I could not believe that he would take such a voyage without letting me know – but in the haste of preparation I had certainly left unopened some private post, and it might well be that some communication of his had been among it. The same circumstance may have resulted in his not receiving the note I sent, hastily scrawled, only the day before to his house in Regent's Park, informing him of my own departure. Well, 'twas all as one.

In an hour, we were pitching on bumpy seas in the channel – but I was delighted to observe my friend had a stomach as firm as myself, and accompanied me without demur to the communal table at which we were to take our meals in company with the two civilian gentlemen accompanying the voyage – Mr Richard Midgely, the artist, and Mr St John Thripp, whose duty it was to write a full description of the areas newly surveyed.

Our companions seemed agreeable enough. Both were of their middle twenties – so without the inexperience of extreme youth or the ponderousness of age. Mr Midgely was much the artist, with fair hair sufficiently long to curl about his open collar, slender, sensitive hands, a pale countenance and lively, bright blue eyes. Mr Thripp was dark, his hair more formally cut, his person more thickly-built, but of a manner perfectly acceptable if a trifle terse. Both seemed sufficiently well educated to be palatable companions – but this we did not have the opportunity to discover, for after fifteen minutes, Mr Thripp grew as pale as Mr Midgely, and the latter even paler; until, the former throwing his hand over his mouth and making a precipitate exit from the cabin, the latter followed him with only a little more ceremony and a little less speed.

We were highly amused at this, and finished a bottle of claret, drinking the health of the two young gentlemen who, whatever achievements they might possess in the field of art and literature, were clearly less seamen than their fellow passengers!

Chapter Three

The Adventures of Andy

Our voyage continued agreeably, although not smoothly, for the waves frequently broke over the forepart of the *Proper Pride*, and sometimes even approached us as we sat on the quarter-deck. At night, however, it was delightful to watch the foaming edges of the waves appearing like lines of phosphoric light, chasing each other; and whenever a wave dashed over the decks, the sparks it contained ran with the water to and fro as the ship rolled from side to side.

Occasionally the weather became positively rough, and on one occasion help was called for as the trunks and other articles broke loose in the cabins and slid backward and forward on the floor. Once, the door of the pigsty was forced open, and the poor animals ran in great consternation about the deck, one having the misfortune to fall head-long down the cabin stairs, the noise of its fall and cries adding to the terror of the scene.

The wind being in general fair, however, we were thankful, among all the restlessness occasioned by the ship's motion, that we were getting fast forward. We saw only a few other vessels – once, on one hoisting English colours, we edged towards her, and found her to be a Poole ship from Newfoundland, bound to Valencia in Spain. Robert, being a native of Poole, found an acquaintance in her captain, and gave him some very welcome information concerning his family, a circumstance which afforded him much pleasure.

At length, flying fish made their first appearance; a shoal of bonettas played about us – though they proved impossible to catch, even though the jolly-boat was launched and the captain and two sailors made to gain for our table some fresh fish, which we were assured would be delicious. But it was not to be.

The dangers of travelling by sea (and not only during stormy weather) were from time to time impressed upon me even in so placid a voyage, for on one occasion certain rocks, marked in our charts as lying to the north of Porto Santo and called the Eight Stones, became an object of some anxiety to the captain, and though their existence is not fully proved, he kept a sharp look-out for them by night and day – for by this time our dead reckoning was so much at variance with the chronometer that by his account there was a hundred, and by Robert's no less than a hundred and forty miles difference between them!

I was at once pleased and frustrated by the sight of land, from time to time – land which I would feign have explored, had it proved possible: for instance the Salvages, generally considered as belonging to the Madeira islands, and uninhabited – but how grand they looked, with the square-looking, jagged precipice of the Piton Rocks; then, the peak of Teneriffe, its summit enveloped in clouds, and Palma, another of the Canary Islands, marvellously grand, with large masses of clouds with shades of a bright blueish grey colour showing through various openings the brilliant orange, purple and greenish tints of the unclouded atmosphere beyond them, and hovering above the western horizon, which down to the edge of the sea glowed with the most vivid gold and crimson hue.

We passed so close to the westward side of Palma that

we could distinctly discern every object on shore, and I longed to set foot there; however, it was impossible. Eight days later, we saw Sal, one of the Cape de Verd islands, with two high peaks and some lower mountains to the north of them. Then on the same day came the island of Bonavista, most picturesque, with several ranges of mountains of beautiful shapes and different heights, some being cones with craters on their rocky summits – and here we had a splendid display of the agility and playfulness of a host of bottle-nosed porpoises, which for nearly half an hour played and frisked about the ship's bows, leaping out of the water, pursuing each other in all directions, tumbling tail over head and performing all kinds of tricks.

It can perhaps be imagined how calming to the nerves was this voyage, when for the first time for many months I was not once troubled by the knowledge that upon the morrow I must pay court to some madam or another, who more likely than not would expect me to perform *coitus* – something which, I was fast concluding, should be the product of true desire rather than becoming as common (as in some parts of society it is) as shaking hands or taking wine with one's dinner.

Robert and I had been sparing of our amorous anecdotes; and my only apprehension of the sexual, if so it can be called, was during the sing-songs which nightly took place among the crew when they congregated upon deck in the cool of the evening, and when verses were heard which though clearly well known to them (for they all joined in the singing with good heart and without book) were unknown to me. I took note of some of them, with the thought of publishing them perhaps in a broadsheet among my friends: I will not reproduce them at length here, but – to give example only of the less disgusting (to spare the blushes of my lady readers) – there was for instance the ballad of Oyster Nan, among the more innocent verses of which were the following:

> As Oyster Nan stood by her tub,
>   To show her vicious inclination,
> She gave her noblest parts a scrub
>   And sighed for want of copulation.
> A vintner of no little fame
>   Who excellent red and white can sell ye
> Beheld the little dirty dame
>   As she stood scratching of her belly.
>
> 'Come in,' says he, 'you silly slut,
>   'Tis now a rare convenient minute;
> I'll lay the itching of your scut
>   Except some greedy devil be in it.'
> With that the flat-capped fubsy smiled,
>   And would have blushed, but that she could not;
> 'Alas!', says she, 'we're soon beguiled
>   By men to do those things we should not.'
>
> From door they went behind the bar
>   As it's by common fame reported,
> And there upon a turkey chair
>   Unseen the loving couple sported.
> But being called by company
>   As he was taking pains to please her,
> 'I'm coming, coming sir,' says he,
>   'My dear, and so am I,' says she, sir.

Then there was a ruder ditty, which began:

> If any man do want a house
>   Be he prince, baronet or squire,
> Or peasant, hardly worth a louse,
>   I can fit his desire.

I have a tenement the which
I'm sure can fit them all;
'Tis seated near a stinking ditch,
 Some call it Cunny Hall.

It stands close by Cunny Alley
At foot of Belly Hill.
This house is freely to be let
 To whomsoever will . . .

But I will not embarrass the fair by repeating the remainder of this scabrous song, amusing enough though it be; and indeed I am continually astonished at the dexterity of the humour inherent in these old songs, which arising from the common people are yet refined by time into something sufficiently witty to amuse the most literate.

To return to my account – a few days after sighting Sal, we encountered the single severe storm which interrupted our otherwise smooth voyage to Cape Town. Joining me upon deck, Robert took one look at some very black clouds which arose in the south east, and with remarkable celerity called the captain, who gave orders to shorten sail. The swiftness with which the clouds came rolling on was terrific, and they brought with them such a sudden gust of wind that the utmost exertion hardly saved the royals and studding-sails from being blown away before they could be taken in. Some mischief was done to the rigging, and we could hardly stand on deck. For about an hour we ran furiously through the water, when another cloud much more black and threatening than the former appeared in the south. Its approach was announced by several claps of thunder of increasing loudness, and we prepared for a heavier squall, when after a quarter of an hour's violent rain, it suddenly fell calm.

Then however our troubles began, for the sea having become extremely agitated by the fury of the former gale, the swell was tremendous; and as there was no wind to carry us forward, the ship being at its mercy plunged very hard. A wave struck her a-stern, broke two of her cabin windows, overstreamed all the books, papers and whatever lay on the lockers, and filled the floor some inches high with water. Fortunately not much injury was done, but we were obliged to put in dead-lights, and glad to retreat on deck out of so hot and dark a dungeon.

As we sat waiting for the cabins to dry out, the sea once more being calm, I could not but note that something was amusing Robert, and asked if I could not be told what it was?

We had (he began) determined to keep from the subject of the fair sex – but I must confess that the recent storm reminded me of one episode which you may find amusing. It occurred just after I had been promoted lieutenant, in the year of '23; and I was serving on the *Canary*, which had put out of Southampton for Boston, in the north of America. We had a number of passengers – not immigrants, but gentleman travelling on business – and one of them attended by his daughter, a Miss Emmeline Grant, who from the first was characteristic in presenting a picture of the most ideal yet distant beauty. Dressed to the highest points of fashion, her hair always neatly in order, she contrived to maintain on sea the dignity and calm which no doubt she exhibited on land. Slender and dark, she appealed most strongly to those masculine instincts in me which at that time – having been aroused at an early age, as I have already described – were still rampant. Yet it was impossible that I should approach her in a corporeal fashion, for though (and I cannot but report it) I was the only presentable young man on board near her own station in life, she maintained the utmost distant courtesy, exchanging merely polite greetings on meeting me upon deck or on the rare occasions when she frequented the common cabin. (Her father, I may say, was a gentleman of corpulent stature, who for the most part kept his cabin, groaning and complaining at the slightest motion of the vessel.)

Our voyage was for some time calm; but on the fifth day up came just such a sudden storm as we have now experienced. I was at the time in the common cabin, and as it happened alone with Miss Grant, who was idly turning the pages of Miss Austen's novel *Sense and Sensibility*. It was warm, and by permission – somewhat coldly given – I had removed my coat and sat in my shirt-sleeves, ostensibly looking out of the port, but in reality covertly admiring the handsome turn of that arm which lay upon the table, the delicate hand whose fingers I could all too clearly imagine performing those tickling tricks which most easily arouse us, and those cherry lips which . . .

But my enjoyable fantasies were interrupted by my seeing just such heavy clouds approaching as announced our recent storm. My experience had taught me what was about to occur – and happily, I knew that both the first lieutenant and the captain were upon deck, so that my presence there would be supererogatory. I rose, stretched myself, and with care not to appear insolent, made my way to that side of the cabin where Miss Grant sat under pretence of consulting the barometer which hung there (and which indeed now registered a sudden, even calamitous, drop).

As I stood slightly behind her, the first squall struck us, and the ship lurched under the sudden onslaught of the wind. The chair in which the fair one sat was flung backwards, so that had I not been expecting some such motion it would have fallen to the deck. As it was, I caught it – or rather, (not entirely by accident) caught the figure which occupied it, my hands naturally falling about her shoulders, and apprehensive even in that moment of the warmth and malleability of the flesh beneath the linen of her fashionable gown.

Even then, her equanimity was disturbed only to the extent of a cry, and she was able to stutter her thanks and rise to her feet – not, I am sure, realising that the vessel's movements were for the time to continue so erratic that only a seaman could be expected to retain control of his balance. The second lurch sent her staggering against me, and I was forced (oh, delightful contrivance!) to throw one arm about her waist and place the other about her upper person, where my palm fell – by what accident I cannot explain – upon one of those charming, swelling breasts whose presence had only been hinted at by the disposition of her gown.

She could not protest – for by this time, the storm was truly upon us, and the ship's movements rendered it impossible for her to walk.

' 'Twould be safest to retire to your cabin, ma'am,' I said; and, by this time being overcome by fear, she tremblingly acquiesced – allowing me to half-carry her from the place and along the short corridor past the door behind which I could hear her father grumbling and cursing. A fumble at her cabin door, and it opened into the small space which for the voyage represented her private quarters.

She was by now in such a state of terror that I felt it incumbent upon me to offer what comfort I could: she should not fear, I suggested, for whatever calamity awaited us – and I must confess that there were some rocky outcrops in the area which were a danger to shipping in such circumstances – I would do my best to contrive her escape; at which she drew me to her with an enthusiasm little short of the passionate, and in doing so actually tore my shirt open, her nails scratching at my skin.

The accident inflamed me even more than the sensation of her body in my arms; yet I was able to exercise sufficient restraint to lay her upon her narrow bunk, and made to go.

'No, sir – Mr Hooke, pray remain!' she cried, and reaching up, clutched at my shirt, tearing it yet further, and this time inserting her hand to grip my shoulder with all the determination of an eager mistress. I judged that by now her fear was such that she merited a greater comfort than mere words could accord, and pausing only to shrug the remains of my shirt from my shoulders, I laid myself by her – or rather, the bunk being so narrow, upon her.

In doing so, a lurch of the vessel so disturbed my balance that I accidentally caught at her dress rather than the edge of the bunk, and in doing so tore her clothing somewhat – revealing, as I could not but notice, an entire sphere, the perfect contours of which, its centre deliciously marked by a rosy bud, would have been most attractive to anyone hard-hearted enough to take advantage of a young person in so advanced a nervous state. As it was, the sensation of our naked flesh meeting in what was tantamount to an embrace seemed to have a calming effect upon Miss Grant – perhaps by offering her a sensation other than fear to occupy her mind. Her eyes – which I have perhaps neglected to mention were dark almost to blackness – met mine in a gaze which seemed delightedly apprehensive, and at the same time I felt her hands, which had been fluttering in the last degree of apprehension, fall upon my back, where they began to move gently as though feeling the texture of my skin, one

then entangling its fingers in my hair while the other –
yes, I could feel it! – descended to my waist, where it
seemed disappointed to be balked of further progress by
the waist of my cursed breeches, which of course I had
had no opportunity to loosen.

The ship had now been turned to run before the wind,
and though its movements were still acute, was clearly
under control. Holding the edge of the bunk with one
hand, and with the other pressed upon the mattress, I
was able to relieve Miss Grant of some of the weight of
my body, which had until that moment been as con-
stricting as it was (I hoped) comforting. I reluctantly
made as if to descend – for with her father in the next
cabin, I had no desire that he (however preoccupied by
his own situation, being by no means deaf) should overhear some complaint by his daughter, and in turn com-
plain to the master.

But a smile now came to the lips of the lady, and
'Stay!' she murmured; 'I would be obliged if you would
remain until all danger is past . . .' And at the same time,
she took advantage of the lightening of the load upon her
body to slip her hands below mine to fumble at my waist –
but fumble fruitlessly, the fastenings of a gentleman's
breeches being, it seemed, unfamiliar to her.

Pressing a kiss upon not unwilling lips, I slipped for a
moment from the bunk and divested myself of my lower
clothing, presenting the lady with what I imagined was
her first view of what I hoped would remove the last
vestiges of her fear. Yet as I did so, she herself removed
her torn dress; and as she dropped it to the floor of the
cabin, to my astonishment reached out to grasp my tool
and to plant a kiss upon its tip, even protruding her
tongue to run it round the flaming and impatient tip.

I guessed from this that Miss Emmeline Grant was less
the cool young virgin than she appeared – which indeed

proved the case, for as far as the strict confines of the cabin would permit, she exercised many a trick that even the experienced whores of Portsmouth had not at their command – or, if they had, had not revealed to me! In short, as the storm gradually subsided, our own tempest grew, so that I had from time to time to place my hand over my companion's mouth lest her cries of pleasure should communicate themselves to the neighbouring cabin.

After many a pleasant contrivance during which she increased my fervour by denying me entrance to the haven at which I aimed, she rose from her knees – having afforded me the most tantalising enjoyment by the gentle and apprehensive sucking of my member – and sitting upon the edge of the bunk, opened her thighs and placed her feet – so narrow was the cabin – against the partition behind me, opening that treasure the dark curtains of which I easily parted, sliding into a cave so warm and liquid with her own delight that at first I was scarcely apprehensive of it. However, that the motion pleased her there could be no doubt; and, seeing that her embrace was perhaps too frictionless to be entirely pleasing to me, she reached down to toy with my cods, to run twin fingers each side of their sack, to tickle my fundament, offer the cheeks of my arse the compliments of her sharp nails, and finally to encircle the base of my engine, so that as it withdrew from her purse, she was able to drum upon it with her fingers in a light but entrancing motion, forcing me by mounting emotion to quicken my movements – which she met with an equal thrusting until it was her turn to stifle my cries with a kiss, stopping almost the back passage of my throat by the insertion of her tongue.

In a moment it was over, and my first fear was that, her emotions being stilled (for the contraction of her muscles had made it clear to me that – as is so rarely the case – our delights had coincided) she would withdraw into that distance from which the storm had drawn her. But no; indeed, reaching for a towel, she wiped from me the sweat with which my exertions had liberally bedewed me, before laying my now shrinking member upon the palm of her hand and cleansing it with some water from the ewer containing the small amount of liquid allowed to each passenger during a day.

The ship was now upon an even keel – after what length of bucking and dancing I knew not, for time had become entirely distorted; and disguising as best I could the state of my torn shirt, I slipped from the cabin. However, I need not say that the introduction made between us by wind and weather was taken up more than once before we sailed into Boston harbour – where a handsome young fellow of about my own age came on board and demanded to be directed to Miss Grant's cabin, and (I could not but observe) was greeted there with enthusiasm – the lady, as she threw her arms about his neck, offering me a pleading glance which I took to be an entreaty to offer her no familiarity of address in the gentleman's presence.

It goes without saying that I did nothing of the sort; learning, in a brief conversation which I contrived when ostensibly assisting her with her luggage, that Mr St Clair and she had been engaged before he left England, and were shortly to be married; whence I inferred the reason why she was not, as I had hastily assumed, a virgin – that indeed the couple had enjoyed each other with some vigour before their separation. I respectfully offered him my congratulations, and was rewarded by the gift of five guineas, offered with some condescension – so that I was highly tempted to reveal . . but no, 'twould have been unkind.

And so, you see (my friend concluded) that sudden storms at sea can be delightful as well as menacing!

The rest of our voyage was unexceptionally calm and restful, the time passing in reading and in sitting upon deck and observing the fishes and birds which played in our wake or soared above us – the most interesting of the latter being the albatrosses, which rose heavily from the water and by degrees mounted up, soaring eventually to a great height, then hovering like kites, wheeling about, and approaching the ship without fear, bidding defiance to those men who sometimes shot at them – something at which I protested, for such marksmanship was exercised only for 'pleasure' – had they been killed, they could not have been fetched from the sea; and had they been fetched were not, I was assured, good eating. However, happily not one of the creatures was ever hit by our men.

Fifty-three days after leaving England, Robert assured me that the day had dawned when we might expect to see the Table Mountain. A sailor was sent to the mast-head to look for land, but the foggy appearance of the horizon prevented his seeing it. By reckoning, we were only forty-five miles off. At ten that night the water had a singular appearance; it looked muddy and white, and was plentifully bestrewed with sparks. The waves, whose foaming had appeared extremely bright, had subsided, and the captain felt some alarm. We hove to; but on sounding, no bottom was found with a line of one hundred and fifty fathoms. We therefore kept under an easy sail all night.

Next day, all at once, the second mate, who had taken his station in the main top, roused us from our dullness by calling out 'Land!' He discovered it among light clouds to the south east. It was the Table Mountain, and some of the adjoining hills. The captain, being called up, expressed his disappointment on finding it lying in that direction – but we gradually made towards the bay, and rather than being disappointed by the ship's slow progress, I was delighted by the view before us: besides the magnificent group of rocky mountains to which the Table Mountain belongs, there appeared further inland a very picturesque range of singular shapes, some with rocky peaks, others flattened, like Table Mountain.

Cape Town itself now came into view. The whiteness of its buildings gives it a cheerful appearance, though the low tower of the Calvinist church, surmounted by a squat, pyramidical steeple, is its only prominent feature. As we moved slowly into harbour, we were boarded by the harbour-master, who demanded the mail-bags. A doctor accompanied him, to examine into the state of health of the crew and passenger: before this has been done, no one is suffered to land. I was surprised that the doctor, not content with questioning me about my health, insisted on a minute examination – including the careful investigation of my private parts, for it appears that the government of the place is eager that no disease of a venereal kind should be established there.

A pilot having brought the ship to an anchorage, I went on shore to enquire about lodgings, and found a small group of people eager to offer accommodation to any passengers on board; myself being the only one, I had the choice among a number of decent-looking bodies, and fell upon a Mrs Disandt, in whose house on Graave Straat I took two rooms, sitting room and bedroom.

Having enjoyed a night's sleep, though somewhat disturbed by a strangeness of the house not moving about in the manner of my recent home, I spent the morning at leisure, unpacking my trunk and disposing the few belongings I had brought with me, but had not been able to air during the voyage. I was happy to be surprised, in the afternoon, by Robert, who had gained leave of absence from the ship for two weeks, and knowing something of the place, offered himself as a guide.

We went immediately forth, after breakfast, to see the town. Passing through several streets, we entered the Governor's Gardens, with avenues planted with oak of luxuriant foliage, skirted on each side by hedges of myrtle. The ground is laid out in squares, enclosed between high hedges. Within a stone fence, several ostriches and other birds, and in a separate building, a lion, lioness and tiger and two or three more wild animals were kept.

Leaving the gardens, we walked to the foot of Table Mountain. Already, before we landed, we had observed a white mist creeping up from the south through the opening between the Devil's Hill and the flat summit of Table Mountain. This had now nearly covered the former, and was fast spreading along the rocky sides and summit of the latter, carrying with it a blast of wind which in a short time grew so strong that we could hardly withstand its force. The change from the most clear, calm and warm weather to storm and fog was almost instantaneous, and before we could reach any kind of shelter we were driven along by the gale, shivering in the cold.

On my remarking that I should be glad to be warm, Robert enquired with some diffidence whether I would welcome warming of a female kind; for, he said, he could take me to a house where for a moderate fee I could – as he put it – disencumber myself of any passions which had mounted during our weeks away from female company.

Though until that moment, I must assert, the idea had not occurred to me, the moment he mentioned it I assented – realising that indeed I was now ready for such relief. On which he grinned, and led me towards the quays, then turning into a narrow alley where a low, white building stood in its own grounds. His knock was answered by a diminutive black boy neatly clad in white shirt and trousers, who led us to a chamber where a large black woman of appearance as cheerful as she was buxom, greeted Robert warmly. On his introducing me, she immediately pressed into my hand a glass of some intoxicant which was pleasantly warming, and went for a moment from the room.

Robert explained to me that this was an establishment which he had frequented upon his two previous visits to Cape Town, and which was highly respectable (as such places go) – attracting a clientele not only from the town, but from places as far afield as Stellenbosch, Zwellendam and even Zeekoegart; though, he said, the Calvinist religion was much against sensuality, human nature being no different here than in countries where other churches attempted to restrain natural instincts, there had always been commerce of a copulatory kind, and the elders now recognised that the provision of such establishments as this meant at the least that the commerce could be controlled (and indeed through payments made to the public coffers, was of assistance in keeping down taxation).

Returning, the plump Madam led us to a large salon in which eight or nine black women were at their ease, and invited us to make our choice.

I should not, of course, have been surprised at the ladies being all of that colour; indeed, should have expected it – for though Robert later explained that there was a less respectable house elsewhere in the town where a couple of white women were to be had, it was the case that the best houses of prostitution in this country were inhabited by ladies of colour, not only (and as I think disreputably) because the strict religion of the white men discouraged them from satisfying their lusts with women of their own race, but because most white women thought the profession beneath contempt, whereas for the blacks it offered perhaps the sole possibility to make a fortune which would keep them and their families in comfort.

I had only once been presented with the spectacle of a black woman before – at Southampton, some years previously; and the sight of such a number was at first bewildering – only in the plethora of choice, for they appeared to me to be in the first degree delightful, open and frank in nature, and (though one or two were more corpulent than was entirely to my taste) of attractive appearance.

Frank whispered to me that one, in particular, was to be recommended; and I accepted his advice – she being a short, slim, pert little creature dressed only in a bright red cloth wound about her loins, her charming breasts bobbing pleasantly as she greeted me and took my arm. Meanwhile, Frank had approached one of her sisters, and we went from the room and up a set of stairs.

I had assumed that we would then go to separate rooms – but to my amazement we were ushered into a sort of dormitory, a room which seemed to occupy the whole of the upper floor of the house, and in which were no less than eight beds, three of which I saw were occupied, for to reach an empty one we had to pass two on which couples were already at the game, while in a far corner another lay apparently asleep, no doubt exhausted by their exertions.

Not being excited by the public observation of my pleasures, I was much tempted to withdraw, though Robert – who clearly had experienced the place before – was already throwing off his clothing. However, my girl, pausing only to drop her single article of attire to the ground, was already unbuttoning my shirt, and (in short) proved so adept in at once disrobing and exciting me that I was soon oblivious of anything but the strong tide of anticipatory delight that was flooding through my veins.

This was again momentarily subdued when my girl – who seemed to go by some such name as Mopsa, though I may have misunderstood it – fetched a cloth wetted with cold water and, soaping it, thoroughly cleansed my private parts; for, the place being free of disease, every professional lady is instructed to take such a precaution. There is no doubt but that it is wise; yet I cannot say that an application of cold water, even in a hot climate, is commensurate with the excitation of amorous proclivity. However, when having completed the task Mopsa found me in something of a shrunken state, she soon found ways of heating the iron once more – and my two months' deprivation of female society was no hindrance in this; so much so, indeed, that in less than half a minute from the moment of my entering her, my passion released itself in a flood – half to my relief, half to my shame; for even with a whore, it is a cheat to deprive the female of at least some satisfaction from congress – while in the case of a professional engagement, the sum paid for satisfaction is almost wasted by so speedy an end!

My companion seemed to sense my disappointment, for she smiled, and gently persuading me to lift myself from her body, turned me so that I lay upon my back with my head resting between her thighs, and began gently to stroke my entire body with the tips of her fingers, touching as gently as a feather my chest, arms, arm-pits, paps, then the area where my instrument, sadly shrunken, lay like a worm – yet under her touch began to swell; and as it happened, the couple upon the bed next to ours – a muscular young man who was perhaps a seaman, or a miner, or at any rate from his appearance one used to manual labour – at that moment chose to engage in a coupling of more than usual interest, the young girl standing upon the bed with her hands clasping the bed-knobs, her legs wide apart, while her companion thrust into her from behind; all this but a few feet from my face, so that I could not but observe (not, I confess, having the strength of mind to turn my eyes away) the spirited thrusting of his pego, his cods positively smacking – so that the sound could distinctly be heard – against her thighs, and his action so vigorous that almost a steam of pleasure arose from their distended and happy parts.

The sight, together with my friend's ministrations, soon revived me; and catching her by the hips I lifted her (she not being of any great size) into the air and lowered her upon my once more ready staff, where with a happy grin she rose and fell in delightful rhythm until once more I gave up my soul with so pleased a cry that it drew applause from my neighbours (now themselves resting from their labours) and from Robert and his companion, who, I supposed, were happy with a single pass, and were now dressing.

It perhaps need not be said that I returned to my lodging through streets cooled by the rain, feeling – after my cruise and my more recent exertions – positively a new man!

Chapter Four

Sophie's Story

The *Flower of Kent* paused only once on her long voyage across the Atlantic, and that was at Lisbon, where we took on cargo, and where I was able to show the city to Frances and the two gentlemen, Mr Thripp and Mr Midgely – for I had spent some time in that place only a few years previously, and was conversant with its delights – though these now comprised a number of new buildings, including a handsome zoological garden.

Our two male companions were pleased, I think, to be able to set foot, however temporarily, upon dry land; for this being their first venture upon the oceans, neither had so far found their 'sea legs', and at the slightest swell were wont to vanish below decks, or if already there to make excuse to go to their cabins, whence, on passing, it was impossible to ignore certain sounds significant of extreme nausea. I could only hope for their sake that they would soon become accustomed to the motions of the sea, for otherwise they were in for a miserable month or so – and we for the deprivation of any male company (the ship's officers choosing to keep themselves apart from the 'civilians', as they called us).

However, our being alone enabled me to get to know my new friend, who I found more and more amiable – but whose life up to that time had been indeed a sad one. Her late husband having had but one connexion with her – and that on their first going to bed (rarely the most satisfactory incident of a maid's amorous life), she had experienced only dreams of sensuality – and those for the most part so abstract as to have been painful rather than pleasant; of men in general she had neither knowledge nor experience, and all my efforts to convey that it was not only for their conversation and social discourse that I prized them, were for the present doomed to disappointment. Sir Douglas had, as I gathered, approached her not only without candle, but swathed in a nightgown, so that the male body was as foreign to her as the coast of Africa; and upon my ever mentioning it, she would shudder and change the subject.

Well, she was still young; and I had hopes that a conversion might be effected – whether with the aid either of Mr Thripp or Mr Midgely, I could not say, though at least by the time we were four or five days out of Lisbon both gentlemen seemed to have accustomed themselves to the movements of the vessel, and – at least while our journey continued, as it had begun, in mild weather – were able to take a more constant place in our little society.

Mr Thripp, as it appeared, was of a gentleman's family from the city, his father being a merchant; his interest was in geography, and he was extremely happy in having been chosen to survey and map some of the islands of the Pacific ocean previously uncommitted to paper. He was not greatly given to conversation, but his silence was contemplative rather than sullen. The heat of the sun was, upon deck, such that he soon begged for our permission to remove his shirt, thus revealing a torso admirably well-set, with shoulders and arms so muscular as to suggest the man of action rather than the scholar: and upon my questioning him, confessed that he had much enjoyment of fisticuffs, and had studied the noble art with Jumping Jack Sydney, the bare-fist champion of

Wapping; the art of self-defence, as he said in one of his brief sentences, being an honourable and often useful one. I was, incidentally, pleased to see that Frances directed many a covert glance in his direction as he sat or lay in the sun, sometimes with a book of charts under his hand, sometimes merely resting; and I could not but suppose that she found something pleasant in the aspect of his robust person.

Mr Midgely was of an entirely opposite character, for he shunned the sun, even paying a seaman to construct for him a little awning or tent, in the shade of which he sat, generally with paper in hand, sketching the ship and the activities of the crew; his only concession to the gradually increasing heat being to unbutton his white shirt, revealing the level platform of an almost equally white breast, sprigs of fair hair only lightly decorating the pale pink paps, almost as tender as those of a budding girl.

He was, however, nothing of an effeminate – as I was pleased to see upon one occasion, when Mr Thripp in play threatened to tear the shirt from him, whereupon Mr Midgely with an incredibly quick and dextrous movement took his friend's arm and with a strange turn at once had him face downward to the deck, his arm up behind his back, and the stronger man at once helpless at the hands of his much frailer companion! I was happy to reflect that the brute strength of the latter together with the dexterity of the former would provide ample protection for two ladies, should the need arise!

It was when we were some weeks out from Lisbon that, coming on deck in the late afternoon, I was surprised to find Frances reclining in what was for her an almost indecorous fashion, her dress falling from one bare shoulder, as Mr Midgely sketched her. She was by no means – as it seemed to me – unconscious of the pleasure of being minutely observed by a person of the opposite sex; or rather, by persons – for not far away, Mr Thripp (ostensibly reading) also observed her closely, and under my gaze stirred uneasily, so that it seemed to me that his discomfort sprang as much from a certain pleasurable 'dis-ease' below the waist as from my noticing his preoccupation.

On our going below to prepare for supper, Frances appeared languorous and thoughtful; and though upon my remarking on Mr Midgely's obvious admiration of her she made nothing of it, I believe that she was by no means displeased. At supper, he was more than usually attentive – being the chatterer of the two – making conversation almost entirely with her, so that were I of a jealous disposition, I might have taken offence at it. As it was, I was delighted, and by turning at every moment to Mr Thripp, encouraged commerce between the other two. (I may say that I got nowhere in provoking Mr Thripp to conversation; though he seemed by no means averse to my own, listening with attentive gravity, and – as it seemed to me – no little pleasure in my company.)

Mr Midgely showed a genuine regret when the evening ended – and Frances was no happier; and on our retiring to the cabin we shared, expressed her pleasure in the evening.

'Well,' I remarked, 'I am happy that you begin to find the company of the other sex more agreeable.'

'I have never found it other than agreeable,' she replied, 'in as far as I have experienced it – which as you know is sparsely enough. It is simply the – the commerce of which we have spoken that I will ever find repugnant.'

' "Ever" is a long word,' I replied, but did not press the matter.

The night was particularly close and warm, and with

that freedom to which I was ever prone – and which in the circumstances of sharing a cabin with a woman friend I had no hesitation in indulging – I threw off the single sheet which was my only cover, and lay entirely unclothed upon the lower bed or 'bunk' – for the ship did not employ hammocks (or not, at least, in our quarters), but large shelves which sprang from the wall or 'bulwark', and which formed our beds, one set above the other; I had taken the lower one, as a courtesy to my friend – in which, when I lay upon it, I had but a few inches of space above me, where my friend lay upon the topmost 'shelf' or bed.

I was conscious, as time passed, that neither of us found it easy to sleep; I could hear Frances moving about, a few inches above me; while in the heat I too found it impossible to do more than rest, and lay watching the shaft of silver light from an almost full moon swing to and fro across the wall of the cabin, where it streamed in through the small window or 'port', as it is called, which provided our only outlook. I was, however, less restless than Frances, and perhaps gave the impression of sleeping – which may have been the explanation for what next occurred; for after a while, I saw my friend's arm appear over the edge of her bunk, hanging down, palm towards me as she lay (I presumed) upon her face.

In a while, with the utmost gentleness, she moved her hand inwards, while in the dim light through lowered lids I saw her face appear over the edge of the bunk, looking toward me (though I could have been but a dim shape to her). Her fingers now fell upon my arm, which they tenderly caressed, then slowly moved inward until they touched the side of my breast, the single feathery tip of a finger reaching its tip, which by now was firm and proud.

I must confess that some weeks without commerce with a gentleman – together, I have no doubt, with my admiration of Mr Thripp's excellent physique – had roused my feelings; so that with no desire to disguise them, and in no doubt of my friend's interest, I immediately reached up, and placing my hand around the back of her neck, planted a kiss upon those delightful lips.

There was a gasp of surprise – though not, I think, of horror; for whatever she had expected, it had not been so overt a gesture. For a moment, she hung back – and then returning my kiss with ardour in a moment slipped from her shelf and climbed upon my own, so narrow that even had we both by now not desired it, the entire lengths of our unclothed bodies were pressed one against the other!

The passion with which Frances now embraced me confirmed my belief that she was as warm-blooded as any young woman of her age; nor, though I neither expected her emotions to be directed exclusively at her own sex, nor (as my friends will confirm) was I myself given entirely to the emotions of Sappho, did I shrink from her expression of it. The tenderness of her embrace, the soft caresses of her hands, the equally gentle fluttering of her lips, were entirely comfortable in the circumstances in which I found myself – nor did I have any hesitation in returning them.

Her person was, as I believe I have stated, less full than my own; so that on my lips descending the slender column of her neck, they found the breast almost of a boy, the spheres no more prominent than shallow saucers – though the firm tips at their centres were drawn into protuberances of pleasurable flesh, which on my softly nipping them with my teeth produced a little wail of pleasure from between Frances's lips.

Her breath came more quickly and more shallowly as

my tongue drew a line from between her breasts to her belly, then, only pausing momently at the dint of her navel, entered the feathery forest below, reaching the shores of that lake where the pivot of pleasure lies; and on my finding, next, that very centre – the tiny pole around which the sensual life revolves – she let out a sudden shriek which was stifled only by her clasping both hands over her mouth – but which she then immediately transferred to the back of my head, clasping it in almost a frenzy, while with gradually increasing pressure I lapped at her body, which in a moment drew itself up (to our danger, in the constricted space) so that her calves positively crossed at my back, her thighs pressing against my cheeks while her whole upper body shook in a spasm of pleasure, after which she relaxed to lie panting beneath me as, temporarily exhausted, I too relaxed, my head lying on the cushion of her swollen, delighted quim.

Her speedy exhaustion was followed by as speedy a recovery – or at least a speedy determination to return the pleasure I had given; for wriggling from beneath me, she now stood at the side of the bunk, the better to enable her to caress my entire body with her hands and lips, which – I suppose through instinct, for it was certainly not through usage – she performed with all the dexterity of a practised lover; indeed, I was able by an exercise of imagination to suppose that it was a man who paid such inspiriting tribute to me (and I must confess that it was towards the handsome Mr Thripp that my mind turned, so that as, with the dextrous application of her digits, my friend brought me off, I almost expected to feel between my thighs the scalding tribute of his approbation).

We both slept well after the interlude; and in the morning spoke not of it – though my friend's blushing look, no less than her careful attention to my every need, told of her admiration – at which, I determined that her attentions should be redirected another way; for while I was pleased to have her as a friend, and by no means distressed by the incident which had occurred, I have never wished to become exclusively the lover of another female – not only because it is not my habit, but because I had seen in the past what jealousies and unpleasantnesses could result from such a situation, when the object is not a confirmed Lesbian.

I therefore set out to throw Frances much into the company of Mr Midgely, who I knew admired her; and finding him alone upon deck one morning, asked him whether he was not pleased at having such a model.

'I hope one day that perhaps you will sit for me,' he replied.

'Certainly, if you wish it,' I said. 'But I am sure that you must find Lady Frances a more admirable model – I have rarely seen a young woman of such grace; and she is more than happy that you should find it agreeable to sketch her. Indeed, in confidence, she told me yesterday that she would not be averse to a more intimate study than you have so far attempted.'

He looked his question; on which, I nodded.

'I am sure,' I said, 'that she would grant you a sitting, unclothed, should you request it; and, you know, we are never overlooked at the corner of the deck reserved for us, the seamen being instructed to avoid it except in the very early morning, when they swab down the deck . . .'

He said nothing, but took my hand and kissed it; and that very evening Frances confided to me that he had asked her, with many stutterings, whether she would permit him to sketch her without clothing, and requested my opinion.

It was something, I said, that was not uncommon in society; ladies who were proud of their bosoms having no hesitation in displaying them in advanced *décolletage*.

'But whereas your bosom is handsome, my own' (she blushingly said) 'entirely lacks proportion and dimension . . .'

However, I was able to assure her that different men had different conceptions of female loveliness, and that it was not to be doubted that to Mr Thripp her person presented an object of the most perfect admiration.

The following morning, feigning a headache, I stayed in the cabin, while Frances (in a state of subdued but evident excitement) made her way onto the deck. In half an hour I could contain my curiosity no longer, and cautiously took myself thither, but turned aside from the usual way, and climbed to the top of the hatchway, to a vantage-point where . . .

But what was this? Someone was there before me! 'Twas Mr Thripp, who was lying upon his stomach, cautiously looking at the scene below him – which, standing, I could see beyond his shoulder. There, my friend reclined upon a number of cushions, in the most perfect state of nature; her upper body raised as she leaned upon one arm, while the other fell along her side so that her hand modestly concealed the chief sign of her womanhood from Mr Midgely, who stood leaning against a railing, his sketchbook in his hand – but with the other hand making, as far as I could see, only the most cursory movements over the paper – a most marked protuberance (if one knew where to look for it) signalling clearly the fact that his interest in the fair beauty was not merely artistic.

In a moment, he stammeringly enquired something – the refreshing breeze carrying his words away – and stepping forward, bent to take Frances' head in his hands, and turn it into a more decorative pose; then taking her arm and lifting it so that her hand fell across her bosom – at which point his self-possession entirely failed him, and falling to his knees, he wrapped her in his arms and planted a kiss upon her lips.

For a moment, I feared that so sudden an action would distress so sensitive a plant; but after the merest hesitation, I saw both arms wind themselves about his neck, her fingers entwining themselves in his hair.

Mr Midgely was, as was his wont, clad in trousers and shirt. The latter was in a moment almost torn from him by my friend, whose frankness in returning his caresses would have made it difficult for any other observer to believe that she had previously been so shy of the approaches of a male – indeed, Mr Thripp, who still lay at my feet ignorant of my presence, could be heard to gasp (no doubt enviously) at it. Frances had, however, no knowledge of the intricacies of gentleman's clothing, and no amount of fumbling permitted her to undo her lover's trousers, and her impatience becoming greater, she began to tug at the waist so forcefully, that Mr Midgely could not but smile, and gently removing her hands, stood for a moment to divest himself of the remainder of his clothing – at which my friend was for a moment, I think, abashed by the unfamiliar sight which confronted her; though Mr Midgely was not so generously provided, as to the instrument of generation, as some men I have observed, neither was his tool so insignificant as to provoke denigration; and a female with no experience, somewhat fearful of the sex, might be forgiven a certain hesitation.

But it was only momentary, and on Mr Midgely once more kneeling, she clasped him again in her arms without the slightest reluctance, and the couple fell to the deck, where their bodies assumed the natural postures of love, legs and arms entwined, breast pressed to breast, belly to belly, and the slow swell of a rhythmic movement already hinting at a storm to come.

I must confess that I was by now somewhat heated;
while Mr Thripp had inserted one hand beneath his
body, and now, stirring as he lay, led me to suppose that
something was making his posture – face downwards
upon the surface of the hatchway – a little uncomfortable. Indeed, fumbling at his waist, in one movement he
turned face upward – revealing that he had unbuttoned,
for protruding from his trousers and encased in his right
hand was an instrument of enviable proportions – for
his palm was entirely incapable of enclosing it completely, and a fiery tip was proudly in view above the
circle of thumb and forefinger.

Meeting my eye, he blushed a fiery red; but before he
could move, I had in one movement thrown my dress
over my head, and sunk to my knees – one upon each
side of his thighs, where gently removing his hand, I
replaced its fingers with the warmth of my lips; a gesture
which seemed to give him some satisfaction, for I heard
him sigh, while he at the same time reached out and
grasped in each hand one of my breasts, the texture of his
rough palms being sufficiently inspiriting to provoke me
into a gentle sucking motion which further increased his
pleasure – so much so that in a moment he gently took
my head in his palms and raised it, shaking his own as
though to convey the message that further caresses of
that kind would lead to too swift a conclusion to the
passage of love on which we had just that moment
embarked.

I stayed for a moment crouched over his body. Below
me, Frances had now turned upon her back, and Mr
Midgely was gently inserting his hands between her
thighs, encouraging her to open them. Her expression
was not a confident one, poised as it was between delight
and concern, her small, even teeth catching at her lower
lip. It was at this moment that she caught sight of me – a

strange sight, no doubt, naked and perched (as it must have seemed) on the body of a man who was no less a new acquaintance to me than Mr Midgely to her. However, I took the opportunity of kissing my hand to her, and smiling in an encouraging fashion; at which she smiled back, and at once acceded to Mr Midgely's request, throwing herself open to his importunity; and in a moment, he had entered heaven – in a movement which seemed to give my friend no distress, for on his beginning those movements which must be familiar even to the tyro, she showed every sign of approbation, reaching down to clasp those somewhat small and delicate white buttocks which rose and fell with a motion as regular as the waves.

By now, Mr Thripp seemed to suggest that he was once more ready for some attention; and indeed with fingers surprisingly tender for one so strong was toying with the lips of my lower mouth, gently parting the hair there, and wriggling so as to bring his tool – now no less lubricated by my saliva than by the liquid signs of his admiration – into juxtaposition with it. Unable to think of any objection to such an ambition, I moved somewhat forward until his instrument lay along the length of my opening, so that parting the lips without entering them, it was as it were lapped by them, meanwhile, dampening my fingers, so stroking and gently kneading it as to provoke low groans of pleasure, then slipping one hand beneath to take his cods in my palm, my index finger meanwhile exploring, below, that most tender area between them and the orifice beneath – when his cries became almost barks of pleasure, while his tool began to jerk in a manner significant of immediate evacuation – which I prevented by grasping it just below the cap and firmly squeezing, which in a moment enabled him to gain control of his emotions.

But now, we were interrupted by a cry, below us, of such a nature as I feared might attract the attention of the ship's crew, at work (no doubt) not far away; and looking down, I saw Mr Midgely's back side thrusting with such energetic wildness as (I could conceive) had brought my friend not once but more than once to that pitch of pleasure which happily, in women, can be provoked in repeated cycles by the attention of a vigorous lover.

This prompted me to offer Mr Thripp at last that satisfaction for which by now he was overdue, and lifting myself upon my knees, I lowered myself upon his still tumescent cock, which through its size (have I remarked before that this was remarkable?) provoked inexpressible feelings of pleasure as it distended that happy ring of flesh which encompassed it, while by moving a little forward I was at the same time able to bring it into contact with the cardinal centre of emotion, against which it moved with a delightful fervour as I raised and lowered myself, while Mr Thripp, eager to convey his satisfaction, explored with eager hands every fleshy surface available to him – slipping them beneath (as I rose) in order to caress the inside of my thighs and buttocks, then (as I fell) conveying them to my breasts, now scarcely less susceptible of delight than my nether regions.

The wave which broke through my body was signalled, no doubt, to him by its contractions; whereupon, thrusting upwards with his arse, he too expired, with (as I felt) a fiery giving forth of essential liquor, and a grip of my upper arms strong enough, as I later discovered, to cause a bruise.

I sank upon him, exhausted, scarcely able to command sufficient energy to lift myself from his body and recline at his side; where, opening my eyes after a while, I met those of Mr Midgely – who, quizzical, lifted an eyebrow in mock surprise; himself satisfied, he had risen and now stood upon a bollard to rest his forearms along the edge of the hatchway, while Frances, more shy, stood a little way off, clutching her dress to her, but nevertheless meeting with a charming impertinence the gaze of Mr Thripp, who though so recently satisfied, like most men could not avert his gaze.

Now that the ecstasy was past, I could not but be conscious of the unwisdom of our situation, for had any sailor ventured, or been dispatched, into the rigging, he could not but have seen us at work; and now that I looked, I could see that indeed one man was at watch in what they term the crow's nest, at the top of the foremast (which, however, was for'ard, or to the front of the vessel, and he was looking in the way the ship was going; so I had hopes had noticed nothing).

However, Mr Thripp and I – and I must now refer to our friends as Dick and St John, for after such familiarity to observe the formal conventions would be ridiculous – quickly descended from our platform to join our friends upon the deck, and the men having arranged some cushions, the four of us lay for a while in the sun, too satiated with pleasure to converse.

I was entirely satisfied by the morning's work – not only in my own enjoyment, after some time, of a passage at arms; but in that my friend had been introduced to the pleasures of congress with a gentleman – for her to have restricted herself to congress with women would have been a shame; and were I to have become the focus of such attentions, 'twould have been extremely tedious, and must have ended in tears.

That Frances had found her experience enjoyable could not be doubted; not that in future she would hesitate to repeat it – for I was amused to see that while I lay in the crook of St John's arm, my head upon his shoulder, she – though in the same attitude, her hair falling upon Dick's shoulders as though it were his own – had allowed her hand to steal upon my lover's thigh, and was almost imperceptibly stroking the black hairs there, and gradually stealing up until the fingers lay upon that crevice between thigh and under-belly – at which his cock, which had lain relaxed and diminished, grew beneath my eyes: not, it is true, to a full stand, but to such an extent that she could not resist laying her hand upon it – at which it bid fair to throw her fingers off by a sudden rearing.

At this point, I met Frances' eyes – who for a moment I believe was prepared for a rebuke; but lowering a single eyebrow, I reassured her, at which she once again began her stroking. Without doubt, St John (lying half-asleep with his eyes closed) had thought it was I who was provoking him, and when, sensuality casting its net once more about his body, he opened those eyes, was astonished to discover the identity of his teaser – and turned to me with just the consternation Frances had shown; but received my wink with the same pleasure, gently raised himself and slipping his arm from beneath my head lifted Frances' hand from its now substantial resting-place, and turning towards her attempted to part her thighs in order to sheath it.

She, however, had other ideas, having observed us; and with a firmness not to be denied pinned him to to the deck, then with a dexterity that was a compliment to her powers of observation, took just such a station as I had displayed (which, while variety is the spice of life, was quite sufficiently pleasing to St John for him not to object to it!).

Meanwhile, Dick, waking from his doze, was astonished at the vision which met him – but fortunately was as disinclined as I to take offence; and meeting my eye, reached out for my hand and pressed a kiss upon its palm – whereat I transferred that palm to another area, and one which immediately reassured me that though a slighter figure than his friend, Dick was not less creditable in virility; at which point, in order to give the occasion some slight variability, I threw up my heels, presenting him with a mark he could not miss – and which, in next to no time, he had pierced with an arrow that straightway took the bull.

Our friends proposed immediately that we should cease to share a cabin with each other, but that we should split into pairs. Not allowing them to reach the stage of discussion who should pair with whom, I immediately disallowed the motions; for as I explained to Frances (when, later, she expressed some disappointment) though nothing could exceed the pleasure of a man's company in bed, when it came to the game – as a sleeping-mate his company was almost always less enjoyable, either from snoring, or pitching and tossing, or from itching, or turning, or commanding every space available – and in the close confines of the shelves or 'bunks' it would be nothing but a pain to accede to what they desired (for nothing would convince me that they would be content to spend their time in their own bunks, once allowed ingress to our cabins).

So it was that for the rest of the voyage we contented ourselves with meeting upon deck, in our secluded corner. We were disturbed by only one person – I found that the child who served as a cabin boy, bringing our food and in general caring for our comfort, was used to observing us from beneath the corner of the awning that hid our part of the deck, for I saw his face peering at us as Dick and I were lying, exhausted, waiting for our friends to conclude their bout, before we repaired for luncheon. Well, little George was no trouble to us – or at least only on one occasion, when discovering me alone in the cabin he attempted a familiarity which I dissuaded him from, for he was only thirteen, and I have never found it necessary to take lovers from the cradle; but I was not unkind, nor did I inform the others, and George spent many happy (and I trust instructive) hours watching us, the frenetic movements of the canvas which concealed him suggesting that he found his own means of relieving any frustration that may have troubled him.

By the time the Atlantic and the Caribbean were crossed, the closest observer would not have suspected that only months before, Frances had never known the pleasure of embracing a lover; indeed, I at one moment found her climbed upon a low piece of rigging and watching the sailors as they bathed in buckets of sea-water hauled up for the purpose. While not able to claim that the view of twenty lusty naked knaves skylarking upon the deck was less than interesting, I was forced to warn her of the complications which would ensue should she have anything to do with any one of them – whereat she reluctantly acquiesced and went in search of whichever of our friends was nearest: for we shared and shared alike, the very difference of temperament and figure proving admirably inviting, so that any suggestion of monotony was never raised.

We were so pleased with the relaxed nature of our daily life that we almost forgot that it must come to an end, and it was with a mixture of pleasure and irritation that, towards the end of one afternoon, we heard a cry from the crow's nest, whence the look-out man announced that the first part of our journey was over; now, we must leave the ship, and traverse the isthmus of Panama.

Chapter Five

The Adventures of Andy

It did not take long to exhaust the pleasures of Cape Town, which – there being no theatre and precious few places of entertainment other than that I have already mentioned – were neither numerous nor remarkable. There were within easy reach of the town, indeed, excellent beaches from which swimming was easy and enjoyable; but when the novelty of this had worn off, together with the pleasure of once more being upon dry land and without the continual chance of storm or danger from the sea, it left me somewhat bored.

However, relief was at hand, for after a week Robert came to me with the news that the sailing of the *Proper Pride* had been delayed by the discovery that some of her timbers had sprung, so that she had had to be laid up for repairs, which would certainly take a se'ennight and possibly longer. He was further at liberty, and wondered whether we might not take the opportunity to see something of the interior of the country.

I was delighted at the prospect, and we immediately made our way to a nearby stables where we hired two admirable steeds, each of which was good (we were assured) for as many miles travel as their riders would be likely to require within the week.

Hearing what we envisaged – that is, an expedition into the country without definite direction or goal – the owner of the stable proposed that we should engage a young man familiar with the country around; for, he said, though in general a peaceful place, there were here and there stretches of land in which robbery and even murder were not entirely unknown.

We happily agreed, and he summoned immediately a young Hottentot called Kenan – his parents being God-fearing Christians, and naming all their children from the Old Testament. Kenny (as we immediately named him) was particularly pleased with this nomenclature, for his Biblical namesake had lived to be 910 years old, a feat which he appeared to believe he could easily equal. He could look forward, then, to almost nine centuries of life, being only fifteen years old – but yet, we were assured, a perfect and intrepid guide.

Our mounts proved lively and mettlesome, and we set out in high spirits, our baggage consisting only of a few blankets and sufficient food and water for a few days – for the people, we were told, were kindly and hospitable, and we would have no difficulty in finding lodging provided we did not get lost (against which contingency Kenny was sufficient insurance).

We took our way through Tygerberg and Reitvalley, Blauberg and Koeberg, then roughly following the line of the Diep River towards Brakfont and Ganzekraal and eventually Groenekloof. The English have made good roads in the immediate neighbourhood of Cape Town and to Simon's Bay; but we soon left them, and plodded through deep sand almost the whole way. No trees, and but few shrubs, adorn the waste, but we noticed many pretty species of heath, and some elegant flowers, unknown to me. The most common plant is the Hottentot fig.

We made easy camps among what bushes we could find, and Kenny insisted on our not tethering the horses but leaving them to seek their supper among the bushes.

This is always done, it seems, when a running stream is in the neighbourhood, or a pool of fresh water. Having lit a fire, the boy spread a mat on the ground, when possible to leeward of a large bush such as the poison-apple, which screened us from wind. Coffee was boiled, of which, with some eggs, cold meat, cakes and milk we made an excellent supper sitting round the fire.

Near Groenekloof the sight of hills afforded us much pleasure, and we were happy to ride into them – low and green hills, where only rabbit holes offered occasional hazard to our horses' hooves. At last, on the fourth day, we came in view of a small poplar wood on the side of a hill, where a stream of clear water gushed down beside the path we were on to fall in a small cascade into a natural rock pool on the far side of which we could see a little cabin. Here, we paused and dismounted, sending Kenny to the cabin to ask permission for us to water our horses.

But as he approached, the door opened (our approach signalled by the barking of a sleek and well-groomed dog tethered in the shade of a tree); and into the sunlight stepped a young woman whose beauty was such that Robert and I could not but exchange glances of unspoken appreciation. Unlike most of the women of the area, she was clearly of northern extraction, her hair (so long that it fell almost to her waist) being almost yellow, shining in the sun; and her face and arms were sufficiently brown to make us suppose that she was not averse to it – as many European women in the country are, who, unless forced to it by the necessity of labour, keep out of it whenever possible, so that their limbs are almost a pasty white.

The young woman greeted us pleasantly, and happily gave us the permission we sought; showing us where we could tether our steeds out of the heat and within reach of a sunken stone trough connected by a runnel to the pool – and inviting us to enter the cabin for some refreshment, which was some excellent home-brewed ale.

Our hostess's name was Mrs van den Heuff – or Helene, as she invited us to address her; she had come to the place with her husband some three years previously, he being sent from Oslo to take charge of a nearby mine.

It must, we remarked, have been a considerable adventure; but was her situation not a lonely one?

'Why,' she replied, 'that is as one makes it. My husband takes me to Cape Town every few months, when I acquire materials for sewing or knitting' – (and indeed the cabin was full of examples of her excellent craftwork) – 'and it is always a pleasure to sketch the countryside and wild life of the place. Yet it is certainly true that I have no near neighbours, and that commerce with others of my station is rare enough.'

We could discern beneath the brave face she put on a wistful memory (as we thought) of the more varied social life of Europe; but said nothing, and drank our beer. It was indeed a pleasure, after some days away from company, to feast our eyes on so charming a female. She was clad in a dress no doubt of her own making – the style plain, though handsomely decorated with embroidery; and I could not but notice, as she sat between me and the single window of the cabin's main room, that it was her only covering, for the material was a thin cotton which revealed her silhouette with utter clarity (something of which Robert was, no doubt, as apprehensive as I).

Mr van den Heuff was, it seemed, occupied at the mine – some three miles distant – by a fall of rock which had obstructed the progress of the diggings, and which she believed would take as much as twenty-four hours to clear. At this, I could not but catch Robert's eye, and was in no doubt that he had caught my thought – that it was not impossible that the lady might welcome a warmer connection with her visitors than the mere exchange of names. But how to come at this? I must confess that I wished Robert miles away – though no further distant, no doubt, than he wished me!

It was by now late afternoon, and the sun was beginning to sink; the air in the room began to cool a little, though it was still sufficiently warm to make it necessary for us, from time to time, to mop our brows.

'Gentlemen,' Mrs van den Heuff said at last, 'at this time of the evening the sun is not dangerous; you might perhaps care to bathe yourselves in our pool? My husband and I use it for the purpose; it is not overlooked. I am happy to make the courtesy of offering it.'

It was a pleasant offer, and we did not hesitate to take it up, plunging in in our shifts and trousers – which no less than ourselves were dusty and stained by the heat of travel. Kenny, awakened from a doze in the shade of the bush, sat up and looked enviously on – being as always careful to make no move without our encouragement, that having been his education; on our signalling to him to join us, he without hesitation threw off his tattered waistcoat and breeches, and dived into the cool depths – the pool at one end being deep enough for this, while at the other the rock rose to two or three feet below the surface, making the place entirely safe and comfortable.

We too, finding our clothes obstructive, and that – as we had been assured – the place was entirely secret, protected on three sides by brush and on the other by the cabin, stripped our wet clothes from us and spread them upon the rock to dry – continuing to gambol like young puppies, enlivened by the coolness and clearness of the water.

I was amused to see that, since we had – when the main glare of the sun was absent – formed the habit of removing our shirts, the upper parts of Robert's body and my own were tanned to a uniform brownness, while below the waist our skins were still white – so that it was as though we wore some tight garment of white silk, though transparent enough to show even the small hairs! Kenny's body, of course, was black – and a deeper black than I had ever seen before, unrelieved by any shading; so that he looked like a deep shadow, leaping and diving and jumping in a permanent silhouette.

Eventually, we had larked enough; and climbing out, lay on the warm, smooth rock – almost too hot, at first, for our bodies; but cooled soon enough by the water dripping from them. There, lulled by the warmth, in a short time we fell asleep, the two of us side by side, while Kenny lay some distance away.

I know not how long I slept, but waking, heard before I opened my eyes a splashing of water the sound of which seemed of a different character than that of the little waterfall at the deep end of the pool. Opening my eyes, I found myself regarding an idyll which any painter would have been pleased to depict: Mrs van den Heuff had come from the cabin and slipped into the pool, where, her hair streaming out about her, she was now floating upon her back.

Her figure, unclothed, was quite as beautiful as I had inferred. Her breasts were perfectly round, no doubt made firm by the coolness of the water; her body, long and slim, was uniformly brown (suggesting that the sun was no stranger to her beauty); her arms and legs handsomely formed, the latter tapered, the trimness of her ankles and calves gradually thickening to thighs plump but strong, between which a muff of yellow accentuated a dark fissure infinitely tempting.

I was lying upon my stomach, a posture of which I was pleased, for my body had not failed to react to the delightfulness of the sight before me, and while the resultant swelling was to some degree uncomfortable, at least it would offer no offence to the lady, should she glance in our direction.

Feeling bound to share my pleasure with Robert, I reached out a cautious hand and by a shrewd pinch awoke him. He lay upon his back, his body relaxed and inert; as he turned his head and met my eyes, I sent a warning glance enjoining silence, but then turning those same eyes, prompted him to look towards the pool. The result almost made me laugh aloud, for in almost as brief a time as it takes to tell, his male part, which had been lying squab and quiescent upon one thigh, stiffened and grew until it lay upon his belly, paying such immediate tribute to the bathing nymph that she would surely have been complimented, had she but seen it!

Ah – but now I realised she had seen it; for on my eyes returning to the pool, they met hers; she had turned from her back, and was now looking directly towards us, merely keeping herself afloat by gentle movements of her arms, her charming breasts just breaking the water and her eyes steadily fixed on our own, while her lips were parted in an enchanting smile.

With a muttered imprecation, Robert turned immediately upon his face, cursing somewhat more loudly as his engorged instrument came into contact with the hard rock. At this, an irresistible laugh was heard, in which we were forced to join – when Helene (as I shall now call her) paddled towards us, and stood in the shallow water, sparkling drops streaming from her body. She then took four steps, and without the least hesitation or apology, lowered herself to the ledge between us – so close that our bodies almost touched.

Her intentions were clear, and if they had not been, were made so by the manner in which she gently laid her hands upon our arses, the fingers conveniently falling just at the point where the separation of the buttocks offered an area of sensitivity so delightful that her feather-like caressing made us stir uncomfortably as our already swollen weapons strove to raise us from our supine positions.

She smiled at this; and seeing it, we had no hesitation in turning – whereat those weapons sprang into the air, offering a salute so vigorous that it expressed all our admiration. Taking the compliment, Helene rose to her knees and began to please us with such careful and sensitive attentions as the most practised whore had never in my experience commanded.

Her left hand upon my breast, her right upon that of my friend, she stroked first our chests, paying charming attention to our paps (the sensitivity of which to a tender caress too many ladies are not apprehensive of), then straying to play with the hairs upon our bellies, and finally – but not too soon – carefully testing the hardness of our throbbing tools, weighing our cods, barely touching the skin of our thighs, which rose into goose-pimples at the touch.

Meanwhile, we could in common courtesy scarcely refrain from paying some attention to our hostess, our own hands moving in parallel over the surface of her body; teasing those apprehensive, thimble-like protuberances which, their pink darkened almost to crimson, stood at the centre of her breasts, then skimming her sides and moving over her thighs – the small muscles of which played charmingly under our fingers, from the effort of supporting her body – and finally reaching that curtain which obscured her sex, where my fingers and my friend's involuntarily met in their mutual, tender testing of the pouting lips, and joined in a search for the knub of delight about which, in concert, they then gently played.

We were as one, too, in reaching down at the same time to seize Helene's hands and remove them from our firing-pieces, lest a premature discharge might have brought proceedings to too speedy an end. She was understanding of this, and no doubt herself wishing to accomplish the final expression of pleasure by something even more agreeable than manual dexterity, threw her leg across my body and in one movement – made easier by a slippery unguent brought down as the result of her former pleasure – embraced my tool to the very hilt; at which I almost fainted with pleasure – opening my eyes only to see that she had guided my friend so that he now stood astride my shoulders, and by the merest inclination of her body, Helene could embrace him with her upper lips in as pleasurable a fashion (I have no doubt) as her lower lips now embraced me.

It now seemed (through what process I know not) as though our three bodies were one body, for my own intense pleasure seemed one with that of my two companions! Of the intensity with which her gently moving loins caressed my own, there could be no doubt; and yet seeing, from a distance of only a few inches, the manner in which she pleasured my friend, it seemed to me that I felt his joy, and that he must feel mine!

As, lifting her body gently, she lifted the lips of her cavity along the length of my prick, so she withdrew her upper lips from that of my friend, leaving behind a shining trail of saliva; as it seemed for a worrying moment that she was about to allow my tool to fall away, so she supported only upon a full lower lip the very tip of my friend's instrument – before, gently closing her upper lip upon it, she pushed the skin away, and when, overcoming the resistance of the ridge about the crown, it fell behind, embraced the velvet cap, now so full as to seem about to burst, with the soft inner surface of her mouth; then – sinking once more upon me – she swallowed Robert's sword, and as the very bones of our secret parts met, her nose buried itself in the bush at the base of his belly, her chin almost knocking against his cods, drawn up now so tightly between his thighs.

It will not surprise the reader to know that it was at almost an identical moment that, as she arched her back in an access of pleasure, I discharged, and my friend – courteously stepping to one side, spent his seed upon the ground. What was more a surprise was an animal howl from the direction of the cabin; and when, glancing that way, I saw a large and hirsute man in an access of rage, I was in no doubt that had polite introductions been a serious prospect, he would have given his name as that of Mr van den Heuff. As it was, however, he contented himself simply with repeating his exclamation of surprise and disapproval before beginning to charge in our direction with an acceleration surprising in one so large.

We were somewhat at a disadvantage, for I was still pinned to the ground by Mrs van den Heuff, while Robert, ridiculously overcome by a sense of shame at his still erect (if speedily shrinking) tool, had turned to one side and was endeavouring to hide himself behind his hands.

Fortunately, one member of the party retained some presence of mind. I had, at one moment of the above engagement, glimpsed Kenny, his eyes a-goggle (the single white things about him), sitting with his back against a tree, watching us with keen attention, but only able to participate in events to the extent of certain manual manipulations of his hidden person. Now, however, he seemed to move in a flash; and fell to the ground in the path of the charging Dane – who stumbled over his body and fell full-length into the pool.

We could have stayed to discuss the matter; we might

even – being two, or perhaps three, to one – have subdued him. But either course would have led to embarrassments, and neglecting the lady (who, if we thought of her at all, we considered perfectly able to explain herself – if, indeed, explanations were not superfluous) were in a moment upon our steeds (which had been cropping the grass contentedly without interest in the copulatory activities of their masters) and away.

It was not a dignified retreat: I was the best horseman of the three, but even I found it moderately difficult to maintain my seat while galloping over rough country on a steed as naked as I (for we had of course unsaddled our horses, and had had no time to resume our own clothes). Robert had hold of the mane with one hand, and with the other was sawing the air wildly, altogether having the air of someone who would much rather be looking to a tops'l in a gale than in the position in which he found himself; while Kenny had simply thrown himself full length along the back of his mount, both hands entwined in her mane, his body knocking so hard against the beast's back that I feared for the preservation of his generative organs.

In a while, it became clear that the Dane had not given chase, there being no sign of dust anywhere behind us. As to the reason, we could only conjecture: perhaps his mount had been too exhausted after a day's riding to be capable of catching us; or perhaps he had injured himself in his fall. At any event, we were relieved to be able to bring our careering chase to its end, and almost fell off our mounts – Robert clutching at his loins, which were sore from the unaccustomed contact with his horse's back.

We were forced to smile at our appearance: our bodies, lathered with sweat (no less from our recent ride than from the previous amorous combat) were now stuck all over with reddish dust, which on our rubbing at it became a sort of mud, so that we looked like peculiarly dishevelled Red Indians.

We lost no time in thanking Kenny for his part in our escape, which he received with relief, apparently fearing that we would be angered that he should have watched our congress with Helene; yet who could have expected an inexperienced boy – for he was little more – to avert his eyes from so interesting a spectacle?

Our good humour was somewhat dampened by his obviously appearing worried, and when we enquired as to the reason, he pointed out what we had been too relieved at our escape to remember: that we were set naked in open country, with not so much as a blanket between us, and the only house anywhere nearby that of a man who must be supposed to be our inveterate enemy. We were also weaponless, and I was somewhat apprehensive of beasts – for I had heard that in Africa were to be found lion and tiger, leopard and wolf, as well as jackal and wild dog (though I did not enquire which might occupy this region, and might be dangerous to us – but the night makes such anxieties keener than in the bright light of day).

'There is but one thing for it,' said Robert at last. 'One of us must return and attempt to recover our belongings.'

I was forced to agree, though the prospect was not an inviting one; for surely Mr van den Heuff would have placed all our things within the confines of the cabin, no doubt expecting us to return for them, his advantage enabling him to lay an ambush which it would be impossible to avoid.

Rather than waiting until the absolute middle of the night, we decided to retrace our steps immediately – happily for us the blackness alleviated by the light of a full moon. That this was equally happy for our enemy, who would be the more easily enabled to see our approach, we were entirely aware.

We had ridden, in our panic, rather further than we had supposed, and it took us almost an hour before we came in sight of the cabin, making our way around it at a discreet distance until the clump of trees which hid the pool also protected us from the sight of anyone within the house (which in any event had no window overlooking the pool, whether from modesty or chance I cannot say).

Tethering the horses to a rocky outcrop some quarter of a mile away we made our way cautiously towards the place, at once distressed by the sharpness of the ground to our unprotected feet (though Kenny trod happily enough) and comforted by the fact that though naked – and already beginning to shiver from the coolness of the night air – the red dust still plastered over our bodies somewhat disguised them, for it was the very colour of the earth we trod.

Peering from the undergrowth, we were eventually able to look across the pool to the cabin, about which there was no sign of movement. Setting Kenny to watch for any movement (on which he was to signal by a whistle), Robert and I skirted the edge of the pool and came to the back of the cabin; then, upon all fours, crawled around its side until we were beneath a window from which a light could be discerned, burning within. It was just at this moment that we heard a strange crack, followed by a stifled cry.

With the utmost care, we raised ourselves until we could look over the sill of the window.

What a sight met our horrified eyes! With his back to us stood the enormous Dane, now stripped to the waist and showing a musculature animal-like in its strength. Facing him, hanging by arms tethered by ropes to a beam, hung the naked body of his wife, her ankles also secured by ropes – one to a large chest, the other to a heavy bench, so that her legs were stretched wide apart, and her whole body open like a huge X, entirely defence-less. From the Dane's right hand hung a rawhide whip, its end lying upon the boards of the floor; and across Helene's body, traced from below the left shoulder across the lower breast and belly to end at the top of the right thigh, lay a thin red line, which here and there began to ooze blood. Her eyes, staring, may or may not have seen us – for their single attribute was fear; and she was denied even the feeble solace of shrieking, for between her lips had been thrust a pad of some material or other, secured in place by twine.

As we watched, the Dane raised his right hand again. The whip was held over his shoulder, its length hanging down behind his back; with an insolent deliberation, he brought his arm back, then swept it forward. The lash fell again upon our friend's defenceless body; that same muffled cry was forced through her gag, while another red line was scored this time from her right shoulder, crossing the former stroke at the top of her belly.

I do not think that either Robert or I knew what we were doing, for next, I was conscious merely of the sound of broken glass – one or other of us (and we never knew which) had seized a small rock from the ground and hurled it at the window, breaking in one of the panes.

The noise, no less than the Dane's furious stare as he turned, brought us to our senses. In a moment, he made for the door, seizing a pistol from a table as he passed. Robert and I broke away, he making around the cabin while I leaped several rocks, finally cowering behind one big enough to shelter me.

I dared not move as I heard the Dane break through

the bushes at the side of the cabin; then there was an explosion which – from the lack of any bullet landing nearby – I took to signal his firing at Robert. Knowing his weapon would hold but two charges, I cautiously peered round the top of the rock, and seeing van den Heuff looking away from me, took a stone and hurled it in his direction. He was, I am happy to say, foolish or angry enough to turn and fire immediately in the direction of the sound; then for a moment stopped, conscious no doubt that he had exhausted his weapon – for he threw it to the ground with an imprecation.

Robert evidently came to the same conclusion as I: that we must show ourselves now, for the Dane must not be permitted to return to the cabin, and there to recharge his weapon. We both broke from cover at the same time.

Van den Heuff was, I believe, confused at the sight. He could have been in no doubt, when he first set eyes upon us, as to what we were: two pale-skinned strangers, probably effete and unaccustomed to combat. Here, however, was a very different sight: two naked savages, liberally daubed with war-paint, and no doubt – as a result of our mingled fear, anger and determination – as wild in the eyes as about the body.

At all events, he stood still for a moment too long, so that Robert, who was nearest him, was able to throw himself at full-length upon him, butting him heavily in the stomach. This must have been hard as iron, for he barely staggered; and in one movement, picked up my unfortunate comrade and threw him upon the ground – only his landing in the midst of a bush preventing the inevitable breaking of several bones.

This gave me seriously to think, and rather than following Robert in precipitate attack, I circled around the man, looking for some weapon with which I could face him – some neglected iron bar, for instance, negligently dropped. No such thing presented itself; and with an awful deliberation, van den Heuff now began to pace slowly towards me – who stood with my back to the pool, and only with precipitate withdrawal as a possible manoeuvre, which I was determined (through pride) not to employ. Robert was still shakily extricating himself from the bush as the Dane came to within a few feet of me, his great hands like shovels, now raised . . .

Then came the most extraordinary sound from one side of us: a sort of banshee yell which sent a shiver through my frame, and even disconcerted my enemy – disconcerted him sufficiently to cause him to take his eyes off me for a moment; when I threw myself at his feet and clutched one of his legs, bent on toppling him to the ground. Instead, I felt myself lifted as though by the trunk of an elephant; yet maintained my grip, and by dint of a great wriggle managed to get the man off balance – who, as he was tottering, suddenly let out a grunt, and fell like a giant tree to the ground, where he lay still.

Looking up in amazement, I saw only the slender body of Kenny standing over us; but on the ground at his feet, a large shovel, the working end of which, I assumed, had made contact with Mr van den Heuff's head.

I lost no time in tying the man up with some rope which Kenny fetched – he being extremely relieved when I reassured him that his prey was not dead, but simply stunned. He was still at the edge of panic, for, he said, should it be known that a black boy had struck down a white man, his fate would be death. At this, I told him at all costs to stay out of van den Heuff's sight, in case he should recover sufficiently to identify him (his former glimpse having been, as I was assured, sufficiently brief to make this impossible).

Meanwhile, with Robert – now, however shakily, back upon his feet – I entered the cabin, and there –

Robert supporting her body while I cut the bonds – we released Helene, and Robert (whose years at sea had occasionally required the employment of slight medical knowledge) dampened a cloth with water, and carefully bathed the raw stripes which crisscrossed her body, before helping her to clothe herself in a simple shift.

There was no need for explanation. It was clearly impossible that she should remain with van den Heuff; and I lost no time in trying to persuade her to escape with us. Yet she declined, and the more we pressed it, the more complete was her refusal. How could she leave her husband, bound, to die? she asked (for it would be some days before anyone would think of coming to the cabin, and in that time the heat would make death certain through lack of water).

But what of herself? we asked. To which at first she replied merely with a shrug – but, being pressed, admitted at last that the situation was not as desperate as we supposed, for we had not been the first gentlemen she had entertained. On the first occasion, her husband had been guilty almost of murdering the man – but then had turned his attention to her, whereupon she had realised that the stripes which he had inflicted upon her in themselves constituted an excitement almost as fierce as the act for which they were a punishment – while Mr van den Heuff, who she insisted was only upon provocation violent to any extreme, himself derived entertainment from beating her, which was an action he never brought to such a pitch that it endangered life.

I was not confident of the truth of this, and neither was Robert – having received sufficiently rough entertainment; however, we were forced to acquiesce in her remaining behind. Yet she insisted on fetching water and helping us to bathe ourselves, even summoning Kenny, for whom she performed the same office. While the excitement of the evening's activities, together with our former enjoyment, rendered us almost impervious to the prospect of bodily pleasure, and even Helene's careful attention to that part of Robert's body rendered tender by the action of his bareback ride (upon his horse, I mean) evoked no carnal response, Kenny's younger body offered no such resistance, and a tool of remarkable, even enviable size, raised itself during the lady's bathing of his body; at which she could scarcely, as it seemed to us, refrain from offering to perform for him the same service as she had rendered Robert, positively licking her lips; but upon seeing our surprise, refrained (if not, I believe, without some regret) from any familiarity other than being particularly careful in cleansing the aforesaid implement – showing so much care, indeed, that poor Kenny's eyes almost started from his head in his efforts to contain his emotion.

Mr van den Heuff was stirring and groaning when we returned to him, so that Robert was forced to strike him once more in order to render him insensible while we dragged him within. We then loosely tied Helene and laid her beside him; the plan being that, when he recovered his senses, she should after a while – allowing us time to escape from the area – loosen her bonds and release her husband.

We bade the lady a not especially loving farewell, our attitude to her being now a mixture of admiration for her physical appetite and a certain disapproval of her conduct (for even moralists as relatively free from inhibition as we could not but reprehend her behaviour). We then rode – properly clothed and with our beasts once more saddled – for twelve hours without stopping, which placed us within half a day's ride of Cape Town, and therefore, we trusted, beyond Mr van den Heuff's reach.

Back in town, we returned the horses; discovering

from a note at my lodgings that the *Proper Pride* was now repaired and ready to sail on the tide, the following day. Kenny, hearing us talk of this, became thoughtful; and later approached us with the plea that he be allowed to come with us as our personal servant, not only relishing possible adventure, but clearly worried that Mr van den Heuff might find him out, when his fate would indeed be a dreadful one.

In short, while it was impossible that an officer of the ship should employ a personal servant (especially a black boy, for I cannot avoid reporting that there is some prejudice against the race among many of the men and even some of the officers of HM Navy) there was nothing to prevent my engaging the lad; and moreover we both felt under a distinct obligation to him for saving us not once, but twice, from probable injury and possible death. I thus engaged with his master, at the stables, and for a sum equivalent to ten shillings became his owner, body and soul, and setting up a small hammock for him in the corner of my already confined quarters, began to teach him those few offices which would make him useful as a personal servant – which, he being bright, cheerful and willing, he was in a very few weeks complete master of.

Chapter Six

Sophie's Story

Upon our arrival at Chagres we immediately made ready for our journey across the isthmus, by land as well as by water, to Panama, where the schooner *Sulphur*, of one hundred and nine tons, was awaiting us. Our baggage was first landed, and before dark re-stowed in a *bongo*, or canoe hollowed out from a single cedar tree, some eighty feet in length and eight feet wide at the stern; this was calculated to carry seventy bales of one hundred and twenty pounds each, and was fitted with arched thatch abaft, and capable of accommodating six passengers – but on this occasion there were only Frances and myself, together with a young surgeon, Dr Stephen Nadge, with Dick and St John, who were much concerned with the safety of their provisions of paper, writing and drawing instruments, and scientific instruments for measurement.

A canoe of our size is generally reckoned to reach Gorgona in sixteen or eighteen hours, and Panama in a further nine, if daylight favours; but this can only be performed by an European, for the natives will take their time in order to increase the sum they may charge for the journey (which is by the hour, and amounts often to as much as eighty-five dollars, and more during the rainy season).

Even during the dry season – when we were travelling – there are delays to large or heavily-laden canoes, from 'rapids' or grounding, which is tedious as much as dangerous. No danger exists in point of highway or sea robbery, and the people in general may be trusted with large sums of money. Part of my baggage, indeed, was missing for eight or ten days, but without apprehension on the part of the residents at Panama, who affirmed that 'it must be safe' – and so it proved, having been delayed by the breaking down of the mules! It was eventually borne to me on the heads of men. One package weighed one hundred and seventy-six pounds!

As our passage was not to commence until dawn, we took up our quarters in a house provided by an Englishman, with the intention of enjoying a preliminary nap – the last we expected on this side of Panama. However, we were disappointed in this, as the whole village assembled nearly beneath our windows and maintained a constant succession of native songs and dancing, accompanied by very discordant music, until dawn, when they dispersed, and we embarked.

The surgeon, Dr Nadge, was a man whose acquaintance I had not had the pleasure of, since he had stayed during the voyage firmly with the crew. He was a young gentleman of perhaps twenty summers, evidently very recently qualified in medicine, with somewhat serious, large, pale eyes peering through thick spectacles – peering at everything in view, as though he expected even inanimate objects in so foreign a place to be endowed with the property of poisoning anyone who came near them.

We quitted the bank, and notwithstanding our ill-founded suspicions, very soon enjoyed a most comfortable sleep under our awning, formed by a thatch of palm leaves covered finally by a painted canvas. Our crew consisted of a *padron* or leader and five rowers, their rate of pay on these occasions being five *reals* each, or two shillings and sixpence *per diem*. Although the cost of this canoe was eighty-five dollars, the return charge, waiting twenty-four hours, was only ten. Any delay beyond twenty-four hours entails a charge of five *reals* a day per man.

Our journey began at a rather slow rate; the men perhaps had not lately worked together, or possibly were fatigued by their dancing exertions of the previous night. They were for the most part very handsome specimens, and I was not surprised when on our stopping at Gatun, about eleven miles from Chagres, to allow them to dine, and where their wives resided, they all vanished, and it was not without much difficulty and by the exertion of the *padron* that they were extricated from connubial embraces and returned to their oars; whereat one man in particular exhibited much sulkiness and ill-humour. On my enquiring the cause, it proved that his wife had been absent from the village, and that therefore he had not had the opportunity of employing her for the purpose he desired.

At about 3 p.m. we moved on, and at sunset came to for the night at a sandy beach, where our crew commenced their culinary operations, having provided themselves with rice and ripe coconuts at Chagres. The coconut, having been grated finely using one of nature's provisions on the banks of the river (i.e. the stem of a plant very closely studded with fine spines), is put into an iron pot, mixed with a small portion of water, and boiled until it becomes milky. It is then strained by another of Dame Nature's utensils, viz. a sieve made of the *Gorgonia flabellum*, or Venus's Fan, and the remains finally squeezed by hand. The milky fluid is boiled with rice, and affords, with the addition of sugar and rice, a very palatable mess.

We were not without music this night, the frogs maintaining a concert in imitation of our friends at Chagres.

Dr Nadge, enquiring what caused the noise, and being answered *serpo* – a term applied to frogs here – thinking it meant a snake, was rather shy of the shore for a time.

Alas, the coconut did not settle well upon my stomach, and soon after retiring to rest I was seized by severe cramps; which Frances thought ill of, and insisted upon sending for Dr Nadge. The young man, appearing, invited her to leave the tent which we shared, so that he could examine me. I explained that I was determined upon my discomfort being merely the product of indigestion, but from one purpose or another he was firm that he should make a full exploration, first pressing my stomach through my dress, then asking me to remove it – which without hesitation (for it is improper to be over-modest in certain circumstances) I did – revealing, of course, my entire body, which he seemed to regard with some admiration, for he held the lamp aloft in his left hand the better to see, while passing his other hand over every surface available to him, including my breasts, asking whether they were sore, and on my replying in the negative nevertheless slightly pinching and squeezing them in order 'to ensure that there was no tenderness.'

I was pretty sure by now that his examination was as much motivated by the warmth of his male feelings as by any medical intelligence; and indeed the pain had now ceased, at which, when I told him, he seemed somewhat disappointed. Nevertheless, 'I am pleased, Mrs Nelham, at that,' he said, 'though it relieves me of the pleasure of regarding one of the most perfect specimens of female beauty it has ever been my privilege to examine. I have dissected many corpses of about your size, ma'am, and . . .'

I interrupted him with an 'Ahem!', at which he excused himself – but proceeding: 'Forgive me – it is merely that my experience outside the dissecting theatre has not prepared me for the sight of so perfect a specimen! If I may say so, the entire appearance of the mammary glands approaches the ideal as far any student could expect to experience it, while the weight and texture' (here he placed his hand upon the underside of my left breast, weighing it as 'twere a pumpkin) 'is of an equally satisfactory nature. The nodules of the aureola, while not darkened as in the condition of pregnancy, are sufficiently rough to the touch' (here he grazed my nipple with his forefinger) 'to assure me that lactation would be plentiful, while the speedy erection of the tissue upon being stimulated' (trembling a fingernail at the tip) 'reveals that the involuntary muscles are in order.'

I could not but note that his eyes turned next to that area of my person which there could be no excuse for examining – no excuse that is, except that which came readily to the lips of a young man in search of knowledge.

'If you will permit me to remark,' he continued, 'even a cursory glance reveals the beautifully shaped and protruding *labia majora*, so often disfigured in woman by an excess of hair; in your case – if you will permit,' – and he here moved one of my legs aside in order to permit himself, bending and holding the lamp nearer, a closer view – 'the growth is handsomely decorative without being obstructive, and indeed the charming gap between the lips (sometimes too firmly closed) is what the textbooks remark upon as desirable but relatively rare.'

The reader may wonder why I permitted such familiarity; yet the young man was a doctor, and his encomiums of my person were so flattering as to persuade me to allow him to continue to praise it!

'Upon parting the lips,' he then went on, setting the lamp on the floor in order the better to see what he was about – and to free his second hand in order to perform the action of which he spoke – 'the *labia minora* are seen to be equally perfect in form, barely hidden by their larger sisters, and at the back fused, if I am not mistaken' (inserting here a forefinger) 'yes – to form the most delightfully constructed *fourchette*.

'I note,' he continued – as, despite myself, I began to feel a certain pleasure at his delicate probing – 'that even such an examination as this, conducted, I assure you, without the least inclination towards the carnal, encourages the blood vessels to do their work efficiently, and engorge the inner lips sufficiently to . . .' But here, he blushed, and broke off – then recovering himself to continue:

'I note that the upper lips of the *labia minora* are not capable entirely of concealing the clitoris, which in this case is also unobstructed by a prepuce – something which' (and his colour rose again, yet he continued) 'I believe is of advantage to women in the matrimonial act. May I ask if this motion is in any way dulled or lacking in sensation?' – he gently moved his finger in a remarkably sensual and enchanting manner, so that I positively wriggled with pleasure.

'I see that it is not,' he said. 'That is most satisfactory, and what I would expect.'

To my amazement, he now stood up, and taking a piece of cloth from his medical case, placed some spirit upon it and cleansed his hands. His tight, white trousers would have revealed perfectly plainly to me any evidence of his arousal. There was none. If I had been flattering myself that his admiration was more than medical, I had been mistaken.

'I am pleased that you are recovered, ma'am,' he said; 'please do not hesitate to regard me as at your command should you in future require assistance of any kind.'

At which he bowed, and withdrew.

On Frances now entering to enquire after my health, I

was, I fear, somewhat sharp with her; and later in the night, when everyone else had fallen into a heavy slumber, I slunk from my tent and made my way to that of our two friends, where I aroused Dick, and pulling him half-protesting from his bed, persuaded him to gratify those feelings which had been aroused by Dr Nadge's arousing but cool actions. One day, I promised myself, that young man should requite me.

At dawn we breakfasted, and then re-commenced our journey with more spirit. At this stage the oars were replaced by long poles shod with iron, similar to those used in our Cambridge punts. A platform consisting of a single plank on each side of the canoe enabled the men to walk about fifteen feet forwards, and with the pole to the shoulder walking aft maintain a rate equal to about two miles per hour against the stream.

Our progress this second day afforded us little variety of amusement save in the appearance of a few alligators and iguanas. Some of the latter were taken by our crew. The eggs of the iguana are much esteemed – every house has strings of them hung up to dry; the children eat them; after which, having filled them with air, they explode them by a blow of the hand, in mock contention, causing a very sharp retort. They are similar to those of the tortoise or turtle, but in size not exceeding those of the pigeon.

The second night we passed in our canoe. The work of the following day became more tedious, owing to the drought which had lowered the level of the river, which frequently compelled us to land. On one occasion, our passage was for some time obstructed by a large tree which had fallen across the stream at its most rapid point. Fortunately, in its fall it had broken away much of the bank, through which the stream, impeded in its former course, had forced a channel, and we effected our passage by this new cut, after some little dexterity on the part of the boatmen, aided by the exertions of the male passengers.

It was on one of the forays ashore that Frances unfortunately ran a thorn into her foot; and one of the crew – the somewhat sullen man who had missed his wife at Gatun – was told to help her; which he did by bending and inviting her to hoist her skirts and sit astride his shoulders, whereupon he stood and carried her easily – though with some damage to her hair from the lower branches of trees. I could not but observe that his hands, at first clutching her thighs above her dress, soon disappeared beneath it – with the comic result that the skirts fell over his shoulders and down his back and sides, and it appeared from the back that Frances was a tall, thin woman of some ten feet in height! The native was now holding her by her naked thighs, and his expression became considerably less sullen, while Frances's similarly appeared sanguine in the extreme, reminding me that the opportunity for sensual enjoyment frequently presented itself under the most impertinent circumstances.

About sunset we got sight of Gorgona, and were shortly afterwards housed for the night; the next day there was some delay in our starting, due to Dr Nadge discovering some plant in the area which he assured us would be valuable in his medical studies, and which he insisted on searching for in quantity for some hours before (after some persuasion) ill-temperedly agreeing to make do with the examples he had by then gathered.

The next thing was that a party from the *Sulphur*, which had been ordered to meet us here, was by the mistake of a guide taken to Cruces, missing us entirely. And then, shortly before sunset, we lost our guide and fell into the wrong road, eventually meeting with shelter for the night where nothing else could be obtained. However, in the morning, by the assistance of a peasant, we were enabled to reach the main road, and about two that evening arrived at Panama.

This city was formerly a place of some note, but about a century ago may have been said to have arrived at its zenith. The remains of the buildings evince wealth, and afford some idea of the extent to which they hoped to carry their improvements. But they are now fast falling into decay. The port is seldom visited by vessels of any size, and the fortifications, which originally were admirably constructed, are rapidly following the fate of the houses. The population is chiefly a mixed race; few Spaniards are to be found. One Englishman, and the American consular agent, comprised all the society we met.

Within three days, we were all settled on board the *Sulphur*, and sailed for a group of islands in the north Pacific which comprise an area of some six thousand square miles, the largest island of which, Hawaii, has an area of over four thousand. Here are some of the world's largest volcanoes, one of which, Kilauea, on Hawaii, has a crater some two miles across, and still smokes regularly, with occasionally a display of pyrotechnics.

Our voyage having passed most pleasantly, it was with some anticipation that we went upon deck at daylight to observe the island as we approached it – heavy clouds alas capping the summits of the remarkable peaks and precluding a clear view. Then came heavy rain; but this offered a remarkable decoration to the view, the numerous cascades resulting from it affording us a very interesting embellishment to the lower scenery, which we were passing within three or four miles. The numerous silver threads of fresh water, sportively displayed, must be seen to be enjoyed! No description can convey the idea of their number and variety, and a sketch including twenty waterfalls within one or two hundred yards would appear almost a burlesque; yet such was the fact.

We steered for Oahu, the island which contains the bulk of the population and the capital; and anchoring, the pilot's boat came off, the pilot being drunk; and on the morning following we went ashore, and Dick and St John set about their work – which meant that Frances and myself were thrown upon our own resources.

I was surprised to hear that the island is ruled by a woman – a virtual queen, Kinau; to whom we sent a message asking whether we could pay our homage, receiving in reply a courteous letter:

'To Mrs Sophia Nelham, in care of the sloop *Sulphur*: Salutation to you, Mrs Nelham, of the British vessel, the stranger beloved. I have received your letter, and I give my consent to your request to visit me.'

This was delivered by a native clad in a scarlet jacket, who offered to convey us that afternoon to the 'palace', where we were assured hospitality would be offered for as long as we cared to remain. We therefore took a package of necessaries, and set off upon horseback, in a little more than an hour reaching a stockade or enclosure within which was a number of large, thatched buildings. On seeing us in the distance, there was a great stir; and when we entered through the gateway it was to find a veritable guard of honour, consisting of militia to the number of over a hundred, all well clad in white uniforms, and forming two ranks through which we passed, nodding and smiling. At the end of this ceremonial avenue stood a body of the Queen's personal guard, remarkably handsome men in scarlet jackets, some few with epaulettes, tinsel, et cetera, their swords raised in homage.

We dismounted and were greeted by the commander

of this guard, who led us then into one of the largest houses or huts, at the entrance of which stood a large native bearing the *kahili* or feathered plume and badge of royalty – constructed of the dark tail-feathers of the cock, resembling somewhat the feathers worn by our regimental bands, but of much greater size – the plume and pole being about eighteen feet long, the plume almost five feet in diameter.

Queen Kinau was a large lady of uncertain years, whom no-one could call especially beautiful, though a flatterer might I suppose refer to her as handsome; she was tall, and of full figure, and her breasts – uncovered, as is the fashion here – were of such dimensions that they must surely be an embarrassment to her in any quick movement.

She had considerable *gravitas*, and on our making deep obeisance, raised us to our feet and greeted us with courtesy, offering us a ceremonial drink (made from I know not what) and some small cakes with the consistency of baked mud, and a taste which may resemble that of such a delicacy!

The Queen spoke only indifferent English, her conversation being restricted to enquiries about the health of Brother King – which we took to mean His Majesty, and answered with reassurances that he, like Her Majesty, would doubtless live for ever.

We were then conducted to a feast, which consisted in part of dubious foodstuffs which we treated with respect, but also of fine roast pork and other meats which were a pleasure to palates too used to salted beef.

By the time the feast had been concluded, and the last of a number of dances (performed by young women of the court) had been concluded, Queen Kinau rose, and took Frances and me by the hand, leading us from the banqueting-house and towards another smaller hall which I presumed contained our sleeping quarters. However, on the curtains at the entrance being drawn so that we could enter, we found ourselves in a large room lit by firelight, upon the floor of which rush matting was laid, with, here and there, piles of rugs, and in the centre a larger pile, at which the Queen gestured with the words: 'Rest you happy.'

We would have expressed our gratitude, had we not been surprised by the fact that the hall was not otherwise empty, but that around its walls stood perhaps a dozen motionless figures, like statues in dark wood – statues of naked males, whose breasts upon close examination could be seen to rise and fall.

The Queen now gestured at these gentlemen, then at us, stretching out her hand, palm upwards, as though she were offering us a gift.

We were uncertain as to our course. Frances whispered softly into my ear, 'Can she mean . . .?' – but Her Majesty must have inferred our doubt, for with a quick gesture she summoned to her side an elderly gentleman whose command of English – while less than perfect – was greater than her own, and of whom she had made use occasionally as interpreter. She spoke sharply to him, who turned then to us with:

'Mrs Queen make offer you take for comfort one brother for night.'

We could not but raise our eyebrows at this; while it would be interesting to be able to report, in England, that I had been the lover of so close a relative of a Queen, I knew not what the diplomatic consequence might be. However, it quickly occurred to me that the word 'brother' was probably an euphemism, and that the men were in fact members of the royal harem (if one may so describe a collection of males).

The Queen was by now becoming somewhat impatient,

and taking Frances by the arm, drew her towards one of the young men, tapping him familiarly upon the breast, smacking his arms and sides, and finally with the gesture of a butcher commending a special joint, reaching out to lift upon the palm of one large hand a personal appliance which though pliant was impressively imposing. Her Majesty then took my friend's hand and closed it upon her own, trapping between the two palms the young man's prick (he, meanwhile, showing no sign of emotion) – and nodded her head towards the pile of rugs at the centre of the hall; whereupon Frances could do nothing but acquiesce in what was more an instruction than a suggestion, and repaired thither, nervously clutching her companion by that part of his anatomy with which the Queen had acquainted her.

It was clear to me that I must follow her example if the Queen was not to be offended, and since there was nothing to choose, as far as I could see, between the gentlemen of the bedchamber (if I may so describe them), went up to the nearest, and – following the example shown me – took him by the appropriate handle and led him, too, to the centre of the room, where I sank to the ground beside my friend.

The Queen was clearly pleased, smiling and nodding; and now spoke again to her elderly courtier, who stepping forward remarked: 'When finished they,' (gesturing at our two companions) 'continue those' (gesturing at the other young men, who remained motionless at their posts). The Queen then swept past us to the door, pausing thoughtfully only at the last moment, and as though in an afterthought reaching out to the man nearest her, and persuading him by the grip of her strong right hand to follow her outside.

So we now found ourselves on a sort of platform, viewed in flickering firelight by a number of Hawaiian gentlemen who stood stiff as guardsmen about the walls, and by two somewhat closer. I must confess that I would have been more dismayed if it had not been clear that Her Majesty had the pick of young manhood for her court – for if in the dim light at the periphery of the hall the young men appeared sufficiently handsome, our two particular friends, now more brightly illuminated, had forms which would be envied by any European – evidently trained to a degree of athleticism, their limbs were well-muscled, their shoulders broad, their hips narrow; and I could not but remark that, while still in repose, their personal parts resembled those of the darker, African race, in that they were particularly large – almost of the thickness of my own wrist.

Frances had clearly noted this, for her eyes were a-goggle; I presumed she had not previously seen an unclad man of colour, and therefore shared the apprehension which I must confess had been my own reaction on setting eyes on one – that any attempt on his part at carnality would split me wide open! However, I knew that it is a characteristic of the native races that when engorged, their instruments gain in strength but not in size; were it not otherwise – were they to swell in proportion to their unexcited size, as our European lovers do, the prospect would indeed be more frightening than delightful.

I whispered a word of encouragement and reassurance, and then, standing, removed my dress – for it was clear that it would be in the highest degree improper and insulting were we to scorn the Queen's gift.

I was amused to see that the discipline which kept the young men at their posts was not unbreakable; presumably the sight of my body was the first they had had of an unclad European – and that they admired it was clear not only from the shining of their eyes, but the stirring not of their arms or legs, but of that part of them incapable of not complimenting a beautiful woman; and when Frances, though still with diffidence, followed my example, I wondered whether the sight of two such wonders (as we were to them) would not entirely shake their discipline!

However, it was our two more intimate companions with whom we were chiefly concerned, and that they were as interested in our appearance as their colleagues was clear from the closeness with which they now began to examine us: persuading us to lie upon the rugs, and themselves kneeling at our sides – but confining their examination to the visual. I must confess that the picture which met our own eyes was not unpleasant. My reader may find it difficult to believe that two ladies could regard with equanimity the prospect of lying unclad within the view of a collection of savages, with two of whom some carnal connection was to be expected; yet the men concerned were by no means unhandsome, nor to the least degree (as far as we could apprehend) uncivilised; and the firelight glinting upon the velvety surface of light brown skins, and the evident admiring interest shown in our own persons, contributed to an atmosphere not in the least degree frightening.

However, after a while I began to wonder whether the night was to be spent in mere mutual admiration, for our two attendants, while continuing to feast their eyes upon us, refrained from any movement towards us; so that Frances whispered, 'Will they never begin?' – being clearly eager for action.

It then occurred to me that it might be courtesy that caused our attendants to remain at a distance. To test the theory, I stretched out my hand and placed it upon the thigh of the young man who still crouched at my side. His response was immediate, in lifting his own hand and placing it upon my thigh, in precise juxtaposition; while on my sliding my palm upwards to his groin, he did the same; and as my fingers met the wiry black hairs at the base of his gadget, so his own paused admiringly at my own muff, before beginning to stroke with a most tender and ingratiating application the area most of interest to him.

Frances, observing this, did not long delay to follow my example, and soon joined her fingers – with difficulty – about the circumference of her admirer's tool, finding with satisfaction that while it still hung pendant, it was of the obduracy of hardwood, and without doubt capable of anything she might hope of it.

There was still, however, some delay; for stretch out our limbs as we might, while our putative lovers were delighted to explore with their fingers what they found, they made no attempt to approach us in the way of congress – though as we caressed them, they clearly grew more and more excited, even to trembling – until my friend's companion, driven as it seemed to an extremity, suddenly seized her by the hips, and in one motion lifted and turned her so that she presented her rump towards him – whereupon without further ado he plunged into her from the rear, so that she cried out at first in surprise and even some pain, but then in increasing pleasure.

I remembered at this point what I had been told by a gentleman of colour who had been employed in a house of resort for ladies which I have described in another place* – that he remembered his father telling him that at home in his native country, only one posture of mating was known, which resembled that of those animals of nature incapable of contriving any other. So without prompting, I adopted the position accepted by my friend, whereupon I immediately was penetrated by the ready weapon of my admirer, which I must admit had a

*Eros in Town

fullness and amplitude equal to any I have experienced elsewhere.

Our admirers were so ready for the fray, so much reduced by their former frustration to a state of expectancy, that our conflict did not last long, for they exhausted their power in only a few minutes. The result was that neither Frances nor I were satisfied, and on our men withdrawing and without much ceremony taking themselves off, we looked at each other in some confusion. However, remembering the words of the Queen's interpreter, I reminded my friend that we were invited, if we wished, to exhaust the capabilities of any or all of the gentlemen before us – and in a moment we had chosen two more, and brought them into the centre of the room, they being not at all disinclined to explore at closer quarters ladies of flesh so invitingly different in colour and texture to that of their own women – and, as far as I had been able to observe, bodies considerably less heavy and unwieldy.

They began at a very early stage to hint that they wished to enjoy the strange fruit; but as I remarked to Frances, it was surely incumbent upon us to educate as well as delight them, and this time we resisted their attempts to turn us onto all fours, instead remaining firmly upon our backs, our thighs stretched invitingly apart – which only seemed to them an invitation to observe us, or at the most to examine with their fingers those parts they so clearly wished to occupy with their very ready pricks.

At last, since they were so clearly at a loss, I reached up to mine, and taking his instrument firmly in my hand, exerted a steady pull which drew him towards me – his face a picture of perplexity, for he clearly did not understand what could follow. At last, balanced as he was at my side and upon the balls of his feet, he lost his balance, and fell upon me, his lower body happily approximating to mine. The unfamiliar sensation of the whole length of his body being pressed against my own was clearly not unpleasant to him, for he began soon to wriggle gently with pleasure, pressing the plane of his breast against my own softer bubbies; and by my side I could see that his companion, observing his pleasure, now laid himself of his own volition along Frances' body, with a commensurate pleasure.

I could feel, now, his masculine part – fully as large as his fellow's – lying against my lower belly, and with some effort (for he was reluctant to remove his flesh from proximity to my own) inserted my hands between us, and by dint of heaving managed to lift him away so far as to insert the tip of the machine between those lips now over-ready to accept it.

He got the idea immediately, for he no sooner felt the engulfing flesh than – no doubt as much from instinct as from design – he began those regular movements which are at once contributors to and the results of pleasure! I could not but observe that Frances was by now the recipient of an equally satisfactory attention – and it was my amusement to note that the attention of the remaining men was so engaged by the unusual sight before them that they had been tempted from their posts and now were gathered about us in a close circle, observing the strange posture in which we were enjoyably poised! Their amusement and excitement was if anything even more acutely aroused when, in order to increase those sensations which were now swiftly mounting to a peak, I threw up my legs and placed their calves firmly upon my rider's shoulders – whereupon, as though disbelieving that their colleague could remain in satisfactory conjunction with so energetic a mount, two of his friends positively lay upon the ground, in order to reassure themselves that congress was indeed still in progress; which, however, must have been confirmed by the shriek which pleasure drew from me as my wellsprings were finally released; and when, a moment later, Frances also signalled the completion of her joy, and our two jockeys, their own rides also rewarded, withdrew from their seats of pleasure, there was a strange subdued rattle of applause – which I saw came from the observers gripping their instruments, no doubt strengthened by the extent of their admiration, and beating a tattoo with them against the flesh of their bellies!

The problem now became that each man was eager to enjoy so strange an experience; but as Frances and I assured ourselves, it was our duty to educate them, and so perhaps to increase the delight of their womenfolk (though this may only have meant Her Majesty, for we never discovered whether these men were reserved only for her); and happily, there being only a dozen of them, it was entirely possible before dawn for us to instruct them all in the rudiments – which included a posture or two in addition to the one which had so impressed them.

They were natural pupils – and so eager that we had some difficulty in persuading them that we could really only accommodate each of them once, for they all wished a repetition, and having shown one of them a trick, all the others wished to try it (indeed, having demonstrated that the tongue could give much pleasure, if adeptly applied to the tender parts, we were amused to see that two of our admirers had withdrawn to the side of the hut and, lying head to tail, were experimenting upon each other – something which may have led to complications upon our leaving!)

Her Majesty did not seem at all surprised to find us somewhat fatigued upon the following morning; indeed I believe that she took this as a compliment. Her elderly courtier, having spoken to one of the harem, then in turn addressed the Queen, waving his hand to encompass the whole band – at which she nodded gravely, and seemed to treat us with a new respect.

Ceremoniously taking our leave, we then returned to the harbour, where we found that the survey of its entrance had been completed – and that stores had been loaded, and the vessel prepared to voyage on to the Society Islands, some way distant, and in particular to the largest island, known as Tahiti.

Chapter Seven

The Adventures of Andy

The long, almost infinite, voyage from Cape Town to India was for me almost idyllic. It was a time of quiet and thoughtful recreation, interspersed with lively conversation with my friend Robert, and in 'civilising' (as I would call it) young Kenny, who in a few weeks – so bright and intelligent was he – became not only an admirable servant but a quick and accomplished student, eager not – certainly – to forget his origins, but to learn as much as possible about English customs, and by hearing of my travels to widen his knowledge of the world.

His upbringing in South Africa had not been unendurable, but had certainly been devoid of what at home we would call comfort; neither was he especially devoted to his people, feeling under no obligation to them – for both his parents had died when he was too young to notice them, and he had been brought up as everyone's (unpaid) servant, and no-one's particular friend.

The race to which he belonged, he told me – having now the opportunity to compare his people not only to Robert and myself, but to the rougher kind of person who formed our crew – was devoted to its own well-being, to the extent that the people were ready to show themselves eager to satisfy their white masters (for this was the relation in which they were held), since this ensured an income of some sort, though meagre. But they are sluggish in performance – unless it is work which positively delights them, when they will work as well as anyone, if for a shorter period of time, for they are very speedily overtaken by boredom.

None of this was the case with Kenny, for even if I made allowances for the strangeness of his situation, and the newness of every experience (for among other things he had never before set foot upon the deck of a ship), he was clearly of a naturally forthcoming and happy disposition. He also clearly regarded me as to some extent friend as well as master, for he did not hesitate to enquire about the incident at the cabin, asking whether all white women were ready to *boum-boum* (as he put it) with gentlemen; and showing perhaps some disappointment when I told him that indeed it was not common, and that Mrs van den Heuff was the exception rather than the rule.

He then asked whether most white women would be as interested in his *pouddha* (as he called his prick) as she; when I was forced to admit that that was possibly the case – but that in the event of his meeting such a woman, it would be best for him to refrain from exhibiting it to her solely on the chance that her enthusiasm would commend him to her. (He was still virgin, I should note, his experience having been confined to some little mutual exhibitionism with female friends of his own age; but having had no instruction in these matters, nor ever having observed coition – the Hottentots being naturally somewhat modest – he had been unable to imagine the act, so that his view of Mrs van den Heuff's congress with Frank and myself had been almost too interesting to him.) Upon his imploring further information I added to the lessons in English, and the rudimentary account of arithmetic which I gave him, a description of female anatomy and the manner in which it is employed in amorous play, which will no doubt at some time be useful to him, and in any event is something no young male should be ignorant of.

So, as I say, the time passed agreeably enough, and in time we set eyes on the Indian coast – the sea-side of Hindustan, uninteresting to excess, being tame and uniform. We did not set ashore, merely viewing the land on the horizon, for we were headed for that small island formerly known as Serendib, but latterly as Ceylon. When that coastline came in view, it was to a degree different from the dull Indian coast, being highly picturesque and romantic, a seeming chaos of hill and dale. The rocky summits of the mountains are thrown into the most fantastic shapes. Impregnable castles, with innumerable turrets, partizans and vantage-points appear to frown defiance.

With the view of benefiting by the land-wind that usually prevails at night even when the most perfect calms are experienced during the day, we kept close to the western shore of the island, which we were thus enabled closely to reconnoitre. At the close of the day a ripple on the face of the placid deep announced the coming of the hoped-for breeze, when a few hours' sailing brought us within sight of the Colombo lighthouse, and when day broke we found ourselves within a few miles of the fort, and in the midst of a fleet of Ceylon canoes – frail barques prevented from capsizing by the attachment of a floating log of wood, termed an outrigger, and attached to the canoes by slightly arched spars of ten or twelve feet in length.

These craft came in great numbers to the ship, with fruit, fish, bread, and pineapples, sold for a *fanam*, or penny-ha'penny; all this food was purchased with great enthusiasm by everyone, the prices seeming miraculously cheap.

In due time we came to anchor in the roads of Colombo, calm as glass, and lost no time in effecting a landing (here I may say that no-one save those who have spent so long a time on board ship can appreciate the luxury of treading again on *terra firma*, Kenny in particular delighting in it – though, we were amused to note, tending to fall over, his legs now expecting dry land to perform the motions of the sea!)

Robert, familiar with the port (he has travelled, in his comparatively short life, to most of the ports favoured by sailors in this part of the world), led us to a house where hospitality would be offered us in exchange for mere coppers – the country being more than usually hospitable to travellers.

A large proportion of the European residents at Colombo live without the walls of the fort, inside which the temperature is much higher than in the less confined suburbs that extend along the seashore. All public offices and the principal buildings are however within the fort, which is therefore the great resort where merchants congregate.

The streets, as in the generality of military towns, run at right angles with each other, and are sufficiently wide and well ventilated. A great portion of the space within the *enceinte* of the fort is occupied by the residence of the governor, or, as it is usually termed, 'the King's House'. This building is long and straggling, but redeems the general character of the surrounding houses, which are for the most part insignificant in appearance and at once destroy the illusive anticipations of Oriental luxury that a *griffin* (and all visitors not resident in the island are known as 'griffins') is apt to cherish.

To a new-comer from Europe, the burning heat of the noontide sun in these latitudes is perhaps less oppressive than to old residents in tropical climes. It has more effect on his constitution, and exposure to the sun is more likely to injure the health of the recruit than that of the veteran. But the actual sense of lassitude and exhaustion is far more sensibly felt by those who have long resided in debilitating climates than by men who, fresh from their native land, bring greater physical powers to contend with the eternal heat.

I discovered, however, during the first night, a chief disadvantage of these climes: a fresh importation of more or less tender flesh is a godsend to the villainous mosquitoes, whose annoyance is formidable. The bite of a mosquito is not painful, and might be borne without repining by any person blessed with a tolerable stock of Christian resignation, were it not that the buzzing of the insect, previous to its attack, induces a feverish restlessness that most effectively murders sleep. If the reader calls to mind the unpleasant feeling which the near approach of a wasp creates, he will easily imagine the nervous anxiety that is experienced by a griffin when he is first aroused by the buzzing salutations of the mosquito.

A speedy recovery from this misery is however helped by the pleasant custom (long may it continue!) of taking a cup of coffee in the morning, as a preliminary to dressing. As you quaff the delicious beverage, all reminiscence of your night's misery fades away, and you rise like a giant refreshed, able to sally forth to enjoy the coolness of the morning air ere the rays of the sun become oppressive.

We were, two days after our arrival, commanded to sup with the Governor and his wife at the fort; and presented ourselves there at seven o'clock, as finely dressed as was possible, our clothes having been in need of pressing and cleaning. Kenny also accompanied us, kitted in a uniform of white cotton, hastily tailored for him in the town.

The party was a small one, consisting of Sir Wormsley Gillard, an amiable buffoon, his wife, a not unhandsome

The Adventures of Andy   119

lady of perhaps forty summers, his nephew, Lieutenant the Hon. Denys Potter, and his *fiancée*, arrived from England only a month before, Miss Jane Petty. She was indeed the single bright spot in the evening, and as I was happily sat at her side (poor Robert left to find what pleasure he might in the conversation of Lady Gillard) I received the benefit of her talk, which however was somewhat depressed.

The burden of her complaint was that while her *fiancé*, Lieutenant Potter, had been attentive and lively on their meeting in London, so that she had had not a moment's doubt, as she informed me, in accepting his proposal of marriage, yet (she continued, and in no subdued tones) she had arrived here to find him enervated, fatigued, weary, stale and altogether not the person she remembered.

'And you know, Mr Archer,' (she said) 'we ladies have expectations of our wooers more than their falling asleep after supper, and snoring until bedtime – and for all I know, after that.'

She accompanied her last words by placing her hand upon my thigh, beneath the table-cloth, and giving it an appreciative squeeze, which resulted in my dropping my spoon into my dish with a clamour which for a moment distracted Lady Gillard from her description of the races which she had attended at Newmarket when on leave in England the previous year. (Robert, I saw, appeared not to be entirely bored by this, and I could not but notice that like Miss Petty, Lady Gillard held her spoon in her left hand, her right being out of view beneath the table – and on the side on which my friend was sitting. He studiously avoided my eye.)

It must be, I said, that Lieutenant Potter's spirits were lowered by too long an acquaintance with the climate, for surely no gentleman would for any other reason disregard such beauty, or fail to pay to it the compliments it demanded?

Colour sprung to Miss Petty's cheeks at this.

'That may be the case, sir,' she said, 'but it does not resolve the problem!' – and moved her hand a little upward.

My compliment to her had been no more than she deserved, and I wondered at her lover's slowness, for her every breath disclosed the upper reaches of a bosom as round and plump as could be desired, while her shoulders – certainly protected from the sun – were of a silken white texture which it was difficult not to salute with a kiss, even in company.

While I took no liberties during supper (I must confess, for fear of once starting, not being able to control myself), Miss Petty felt under no such constraint, and no doubt seeing my admiration in my eyes transferred her hand in time to the bifurcation of my breeches, where she was easily able to reassure herself that my admiration was something more than verbal.

On supper ending, it was with reluctance that she rose from the table in company with Lady Gillard, leaving Robert and myself to be entertained by indifferent port wine, the somnambulant ramblings of Sir Wormsley and (indeed, indeed) the snores of Lieutenant the Hon. Denys, who almost immediately fell asleep over his glass.

After ten minutes of this, even I began to feel positively lethargic, when the door opened and Lady Gillard appeared.

'My dear Lieutenant,' she said to Robert, 'now is the time for me to show you the library! – while Miss Potter is to claim a promise of Mr Archer to accompany her for a stroll upon the fort ramparts.'

I had made no such promise, but the reader will not be surprised to know that I prepared myself instantly to fulfil it; and Robert was no sluggard either, taking my arm as we left the room together, and whispering into my ear, 'Go it, old fellow!' – to which I had no opportunity of replying. Kenny, we left looking excessively dull, standing near to the chairs where the Governor and his aide now slumbered like children.

Miss Petty was waiting for me along the corridor, and without speaking took my arm and led me up a flight of stairs and through a doorway into the darkness, where we found ourselves upon the battlements of the fort, lit only dimly by reflected light. The occasional buzzing of a mosquito reminded me of my enemy; but I was far more intrigued by my human companion, who sure-footedly led me along the ramparts to where a small gun-embrasure stood; into this, she retired, drawing me after her, and in an instant pressed upon my lips a kiss which was so lascivious and drawn-out that I envied the Lieutenant possession of the girl, and pitied him that the climate had evidently withdrawn from him the capacity to appreciate her.

After a while, possibly through lack of breath, she withdrew her lips from mine with a great sigh, and drew away. When I attempted to follow, I felt her hand upon my breast, preventing me; then heard a rustling, the meaning of which became clear when she again advanced, and on my putting my arms about her proved to have slipped from her gown and to be bare as a needle.

While I was deprived of the opportunity – it being light enough only to apprehend most dimly her shape – of confirming with my eyes the beauty of form hinted by what I had seen of it, my lips soon discovered the softness of her breast, punctuated only by eager tips my tongue's tribute to which resulted in a muffled cry of pleasure and a fumbling of hands at my waist.

Its being dark made her efforts in that direction

nugatory, and I was forced for a moment to withdraw while I threw off my lower clothing – and indeed, for good measure, my coat and shirt; to receive now an onslaught so furious as to make me stagger back, my unclothed back coming into somewhat painful contact with the rough stone of the embrasure.

My accomplice was now so eager (to what a degree of frustration the heat will raise an unsatisfied female can scarcely be imagined by those who only know cooler climes) as to require immediate satisfaction, and to ensure my readiness, slipping from my arms she fell to her knees, and in a moment I felt her lips close upon my member, while her hands, passing behind me, clutched at my arse with the most eager grasp; I have never before nor since experienced such eagerness as Miss Petty now showed, her lips moving with such closeness and firmness, her head bobbing so readily, that before I knew it the world had ended for me – and, I feared, for her.

However, she was not a whit dismayed, rising to her feet, and stroking the whole of my body, as it were, with her own; so that in less time than I would have thought possible, I was revived – at which, retreating only a step, she found with her hands a ledge at her waist's height, and with a little jump settling upon it was able to throw her thighs wide open, gripping with both hands my newly restored prick and guiding it home.

I am happy to report that my determination to prove worthy of the honour was now rewarded by a process more happily prolonged, and it was only after she had squealed appreciation no less than three times that I permitted myself another and final approbation of her beauty; after which, in silence, we resumed our clothing.

As we returned to the fort, she took my arm, and with a kiss upon my cheek, asked me to be discreet.

'I fear that I have always been hot-blooded,' she said,

'and in England several opportunities for pleasure were entirely enjoyed by Denys and myself, so that I have been the less able to tolerate his neglect since I came here.'

'I am sure that time will cure the situation', I said (though not entirely confident of it), 'and in the meantime your confidence and generosity will of course be respected.'

We now entered the sitting-room of the fort, where Lady Gillard was sitting upon a sopha, looking like the cat that had had the cream; while Robert, upon a chair nearby, himself seemed not out of temper. The two other gentlemen had recovered sufficiently to drag themselves from the dining-room to comfortable armchairs, from which they made a half-gesture of rising as we bade the company goodnight, Miss Petty in particular stressing the fact that she hoped that I would count upon her to show me any of those parts (of Colombo, it was understood) with which I might wish to be more closely acquainted.

As we made our way to our lodgings, Robert confirmed my suspicions that Lady Gillard had, no less than Miss Petty, offered him certain corporeal satisfactions ('actually,' he said, 'in the comfort of her own *boudoir*') – and that any slight disadvantage which might have been expected to accrue from her more advanced age and corpulence was far outweighed by her voracity.

While by no means determining not to call upon these ladies again, we devoted ourselves the next day to exploring that part of the town given over to the natives – the *Pettah*, or black town, in whose streets may be observed people of every possible complexion between the fair European and the sable negro. This variety is, I am told, the result of connections (in marriage or otherwise) between the Dutch and more particularly the Portuguese colonists and the local people.

Those who are a mixture of Dutch and Ceylonese blood are particularly honest and industrious, and universally respected.

The *Pettah* extends three or four miles from the fort, and is inhabited by at least fifty thousand people who live about the shores of the lake, which, though of insignificant breadth, is of considerable length. Pleasure-boats skim over its surface, adding to the animation of the scene and affording the means of enjoying aquatic excursions, which above all others provide the most delightful recreation in the tropics.

I was as delighted by the scene as Robert, whose previous visits to the place had by no means diminished his pleasure in it. The part of the *Pettah* which borders the lake was particularly pleasant in the evening, and we spent several relaxing hours there, particularly at a house of pleasure of which he knew, where the enjoyment of physical recreation combined with excellent local dishes and wines, taken in the open air (where flaming torches deterred our old friends the mosquitoes from too much participation in the proceedings) made our life enjoyable.

Robert had now some duties about the ship, but suggested that Kenny and I should make excursion into other parts of the island, since the *Proper Pride* would be some three weeks before again setting to sea (some more repairs being necessary: a matter which a little concerned me, although Robert assured me that though an ancient vessel, she was perfectly seaworthy).

I therefore determined to travel to Kandy, a town in the Central Province, on the Mahaweli Ganga some sixty miles from Colombo at a height of 1,600 feet, and famous for a temple in which is preserved a tooth of the Buddha: the place is, of course, a British possession.

Between Colombo and Kandy, a coach service has for some years been established, and the journey is performed in twelve hours, beginning at five o'clock in the morning. Were this performed through the heat of the day, it would be to the last degree enervating; but an hour is allowed at a halfway mark for refreshment. At eleven o'clock the coach pulled up upon the shore, when its occupants (two European couples besides myself, though none English) descended, walked to the shore, divested themselves of their clothing and took a most refreshing dip in the ocean – refreshing, I know, because of course Kenny and I followed their example. It was notable that there was a complete lack of unnatural modesty in the travellers, the gentlemen and ladies only taking care to leave a gap of some few feet, for courtesy, between the groups, but taking no care to hide any part of their bodies from each other – though of course not positively gazing at each other; so that I had to administer a sharp reprimand to Kenny, whose interest in the unclothed bodies of the ladies could not be disguised and might have given offence.

After bathing, we sat down to an *al fresco* breakfast served in the shade of awnings stretched in front of a simple but perfectly adequate rest-house.

Now the coach began to ascend the lower range of the Kandian hills, and the country – which hitherto had had a flat or slightly undulating appearance – became at every step more wild and romantic. The features of the landscape are strikingly dissimilar to the fair level aspect of England, especially in the near vicinity of Kandy, where the road winds through minor passes at the foot of the hills, some of which are extremely beautiful, and then commences to ascend the grand pass of Cadaganava – the length of the road from the foot to the summit of the pass being something more than three miles, and including the most magnificent view of the country stretching towards Colombo.

At Paradinia, a village four miles from Kandy, the Colombo road meets the river Mahavilaganga, where there has recently been raised by Colonel Fraser, the deputy quartermaster general to the British forces in Ceylon, a single-arched bridge of beautiful satin-wood. The local people, relying on their ancient tales and legends, had formed an opinion that the bridging of the river was impracticable, and with this persuasion were in the habit of daily assembling to gaze on the gradual progress of the work, and to laugh to scorn the impotent labours of the *pale faces*; but when, to their amazement, the bridge was found to stand, their admiration knew no bounds, and they looked with fear and wonder on the Europeans who had brought to a successful termination an undertaking considered by them beyond the power of man.

On approaching Kandy, the lake, embosomed within encircling mountains that on every side rise to elevations varying from four hundred to two thousand feet, is the first object which meets the eye of the traveller. Bungalows and villas stud its margin, giving an animated appearance to the landscape, and relieving the stern grandeur of the rugged heights which repose their shadows in the waters that bathe their feet.

The coach traverses the small town and deposits the wayfarer at an hotel that has for some time been established in this happy valley for the especial benefit of invalids and others. Here, I took a charming room, with another next door for Kenny (the manager of the hotel being somewhat surprised that a servant should have a room of his own, rather than existing as he might, generally in the open air beneath his master's windows). After a restful night, we set out to discover the town.

Kandy, when I came to explore it, was not especially notable, consisting of long, straggling ranges of paltry houses, here and there interspersed with a few superior buildings. All the desirable residences are to be found in the suburbs, which extend to a considerable distance on every side, and contain several pretty sites whereon divers bungalows are erected. The late King's palace here is a sad disappointment, the Europeans having modernised and 'improved' it so that it bears an appearance totally different from that which in the palmy days of royalty was wont to dazzle the eyes of the natives. The only part which retains some grandeur is the harem, where secluded ladies once concealed their charms from all save their liege lord and sovereign. In the front of the harem the sun and all the stars of the firmament are carved in stone, and produce an extremely striking and oriental effect.

You enter the edifice through a massive and rather grand archway, and after ascending two or three flights of stone steps and passing through sundry antechambers reach the hall of audience – which, alas, has now been metamorphosed into a criminal court and chapel, the judge's desk making an admirable pulpit; here, the romantic aspect of the place is greatly abated by the presence of anomalies.

The temples of Kandy are, however, its principal feature – especially the Delada Malegawa, which contains the tooth of the Buddha, deposited in a small golden case the exterior of which is completely covered with precious stones and pearls of immense value, fitted into a similar but somewhat larger case called a *karandua*; there are five of these *karanduas*, four of which are in this manner successively embedded!

I was somewhat disappointed to find that women take no prominent part in the ceremonies of Buddhaical worship. The European infidel who anticipates the happiness of meeting the Cingalese fair at the temples will generally be disappointed. The voice of the charmer is in these sacred edifices dispensed with, and in its stead the sound of barbaric horns and drums clangs discordantly on the offended ear. The clamour arising from Kandian temples can be fully appreciated only by those who have had the misfortune of residing within hearing. Each drum seems to beat without the slightest regard to time, and in utter defiance of all the laws of melody. The monotonous din this produces is occasionally enlivened by a horrid squeak from a native instrument which rejoices in the euphonious name of *horanawa*.

Nevertheless, women are certainly present around the temples, and on grand occasions muster in force, and add much to the interest of the *parraharra* and other national processions. The Cingalese women have generally good figures, being short and slight, but for the most part handsomely formed, the best of them being beauteous maidens whose charms are almost above criticism. On my remarking upon this to the manager of the hotel, an amiable gentleman, he showed me an account by a Kandian chief to Dr Davy, a late writer on Ceylon, which will interest all who profess themselves connoisseurs in female loveliness:

'Her hair should be voluminous, like the tail of the peacock, long, reaching to the knees, and terminating in graceful curls; her eyebrows should resemble the rainbow; her eyes the blue sapphire and the petals of the Manilla flower. Her nose should be like the bill of the hawk. Her lips should be bright and red, like coral on the young leaf of the iron-tree. Her teeth should be small, regular and closely set, and like jasmine buds. Her neck should be large and round, resembling the *benigodea*. Her chest should be capacious; her breasts firm and conical, like the yellow coconut; and her waist small, almost small enough to be clasped by the hand. Her lips should be wide; her limbs tapering; the soles of her feet without any hollow; and the surface of her body in general soft, delicate, smooth and rounded, without the asperities of projecting bones and sinews.'

Was there any means (I asked as tactfully as possible) by which I could confirm that promising description? For the ladies I saw about the streets were for the most part too well-covered by their long, flowing dresses for their figures to be studied – though, indeed, they seemed to have, as far as their faces were concerned, a dusky beauty which I do not remember to have seen equalled in the East – with classically low foreheads shaded by luxuriant masses of jet black hair, Grecian noses and short upper lips all of which were perfect and as a whole incomparable.

Mr Srivastav entirely understood my wish to pursue my studies, and directed me to a house in the suburbs – once the property of a government official, but now given over to entertainment; and thence I took myself that very evening, having encouraged Kenny to take his ease during the evening with a book of English grammar with which I had provided him.

I was received most courteously – unusually, by a male manager, for in this part of the world that is the natural state of things, rather than such houses being governed entirely by women, which is more familiar to us.

The gentleman first gave me a beautifully cool drink of some liquid whose nature was as obscure as its purpose, though from a sensual lethargy which shortly invaded me, I believe that it may be directed at calming somewhat the desires of any gentlemen visiting the place who might otherwise prove damagingly energetic.

I was then taken to a room occupied by a number of ladies, all of a pretty youthful appearance, and all of whom appeared more formed for love than for command, for in their large and liquid eyes could clearly be seen (as I took it) the languor and apathy that pervaded the soul within.

Choosing one of these was a difficult matter, since all were fully covered from head to foot; however, my eyes eventually were locked to those of one of them – for no reason other than perhaps some natural sympathy – and when I held out my hand she seemed happy enough to take it, gravely inclining her head, and leading me to a room lit by a single lamp and furnished merely by a large, low couch upon which a fresh white sheet had been thrown, and by the accoutrements of cleanliness in one corner.

I immediately disrobed; but she, somewhat to my disappointment, failed to do so – and on my approaching her with the idea of assisting her (if that was the custom) she merely took my hand once more and led me to a large bowl of water, upon the surface of which some petals of a flower unknown to me floated; and with a cloth and some unguent resembling our soap, washed me all over, leaving me – I must confess – delightfully refreshed; if, alas, the exercise left me in an entirely un-amorous condition, my private part resembling rather an acorn than an oak, which I hoped would not disappoint her (for all I know, the Cingalese men shared with their darker neighbours the property of appearing, even when relaxed, larger than most Europeans).

However, she showed no sign of it, but took me once more by the hand and leading me to the couch, encouraged me to lie upon it; when she retired and made her way to the side of the room, where I saw what appeared to be a window, obstructed by a closely-woven wicker shade or guard, to which she approached her lips and seemed to whisper something – when from, I supposed, another room there came through the obscured aperture the pure and serpentine notes of a kind of flute, to the music of which my companion now began to dance with that extraordinary grace which no European seems able to command, her arms appearing to have no bone within them, so marvellously did they curve and wave, and her body moving with wonderful musicality, so that each change in timbre or key in the music seemed matched by an individual movement.

This was so curious and notable that for a moment I forgot where I was and for what purpose I had come thither; yet now she slipped her garment from her shoulders, showing them fine, the skin lustrous and golden in the lamplight; then, by a sleight of hand which was remarkable, she used her robe as a tempter's weapon, by a twitch of her hands moving it, as she danced, gradually to reveal more and more of her body, so that I had first a glimpse of a rounded calf, then of the lower part of a thigh; first of the fleshy upper half of the sphere of a breast, then of the shadow of a nipple, then of the whole breast – concealed now not at all by the robe, which had dropped to the ground, but by the thick curtain of her hair, which she skilfully deployed, much as a European dancer might use a veil or a fan; and her movements still so married to the sound of the flute that my apprehension was a mingling of wonder, admiration and increasing lust.

That the latter emotion should gradually overcome the others was of course the dancer's business, which occurred in a gradation of slowly rising passion that instilled the keenest apprehension of pleasure to come. After what seemed hours of skilful provocation, she was naked, and I saw that – whether in accordance with religious custom or for what other reason, I knew not – her body was entirely depilated, the delectable nooks

beneath her arms shaded only by the dusk, and that
source of pleasure where I hoped, soon, to graze, entirely
revealed, its lips full and generous, perhaps somewhat
darker than in European women, still partly obscured by
the dim light and by the dancer's motions, so that more
and more I yearned for the opportunity to explore her
body – yet was unable to bring myself to break the spell
laid by the music and her motions.

Now, she began to approach the couch, while I still lay
under a strange kind of spell, quite incapable of
movement – though I must admit that the inhibition did
not apply to one part of my body, which seemed now to
have a life of its own, and was nodding and bowing in
apparent response to my companion's movements. But I
could no more have broken the enchantment in order to
embrace her, than I could have borne to leave the room!
Instead, I lay supine as she came nearer and nearer, and
in a moment felt her fingers begin to flutter over my body,
and her hair, as she bent over me, to brush it, falling
upon my breast, my belly, my thighs – my engorged
member ploughing through it like the prow of a ship
through ocean waves!

I was by now in such ecstasy that I was literally
entranced, and closing my eyes sank into a well of sensuality, when the sensations I felt seemed positively to
transcend feeling and become something else – some all-
engrossing spirit of carnality which lifted me into a realm
of sheer distilled passion such as it is beyond my pen to
describe. I knew, somewhere in my mind, that my body
was being caressed, that my companion's fingers were
playing over my body, even that her lips were now upon
it, approaching and engulfing my manhood; yet I was
beyond and above carnality, raised to a sphere in which
bodily and spiritual pleasure were one. I felt my entire self
rising and rising in a great parabola of pleasure – then,

suddenly, there seemed a giant, painless explosion – and I was recalled to life.

I found myself lying upon the couch, the clear signs of pleasure upon my belly and chest; the music had ceased, and my companion was already preparing with cloths and water to cleanse my body. She might, for all I knew or had done, be a virgin; for I had certainly not penetrated her – nor had I so much as touched her body with my hands (much as I had been anticipating that pleasure).

Yet I cannot say that I was disappointed – indeed, I felt none of the sadness which the classic author has recorded as man's lot after indulging in the passion. On the contrary, I was entirely at peace; I felt as I feel after a splendid meal during which I have refrained from over-indulgence. I even felt strangely at one with the world, as though I had in some way participated in a celebration of the best in human nature. I remembered what my friend Sophie had told me of her experience, on the island of Malta, of the Tantric religion of India*, and concluded that the incident which had just occurred must partake of something of the same nature.

Having helped me to dress (herself now once more modestly covered from head to foot), my companion made a bow and conducted me to the reception room, where the gentleman who had received me asked most courteously whether I had been satisfied at my reception, and received from me a payment remarkable by its modesty.

As I left, I saw nearby two figures, one of which seemed familiar; and on cautiously approaching saw that while one of them was an unknown young man carrying a kind of flute, the other was none other than young Kenny – who was passing the other a number of

---

*which she has recounted in our volume *Eros on the Grand Tour*

clinking coins. I could only draw one inference from this: that he had followed me, and had bribed the musician to allow him to observe, through the wicket, what I had been about.

Well, curiosity is the normal and natural concomitant of youth, and I did not feel inclined to punish him when on returning to the hotel I called to him, and he appeared, clutching his grammar, extremely breathless (having no doubt run all the way back in order to be able to greet me!) He was at the age when the discovery of his masculinity can be troubling and obscure, and no doubt it would be kind in me to arrange that he should be divested of his virginity at some stage in the not too far distant future. I could not trouble myself about that, however, at that moment; for I was suddenly deadly tired, and scarcely troubling to unclothe myself, fell upon my bed in a deep sleep.

Chapter Eight

Sophie's Story

I do not intend to weary the reader by accounts of our daily life upon the *Sulphur* as we made from one island to another; that would be supererogatory, for one day upon shipboard is much like the next. However, on the present stage of our voyage, there was one incident which may perhaps be of interest.

The truth is that I was becoming more and more irritated by our physician, Dr Nadge. It was not that he was offensive – nor did I mind his not being particularly pleasant; it cannot be expected that we should find the whole of mankind pleasing. What made his presence a constant irritation was his entirely ignoring me – and not only myself, but Frances. He appeared the complete misogynist – and St John indeed reported to me that on several occasions he had grumbled that the present expedition was no place for ladies, and that it was entirely improper that we should have been allowed to purchase our places on board.

As I have said, he gave no outward offence; yet simply responded to any greeting of ours by the curtest nod which could be concomitant with bare politeness, and on our approaching any part of the deck which he occupied (even if he was engaged in reading, or merely staring at the ocean) he would move away, with the slightest inclination of the head to show that he recognised our presence – and that indeed it was that presence which forced him to retire!

Was he perhaps effeminate? He had certainly shown during his examination of my person on the journey to Panama that he was not entirely indifferent to the sex – yet perhaps that interest was indeed merely medical? He had, after all, compared my body to a dissected corpse! I determined to discover, once and for all, his inclination – and to that end engaged my friends in a plot.

As I think I have already mentioned, it is the custom on board ship that early in the morning the crew should refresh their bodies by hauling buckets of water to the deck, and there cleanse themselves – an occasion for high spirits and play, apart from satisfying the necessities of hygiene. Frances and I had the habit of imitating this custom – not, of course, upon the same part of the deck, but that portion of it which was set aside for us, and guarded from inquisitive eyes by an awning. Dick and St John were entirely aware of this; they would sometimes indeed join us, and very welcome were their strong arms in heaving heavily laden buckets to the deck. However, Dr Nadge never appeared on such occasions – nor did he participate in the crew's ablutions (which we must have been aware of, for I confess that Frances and I had contrived by means of mounting to a particular vantage-point to overlook that part of the deck where the commonalty assembled, the sight of such a gathering of well-set-up young men in a state of nature being naturally interesting to us).

It was not for some time that we discovered that it was the physician's custom to observe from his cabin, the door of which commanded a view of the passage or gangway from our own quarters to the deck, when we retired from making our toilet, and would then slip up to the deck to wash himself during the period when we were making ourselves ready to break our fast.

On my confessing to Dick and St John what I had in mind, they happily agreed to help – Dr Nadge's lack of popularity being general; and the preparations having been made, Frances and I made our way to the deck rather earlier than usual, one fine morning, and having made our ablutions, returned to our cabin – not failing to observe in passing that Nadge's door was a crack ajar, and making conversation as we went, to ensure that he was aware of our retirement. Then, after a few minutes' pause, we returned quietly the way we had come.

We had timed our return aright: there was the physician, having removed his clothing, standing over a pail of sea-water and busily scrubbing his body with a rough cloth and the help of some of that special soap devised for use with salt water (and not particularly efficacious, I may report).

Compared to the physique of our seamen, whose skins were tanned with exposure to the sun and whose muscles were developed and strengthened by bodily labour, I cannot report that Dr Nadge displayed a figure calculated much to raise the temperature of the observant female. His skin was paper-white, the sparse black hairs upon his body therefore particularly notable and giving him rather the aspect of a half-plucked chicken. His arms and legs were thin, his flanks and buttocks appearing to consist of bones scarcely hung with flesh; between his legs, certainly, hung the usual masculine appurtenances – but the bollocks swung in a loose pouch below a prick so insignificant as to invoke laughter rather than admiration or even interest (though it must be remembered that he was engaged in sluicing his body with cold water at the time of this observation, an action which could certainly not have been counted on to enhance the outward advertisement of masculinity).

We waited, finding it difficult, I confess, not to

advertise our presence by laughter, until he had dried himself with a towel and had reached for his clothes – when we suddenly left our hiding-place and with a push succeeded in throwing him, with not too much violence, to the deck at that part of it which we had designed for his fall – and where lay, apparently without purpose, two ends of rope which our friends had previously supplied, tightly secured to two rings at the bottom of the mizzenmast.

Such was Dr Nadge's surprise that we were able without difficulty to secure his wrists with the ropes, so that though in a fury he wriggled and threshed and kicked, he was unable to release himself; and after a few moments, red in the face – whether with fury or embarrassment or a mixture of the two, I am unable to say – lay still.

Collecting himself, he opened his mouth to let out a cry – when I held up my hand.

'My friend,' I said, 'consider, before you summon help, who will come at your call: perhaps one of the common seamen – in which event your plight will in a moment be all round the ship, having it may be no very satisfactory effect upon the respect with which the company should regard its surgeon. Mr Midgely and Mr Thripp are out of earshot' (in fact, we had merely informed them of our plan; and I was by no means sure that they were not in fact overlooking the scene from some concealed vantage-point). 'It would perhaps be best that you remain silent and hear us.'

'Wh-what do you want of me?' he stammered.

'Stephen,' breathed my friend, approaching the physician's reclining form and placing a hand upon one arm – at which he shuddered like a wild colt at its first experience of a human touch – 'if I may call you by your forename: Stephen, you will know that we have been upon this journey for some months now, and confined to the society of men, but because of the canons of normal behaviour deprived of any but the most distant contact with them.' (I almost blushed at the lie!)

'We have regarded you with increasing admiration – your every movement has been a flaming torch to our desires' – how I maintained a serious aspect is beyond me – 'yet you have been distant and severe. But our deprivation, together with the heat of these tropic latitudes, has made us desperate: in short, we have been forced to this ruse in order that . . .'

But here she broke off, as though unable to continue, instead bending over Nadge to press a soft kiss upon his right pap. The man was in an agony of continued fury, and began to thresh his legs about to such an extent that we were positively thrown to the deck – at which point I am sure that I heard ill-suppressed laughter from our friends, and presumed that they were indeed looking on from some concealed vantage-point.

The sun was now thoroughly risen, and was gilding the deck with light – and also laying down the warm foundations of the usual tropical heat. Standing, we looked at each other, then standing one upon each side of our victim, unclothed ourselves by removing the single garment in which we were dressed. At the first sign – on our bending to lift the hems of our gowns – the pinioned physician screwed his eyes tightly; yet I am sure that in a moment I saw his eyelids flicker, and from the fact inferred that he had been unable after all to resist the temptation to look.

The sight however had no enlarging effect upon our victim's personal attributes, which lay between his crossed legs like three small knubs of flesh, one almost indistinguishable from the other! Bending, I laid my hand upon them – with the result that Dr Nadge's legs shut up like a trap, his knees positively rattling against his chest, and almost trapping my hand. I conveyed this immediately to his fundament – but there was nothing to be found there, his organs of generation being hidden by his upraised thighs.

Frances and I were forced now to take an ankle each, and pull with all our force; which resulted – the physician not being a strong man – in our straightening his legs, which Frances then lay upon, holding them to the ground in an outstretched position.

'My dear,' I said, 'allow me to take your place. Youth must ever have the first bite of the cherry.'

'Not at all, my dear Sophia,' she replied. 'The elder, whose appetite must of necessity be the greater, should take precedence . . .'

Dr Nadge was now looking quite desperate; but there was no escape for him, and kneeling at his side, I now bent over him (my breasts brushing his panting belly) and began to caress his still insignificant parts with lips and tongue. I was confident that even were he the most inveterate bugger, he could not but respond to such attentions – for I have observed in the past that they have much the same effect upon all manner of people, being the natural concomitants of love-making, whether between man and woman, woman and woman or man and man. And indeed, the result was immediate.

More immediate, in fact, than I could have guessed – for in a matter of seconds I felt the physician's tool expand between my lips, changing from the dimensions of a peascod to – well, I lack the simile which could describe the dimensions of his instrument when it was extended, or distended, to the full – for my lips could scarcely contain its head, while the column beneath seemed almost to exceed the diameter of his wrist in thickness, while it must have been at least nine or ten inches in length from tip to root (where, incidentally, his cods were now drawn up in a businesslike sac which seemed to signal readiness for copulation).

I involuntarily withdrew my lips, in order that my eyes could confirm what my other astonished senses reported; and Frances, seeing what had occurred, let out a surprised gasp. We both turned to look Dr Nadge in the face; he blushed still, but yet I seemed to discern a certain pride when Frances remarked, 'Dr Stephen, what have you hidden from us!' – and reached over to test with her fingers whether what she saw was indeed corporeal. As her fingers closed around taut flesh, she stirred – for, whether involuntarily or no, the physician's thighs were now straining to part, and as she lifted her body they indeed threw themselves apart, enabling us to come at their inner surface, softly to embrace his cods, and to titillate with a fingertip the entrance to his back passage, at which his entire body jerked as though an electric shock had passed through it – though I imagine with pleasure, for that amazing instrument which now lay parallel with his belly seemed if anything to grow still larger as a result.

I could no longer restrain my curiosity: could so vast an instrument actually be sheathed in its proper receptacle, without injury? It was an experiment that would certainly be pleasant to conduct, and half rising I threw one leg over our victim's recumbent body, and crouching brought its tip into juxtaposition with those other lips which were ready, now, to attempt to caress it with an enthusiasm more than equal to the former.

At first, it seemed impossible. What seemed a complete distension of my parts was insufficient to receive him, and the effort was such indeed as to pain me. As I winced away, Dr Nadge, with utter calmness, said: 'Perhaps a little lubrication would be of assistance. Might I suggest the application of saliva, in the absence any more oily substance . . .?'

Taking his advice, I spat into my hand, and with it wetted the already shining red head of his prick; when, once more lowering myself upon it, I succeeded in its insertion, and indeed in swallowing it to within perhaps an inch of its root, when its length – the tip seeming to press against my very breastbone – precluded further descent. On my commencing to rise and fall upon this fleshy spit, every inch of it seemed to irritate and thus stimulate, my lower lips being positively drawn outward upon my rising, and returned inward by my fall.

Nevertheless, though the resulting friction was certainly inspiriting, and in consequence of his size, unusual, I cannot say that the sensation was particularly pleasurable, and after a time this must have been clear to our captive, for still with the same coolness, he spoke again:

'I observe that your satisfaction falls short of the ideal; and observe that this is because of the lack of stimulation to the clitoris. If you would be so good as to release my hands . . .'

I had no idea what he meant, the medical term for the man in the boat being then obscure to me; but Dr Nadge's being so calm suggested to me that it would now be safe to unbind him, and I signalled to Frances to loosen his bonds; which she did. He then moistened a thumb at his lips, and placed it so that as I continued my motion, he could, at first almost imperceptibly, then more roughly, stimulate that nodule of flesh which in we females is the counterpart of the prick.

Here was an immediate improvement; for the combination of such a provocation with that of the formidable size and strength of his organ brought me almost in an instant to my climax; at which, still with the same exact poise, he suggested that I should resign my seat to my friend – Frances having by now been reduced to paroxysms of envy.

His tool being thoroughly slippery with that sebaceous liquid which had been the product of my enthusiasm, her difficulty in accepting it was somewhat lessened – despite the fact that she was less generously open to male importunity than I. Paying her the compliment of the same attention as he had paid me, he otherwise remained supine – and now that I could more coolly observe him, it was plain to me that despite his instrument remaining erect, he was taking little pleasure in the proceedings – his breathing was regular, his colour still pale, his face unflushed; his body shaken only by the consequence of my friend, in an access of pleasure, positively battering his loins with her buttocks as she bounced upon him.

On her reaching a conclusion, he courteously helped her to dismount – revealing a tool which was still perfectly erect, but as to its tip, dry as a bone; he had certainly not partaken of our own pleasure. I was about to remark upon this, and to enquire whether we could indulge any special taste which would enable him to be satisfied, when catching at my intention and sitting up, he merely remarked, 'I trust, madam, that now your curiosity and your lust have been at once satisfied, our former somewhat distant relationship can be maintained? I will of course be glad to attend to you in any illness, but must request no further attentions of this kind, on pain of my invoking the protection of the captain. I may say that I would not hesitate to do so; I am long past embarrassment in this matter. I would, however, hesitate to expose ladies to comment, and this will remain a matter strictly between us, unless you choose to make it public.'

He stood up, his prick already beginning to return to its former insignificance.

'I will now retire; I am sure you will wish to refresh yourself before replacing your clothing.'

He nodded, and with a dignity extraordinary in a man clad only in his skin and bearing his clothes under his arm, returned to his cabin.

Frances and I looked at each other without comment; nor was the matter ever commented on between us and our two friends. I cannot say under what form of constraint Dr Nadge was that he should behave so; but my experience of the habits of gentlemen in the matter of love has taught me that there are many different shades of behaviour no two of which are alike and some of which are so strange as to defy explanation, and I took his to be one of them. The incident at least proved useful in being a lesson to my less experienced friend – so impressed, in the first moment, by the sight of so alarmingly large a weapon – that, as women have discovered throughout the ages, it is not so much the size or shape of the instrument as the efficaciousness of its possessor's skill that can convey to the willing female the pleasure she seeks!

The remainder of our voyage to the neighbourhood of Fiji took place in placidity; and on our arrival between the latitudes of 15° 30′ and 20° 30′ south and the longitudes of 177° east and 178° west found what was surprising to me – that a number of islands extends over about 40,000 square miles of the South Pacific, forming a connecting link between the abodes of the Malayan and Papuan races which inhabit the widely-spread Polynesia.

Never having had cause to write the name of the place, I found in making my notes (which is my custom, in order that I might have a proper recollection for the time when I prepare these journals) that the islands are written in a wide variety of ways – including Fegee, Fejee, Feegee, Feeje, Fidje, Fidshi, Feigee, and so forth – the correct forms being Fiji, the name in the windward parts of the group and Viti, in the leeward parts.

Our vessel cruised for some time among the islands, in order that they might be noted and surveyed. Some are unusually attractive – Yathata and Vatuvara, for instance, with their circlets of cocoa-nut trees, the foliage of pristine vigour and perennial green belted with white sand. The other islands to windward are of volcanic formation, Vulanga appearing as if its centre had been blown out by violent explosions, leaving only a rim encircling a dark blue sheet of water studded with scoriaceous islets enamelled with green.

At our request we were taken ashore across this lagoon by one of the natives – and very welcome were its quiet waters after the stormy peril outside. A mountainous surf opposed the strong current which forced its way through the intricate passage, causing a most terrific wind and commotion, in the midst of which the large canoe in which we were carried was tossed about like a splinter! The excitement was intense, the manly voice of Tubou Toutai, our pilot, issuing his commands amid the thunder of the breakers, the men straining with the labour of driving the canoe in its heaving bed of foam, the anxiety which showed itself on every face – all were in broad contrast to the feeling of security, the easy progress and undisturbed repose which were attained the moment the interior of the basin was reached.

But when we set foot on Vulanga, we found it almost barren, with little growing – neither the yam nor the banana repay culture on so bare a place; only small roots, with fish (which abound here) and *yavato* (a large wood maggot) give food to the inhabitants of four villages.

The island of Mothe, however, is very fruitful, and Totoya, Moala, Nairai, Koro, Ngau and Mbengga all have their peculiar charm; Matuku is pre-eminent for loveliness where all are lovely, while Mbau is the most striking of the islands, with a town covering a great part of the island with irregularly placed houses of all sizes, and tall temples with projecting ridge-poles, interspersed with unsightly canoe-sheds.

It was at Taviuni, however – commonly called Somosomo from its chief town being the residence of the ruling chiefs – that we dropped anchor. This is a fine place, about twenty-five miles long, with a coast of sixty miles, and consists of one vast mountain, gradually rising to a central ridge of 2,100 feet. Fleecy clouds generally hide its summit, where stretches a considerable lake, pouring through an outlet to the west a stream which, after tumbling and dashing along its narrow bed, glides quietly through the chief town, furnishing it with a good supply of fresh water; a smaller outlet to the east discharges enough water to form a small but beautiful cascade.

Thence we were taken by a young man, Thakombau, recommended to us as a guide. We had set foot on shore with some diffidence, having heard of the inhabitants as practising cannibals, and having no special wish to arrive at an early date upon a chief's table as a joint of 'long pork', which is what they call human flesh, its taste being somewhat like that of pig.

However, though within the memory of men yet living the Fijians engaged with furious approbation in war and the murderous customs of heathenism, those which we met were nothing if not agreeable.

The natives are generally above the middle height, well made, and of great variety of figure, the men being large, powerful and muscular, somewhat narrow across the loins, and mostly with broad chests and strong, sinewy arms. These facts are readily ascertainable, from their wearing little or no clothing; for though the single missionary upon the island continually attempts to teach them the virtues of clothing, these they resolutely decline to recognise. Some of the younger women indeed wear a brief twist of cloth about their loins, but should this become dislodged in some game – many of which are robust – this is taken to be of no account, and no more trouble is taken to recover it than should a European lady drop an old handkerchief!

The place to which Thakombau escorted Frances and me was nothing if not charming: a stretch of clean, white sand of the finest grains was spread between the edge of the palm forest and the sea, while a deep natural pool fed by the cascading stream stood at its centre like a pearl in an oyster. Here, perhaps thirty youths and maidens were disporting themselves – some diving or swimming, clambering out of the pool again and again either to mount to the top of an overhanging rock and dive into the pool, or climbing upwards through the stream to slide with the waters down the time-polished channel, with the shouts and laughter of innocent children.

Others were engaged in games and sports – some closely resembling our 'hide and seek' or 'blind man's buff'; some of the young men engaged in *veiyama* or sham fighting, or in *veimoli*, or pelting each other with bitter oranges. Others wrestled or raced, the prize being a kiss from a chosen onlooker – which I suspected led to more than a slight familiarity, for from time to time a couple would slip away down a particular pathway between the palms.

Seeing my eyes follow these escapers, Thakombau motioned us to follow him down the same path, which we did with some little misgiving – but for no good reason, for he merely wished to show us the clearing where palm awnings had been erected over raised platforms of some kind of soft material, upon which (as I had guessed) those lovers who had escaped from the beach lay conducting their *amours* – in full view of each other, but with that joy and eagerness as well as an entire lack of self-consciousness or modesty, which our missionaries ever condemn as filthy and wicked.

We could not resist stripping to enjoy the coolness of the fresh water; which we did without any attention being paid to us other than a kindly interest – and if we would not have been entirely averse to a warmer greeting from some of the young men who were happy to stretch out a hand to help us in or out of the pool, we were disappointed; even when my hand accidentally came into contact with the upper thigh of one of them, these boys (while I believe admiring the whiteness of our bodies, which surely must have been somewhat unfamiliar to them) treated us only with the consideration we would have received at a polite evening party in London; or perhaps, more.

We were invited, two days later, together with Dick and St John, to a ceremonial dinner given by the King of Fiji, Tui Nayou. When we arrived outside the large hut which passed as his palace, we saw collected a spectacular crowd of courtiers, all ceremonially attired. These were the only clothed Fijians I had yet seen, and it was clear that they kept their robes for particular occasions.

The men wore a kind of sash of white, brown or figured *masi*, varying in length from three or a hundred yards long! – though six or ten is the usual measure. This sash is passed between the legs and wound two or three times round the loins, securing one end in front, so as to fall over to the knees like a curtain; the end behind is fastened in a bunch, or left to trail on the ground. The women are not allowed to use *masi*, but wear a *liku* or fringed band tied on the right hand side and often long enough to form a train.

The turban, consisting of a gauze-like scarf of very

fine white *masi* from four to six feet long, is worn by all
Fijians who can lay claim to respectability, except such
as are forbidden its use, the headdress fastened by a neat
bow in front or tied in a tassel-knot on the top of the
head. But it must not and does not interfere with the
heads themselves, for on no other part of his body does
the Fijian expend so much time, pains and skill. Most of
the chiefs have a hairdresser to whose care his master's
head is entrusted, often demanding daily attention. The
best *coiffures* have a surprising and almost geometrical
accuracy of outline, combined with a round softness of
surface and uniformity of dye, which display extraordinary care; they seem to be carved out of some solid substance, and are coloured jet black, blue black, ashy white
and several shades of red. Among the young people
bright red and flaxen are in favour.

When we had settled into our places, we had time to
examine the thirty or forty people nearest us, and therefore I supposed of most considerable importance – and
saw that they, besides the most imaginative hair-
sculptures, had other decorations – for their bodies
(those of both men and women) were decorated with
paint – mostly vermilion, applied in spots, stripes and
patches, their almost naked bodies forming ideal can-
vases for a strange art. They also wore as decorations
white and pink armlets and others made of black wiry
roots or white cowries, ivory and shell finger-rings, knee
and ankle bands with a rose-shaped knot, ivory, tor-
toiseshell, dogs' teeth, bats' jaws, snake vertebrae,
native beads ground out of shells and foreign beads of
glass are formed into necklaces. Breast ornaments are
pearl-shells large as a dessert-plate, plain or edged with
ivory, orange and white cowries and crescents or circles
formed by a boar's tusk.

Seeing this grandeur, we wondered what splendour

would deck the body of Tui Nayou. But when he appeared, to our astonishment – walking between two fine warriors every inch of whose bodies was decorated – he was entirely naked: and more, his member – of generous dimensions – was fully extended, as though he was approaching the bed of a mistress. (We learned, later, that on meeting for the first time honoured guests, or those he wishes to impress, the King is aroused, with the help of two well-practised maidens; the result of which exercise is directed at impressing enemies and friends alike – an ambition which I am bound to say was on this occasion fully achieved.)

Tui Nayou was extremely good-looking, tall, well-made and athletic, graceful and easy in his carriage, and exhibiting much intelligence both in his expression of countenance and manners. It was impossible not to admire his appearance: he was of large, almost gigantic size, his limbs beautifully formed and proportioned; his countenance was agreeable and intelligent, while his immense head of hair, covered and concealed with gauze, smoke-dried and slightly tinged with brown, gave him altogether the appearance of an eastern Sultan.

As I have said, no garments concealed his magnificent body, the skin of which was of a clear but decided black; he came towards us, bowed, then taking his seat between us took one of our hands in each of his own and conveyed them to his still extended staff (the touch of which was like that of an ebony wand covered with velvet), then replaced them in our laps – the normal form of greeting the most honoured guests. It is considered not only proper but essential that this greeting should be performed before there is any diminution in the proportions of the instrument in question, for such would be considered not only insulting to the guests but a source of shame to His Majesty.

On this occasion the question did not arise, and though I wish to take no credit unless it is due, it may be (and later events tended to confirm the suspicion) that both Frances and myself were objects sufficiently interesting to prolong the King's interest; we had taken from our cabins two of our most handsome dresses, and these – concealing, yet without undue modesty, those parts which in Fijian beauties were commonly on view – tickled His Majesty's imagination to a degree which warmed him.

However, he was the ideal host; pausing only to salute us with his eyes – which were large and sparkling and betrayed without concealment his admiration – he made a gesture, and a procession of servants brought on the feast with which we were now amply regaled.

Chapter Nine

The Adventures of Andy

No station in Ceylon is more fortunate than Kandy in the beauty of the surrounding country. Of the many magnificent views in the island, that of the Doombera Plains, in the immediate vicinity of the station, is the most worthy of the notice of the tourist. The plains comprise a vast extent of beautifully undulating country, dotted here and there with groups of large and majestic trees, the intervals between which are open and entirely free from jungle. The whole bears a striking resemblance to an English park on an immense scale.

Through the midst of this perfectly admirable scenery rolls the River Mahavilaganga. Being much interrupted with rocks and shoals, no boats appear on its majestic stream, and the lonely river wanders sullenly through a region that seems to sympathise with and share in its solitude. The dark and lofty cone of the extinct volcano, the Hoonnisagiria, which attains an altitude of six thousand feet, raises itself up in the distance, and, supported by a rugged and elevated range of mountains that fill up the background, lends an additional charm and grandeur to this enchanting scene.

However, the time coming for us to travel on – if we were to see something more of the country before retracing our steps to the coast – we took the road for Newera Ellia, a *station sanitaire* to which all invalids fly in search of the health which might elude them in the less elevated districts of the island. A coach was fortunately travelling thither with supplies, and we were enabled to purchase seats upon it.

We left Kandy and followed the course of the valley of the Mahavilaganga until we arrived at the little village of Gampola, where there was a rest-house commanding a view of the distant blue mountains which we were about to ascend. This was not a particularly elegant abode, for it contained only a few dirty and rickety chairs and tables, and when one had carefully counted them, and observed that four bare whitewashed walls enclosed this furniture, nothing remained to be noted or commented upon. Mine host did not attempt to apologise for the undeniable deficiencies of his culinary establishment. 'There was milk this morning' and 'there had been fowls for sale' were the only words of consolation which we could wring from him.

However, a decent curry with some fruit and eggs was eventually set before us, and having eaten it, we counted ourselves contented. The house was on the left bank of the Mahavilaganga, which at that point is confined and rapid. The next day, we crossed it by means of a tolerable ferry-boat, which did duty for a bridge. We then mounted a road through the steep Atabagge Pass, pausing for the night at the Pusilava rest-house, almost one thousand two hundred feet above Kandy.

The temperature was now delightful, partaking neither of the intense heat of the low country nor of the bitter keen mountain air of the lofty plains of Newera Ellia. Indeed, Pusilava is counted most salubrious, and invalids who dread the sudden transition from the sultriness of the atmosphere of the valleys to the extreme chilliness on the mountain frequently establish themselves at this halfway house, which enjoys the bracing breezes without the frosts of the temperate zones.

We found a small group of ladies and gentlemen in residence here: a husband and wife, German by birth, who kept themselves apart from the rest; an elderly Major, retired from the Service, who seemed to have decided to pass the remainder of his days here; a young and somewhat vulgar Englishman who approached me with such freedom that I had to freeze him off, and a somewhat more mysterious lady who I was informed was English, but who appeared only in the distance, and when I made an attempt to approach her, vanished through the nearest doorway.

After I had enjoyed an evening meal, I walked out upon a balcony which commanded a view of the landscape below, looking towards the coast (which was, however, long out of sight). There, I found the mysterious lady standing at its far end, where there was no means of escape; and though she started and looked about her as though for a moment she contemplated throwing herself from the height rather than exchanging words with a stranger, she merely drew a shawl more closely about her and remained, silently contemplating the scenery.

After a while, I drew a little nearer, and ventured the comment that it was a fine evening (which, though not perhaps a remark of such cutting wit as to make an effect in a London drawing-room, I thought perhaps sufficient to establish a *rapport* between two English travellers at so remote a spot).

She indeed seemed slightly interested to hear what I took to be her native tongue, but confined her reply to a simple assent.

I will not detail the degrees by which I drew her into conversation, except to say that the procedure employed very considerable skills; however, I did eventually learn that she was Mrs Walter Fitzpatrick, the wife of a Colonel of the regiment stationed at the fort at Colombo, and therefore knew the Commander and his wife – which made our conversation a little easier.

Upon my hoping that it was no serious illness that brought her to Pusilava, she shrugged it off with some comment about 'a nervous condition', and passed on to asking about my travels.

I was happy to relate to her those incidents which could properly be described to a woman upon so slight an acquaintance. By now she had drawn a little nearer, and I could see that she was of no common beauty – though of a certain age (she must have been certainly over forty years). She was slender, and when her shawl was allowed to slip so that it no longer concealed her neck and shoulders, it could be seen that age had not burdened her with a greater store of wrinkles than might have been expected – indeed, if anything, with fewer.

I had by now decided to play the game of seeing just how far I could ingratiate myself with the lady, in order to discover why she was truly here, alone in so remote a spot; I flattered myself that my experience of the sex would enable me to do so without offence – and indeed, by a certain frankness about a sister of mine, whose name and condition I invented, and who had suffered from the deception of a lover and thus been driven into extremes of melancholy which had resulted eventually in her being confined to her room for over a year, finally drew from Mrs Fitzpatrick the admission that as I had guessed (for it is more common than not in such cases) her present circumstances arose from the neglect of a lover.

That strange circumstance which often persuades us to unburden ourselves to a stranger – especially when we believe that we shall see them but once – led her finally to confess that, not long after travelling to Colombo to join her husband, she had taken a lover.

'My condition was a melancholy one,' she said, 'for my husband, some years my senior, had given up all interest in the conjugal pleasures of married life; and the climate being such as to warm the spirits, I found myself singularly troubled by his neglect.'

I nodded agreement.

'It would only be natural under such circumstances, ma'am, that you should not resist the blandishments of any young man fortunate enough to encounter one so beautiful . . .'

She blushed with pleasure – but perhaps also for another reason, for 'I must admit,' said she, 'that the blandishments were upon my side, and in other circumstances might have been considered reprehensible. My husband employed as a personal servant a young man – no, to be honest, a boy – who was the son of a former officer and his wife, both of whom had been carried off some years previously, with the fever.

'He was now a lad of sixteen, tall and handsome for his years, but so much a part of my husband's daily life that he thought of him merely as a piece of useful furniture, and without considering had ordered him to fetch in my morning coffee, which I was in the habit of taking in bed, before rising. In short . . .'

She blushed again.

'Say no more, dear lady,' I said. 'Who could not understand or pardon a lady in such circumstances, and who could not envy a lad whose introduction to the delights of love should be through the agency of so amiable and handsome a partner?'

'I know not about your last statement,' she replied, 'though the boy seemed by no means unhappy; however, I am in a position to tell you with some certainty who might not pardon the circumstance, and that is Major Fitzpatrick, for coming upon us one morning when he returned to his quarters for some article which he mislaid, and finding us abed, he was thrown into the most extraordinary paroxysm of rage – unreasonable, as I pointed out, in one who had by no means shown himself eager for those favours which my young companion had just enjoyed.'

I remained sympathetically silent.

'And so you find me here, sir,' she said bitterly, 'deprived of all civilised company, and not least' (at which she drew near) 'of those services for which I fear my young friend is now suffering.'

There followed a pause. The reader will no doubt wonder why I did not follow the lead which her narrative had given; but truth to tell I was not in the mood, nor did the lady appeal especially to my appetite, somewhat jaded as it was by a combination of the travel (which had tired me), my recent enjoyment of the favours of a particularly handsome young lady the peculiar keenness of whose attentions I have described, and perhaps of the unusual altitude, which seemed to have the effect of somewhat thinning my blood.

At all events, even my new friend's loosening of her shawl, revealing the swelling of a pair of breasts upon whose round firmness the years had not yet left a mark, did not warm me. Perhaps sensing this, she drew a little away once more, and after a while:

'I notice that you have an unusual servant accompanying you.'

By this she must have meant young Kenny, who I always had serve me at table, though otherwise he was more companion than slave. I explained the circumstances under which he accompanied me.

She had never, she said, seen a young man so dark of skin (the voyage to Colombo alone constituted the extent of her travels outside England).

'Does he . . is he . . .'

I smiled encouragingly.

'Is the skin of his person entirely as dark as his face?' she finally asked.

'Certainly,' was my reply.

'And . . .' – she hesitated again – 'forgive the familiarity, but I have heard that the secret parts of negroes are of immense proportions . . .'

I replied that the relationship between us was not one which had allowed me to confirm or deny that supposition – at which she blushed more deeply than hitherto, and hastily denied supposing any such thing. I smilingly assured her that I had not supposed she meant it (being sufficiently confirmed in my masculinity to doubt whether I would give any lady the impression of being a nance).

An idea, however, now occurred to me.

'I feel sorry for the lad,' I said.

Why? she enquired.

He was in much the same case as the young man she had befriended at Colombo (I remarked); for though when I took him from Africa he was only beginning to show an interest in the other sex, that interest had now become keen – and told her how I had discovered him spying upon me at Kandy; yet that I did not wish his first experience of love to be with a lady whose favours could be purchased – for that might give him quite the wrong opinion of the sex; better he should wait until circumstance presented him with the opportunity of achieving bliss in the arms of a woman for whom the act itself, rather than financial reward, should be its own excuse.

There was for a moment another pause. Then, hesitantly, 'I hesitate to offer, lest you should consider me forward,' said Mrs Fitzpatrick, 'but I have ever had an interest in the education of the young, and feel especially that it is the duty of those of us fortunate enough to be born members of the greatest country in the world to show kindness towards those less fortunate; so should you feel able to recommend it . . I mean, should you opine . . if it might be the case that . . .'

I took her hand and pressed it.

'My gratitude would only be exceeded by that of young Kenny,' I said, and thereupon we made certain arrangements.

Taking leave, I then went in search of the boy, who I found sitting alone, and half asleep, in his room (a small one opening upon my own), and telling him that I was retiring early to bed, asked him to fetch me, in ten minutes, some fruit to my bedside. Without suspicion, though this was somewhat unusual, he concurred, and left the room. Allowing him a moment or two, I then knocked softly upon the door of Mrs Fitzpatrick, not far down the passage from my quarters, whereupon she slipped from it and accompanied me to my bedroom, where without false modesty she removed the single garment she wore, and laid herself upon the bed – whereupon I must confess that for a moment I regretted not having assured a banquet for myself, for she was a handsome woman indeed, somewhat plump, but to an enticing cosiness rather than fatness, her dark hair, now loosened, falling about her shoulders to enhance rather than conceal those rosy-tipped breasts which positively invited the tribute of a kiss.

However, with a smile I persuaded myself to leave the room, and went into Kenny's quarters, where I must confess I stationed myself at the chink of the door, being entirely unable to deprive myself of the sight of the comedy which was about to commence.

In a while, Kenny appeared, bearing the dish of fruit with such care that he did not look up until he was almost at the side of the bed; when, placing the dish upon a table, he raised his eyes to be confronted not by the familiar figure of his master, but that of an entirely unknown lady, naked as a nut!

Mrs Fitzpatrick was now pretending to be asleep, and though a moment's thought might have shown the boy that this was mere acting (for he had scarcely been absent for long enough for a lady to have entered the room, undressed, and fallen into a slumber) he was in no condition for calm reason, and stood transfixed; then, looking around to make sure that no-one else was present (or perhaps merely to confirm that he had not entered a strange room by mistake), he approached the bed a little more nearly, in order to inspect its burden.

The sight was one which certainly did not displease him, though his interest was no doubt prompted as much by unfamiliarity (and thus curiosity) as by carnal prompting; though this was clearly not far behind, for it was soon clear that his interest was most strongly focused (as who could doubt it?) upon those parts of the female anatomy most unfamiliar to him (which admittedly consisted of every area below the neck).

The lady's pose was such as to conceal only the most intimate part of her body; her bosom was entirely open to view, and was so delightful a sight that I could not blame the boy for clearly wishing to caress it – for he advanced his hand to within an inch or so of its smooth and glowing surface; then drawing back, as if nervous of discovery. His eyes then slid the length of the lady's body, pausing at that place where a single hand, curved like a shell, lay just over the velvet mound whose secret grotto he found curiously interesting.

I now discerned by the merest fluttering of her eyelashes that Mrs Fitzpatrick herself could scarcely resist the temptation to observe his reaction – which, unconsciously, had been to carry one of his hands to that area where the sight before him had concentrated its effect; and her seeing this no doubt made it impossible for her any longer to counterfeit sleep, for now her eyes opened wide, and smilingly she removed that concealing hand, stretching it out towards the boy, who gave a great start, and was clearly torn between the instinct to run and the compulsion to remain – especially since he was now able to glimpse that prize which all nature prompted him to advance toward.

The twin instincts resulted in his being rooted to the spot, which enabled the lady, raising herself from her reclining position, to take hold of his arm and gently draw him towards the bed; whereupon he advanced as in a trance comprising a mixture of pleasure and fear – the latter however clearly predominating as the lady, taking his hand, placed it upon her bosom – whereupon with the only instinct he knew, no doubt inspired by a dim memory of his infant days, he seized and fixed upon it with his lips, his sudden passionate gesture causing the lady to throw back her head in a positive ecstasy of pleasure – insufficiently keen however to satisfy her, for as he sprawled face downward across the bed at her side, she contrived to slide one hand under the waistband of his trousers and to clutch at his back side – which in a moment he became aware of, and lifting his head looked at her with such surprise that she was forced to laugh (and indeed his expression so comically combined amazement, pleasure and hope that I almost gave myself away by audible laughter).

He was still at the first too nervous to make any gesture not prompted by madam, who must persuade him to allow her to draw his shirt over his head, and then his trousers down from his hips – which was made no easier by his determination to remain lying upon his face, I suppose for the reason that he believed she might be offended by the state to which her attentions had now (without doubt) roused him.

Mrs Fitzpatrick, as I knew, was not to be satisfied by this, for she was now in the way of discovering whether the rumours (and, I dare say, her hopes) of the difference between the white and black races as to the proportions of their Parts, were true or false. This she attempted to ascertain by forcing him to turn, which he continued to deny until by tickling his arse she made him wriggle with pleasure and (I suspected) the pain of the constriction of his member between his belly and the bed; when finally she overcame his shyness by the simple measure of taking his hand in hers and conveying it between her own thighs, whereupon he finally realised that her eagerness balanced his own, and raised himself that he might more closely inspect the prize – thus making the revelation she desired.

The sight entirely satisfied her, a fact which she signalled by taking the exhibited prize between her hands to ascertain (I supposed) whether its size was equalled by its rigidity, which she clearly discovered to be the case by passing her fingers around and about the shining black cannon – which, however, being as sensitively cocked as might have been expected in the case of a youngster whose first experience this was of being abed with a lovely female, now disappointed her by discharging!

The paroxysm was clearly delightful to Kenny (by his squeak of pleasure), nor though one might have expected instinct to tell him otherwise, was he ashamed of it – for all he knew, the digital caresses might have been all he could expect of a lady!

Fortunately, Mrs Fitzpatrick was sufficiently understanding not to be angry – or else realised that in a boy of his age, the embarrassment would be entirely temporary;

she simply lay back (though with a sigh) and encouraged the boy to satisfy his curiosity as to the composition of the female anatomy, which he did with increasing interest, particularly as to that part new to him (as the bosom was not, though among the many he had seen in Africa, where the upper part of the body was frequently uncovered, none had been white – and he frequently applied his tongue to the skin in order to discover whether its surface, marbled with the most delicate blue veins, was of a natural colour).

She did not, now, remain still, but – with a view no doubt to returning him to full vigour – began to apply herself to entertaining him, which she did with such attention that it was clear that she received as much pleasure as she gave by pinching his paps with her fingernails, passing her hands along his body, from his armpits, where small, tight black curls grew, to his flanks then around to the tight cheeks of his arse, which they gently parted in order to tickle his fundament before weighing those spheres which drew themselves tightly into his groin upon receiving for the first time such tender attentions.

On ascertaining by touch that his prick, which had diminished only in strength rather than in size, was again achieving a certain body by the renewed pumping of his young blood, she astonished him further by applying her lips to its remarkable length, drawing them along its length from base to tip with a tender insistence that conveyed an obvious longing for the moment when it once more attained sufficient inflexibility to be put to its proper use.

Nor was the moment long delayed when that was the case: yet there was still delay, for prompted by her own actions, he now bent to test her lower region, first with inquisitive fingers, then with lips – sipping as at a cup, and not dissatisfied either with the experience or with his new friend's reaction (which was to begin once more to caress that part of him which had already recovered from its too quick expression of interest) – he brought madam soon to a pitch at which she could no longer refrain from that full enjoyment which had been denied her (I supposed) since her departure from Colombo.

Throwing her thighs even more widely apart, she gripped Kenny by the upper arms and drew him up between them until his now once more ready weapon was at the breach; when its softness called to those instincts too deeply embodied in the male to be denied, and – from a vantage-point perfectly set for the view – I saw the ramrod disappear into the barrel (to return to the military simile which her story irresistibly led me to), where in a moment it began those movements which come naturally at such a time.

It was with some surprise that I remarked that the boy was able to maintain himself in the saddle for considerably longer than I would have expected; it may be that this is concomitant with the black races – or simply that Mrs Fitzpatrick was fortunate in her young lover; at all events, it was not until, with a cry sufficiently loud (I feared) to attract the attention of the servants, she threw her legs about his waist with such a convulsion that he was positively lifted into the air, that – with the surprise, perhaps, or simply the motion – he made a final thrust and himself gave half a shout, half a gasp of satisfaction, whereafter they lay in panting pleasure upon the bed.

I now felt it time to reveal myself, entering the room to pour them two glasses of water, of which they were glad (though Kenny at first clearly believed that his being found in such company might be displeasing to me). I found that my observation of their pleasure, though undertaken more from curiosity as to Kenny's reactions than for any other reason, had resulted in my own emotions being somewhat roused; and, in short, by the motion of an eyebrow, enquired whether there would be objection to my contributing to the sum of the lady's happiness; to which her reply was to move a little to one side, whereupon I doffed my clothes, ignoring the half-concealed giggle with which Kenny greeted the unequivocal sign of my interest presented by a weapon which – while, I must confess, not of a dimension even of so young a black man – was such as to indicate my readiness for an embrace which the lady was not slow to permit, and which she returned by receiving me with every indication of pleasure.

Though I could not doubt that he had watched my passage with the young lady at Kandy, this was the first time that Kenny had observed a couple in that intimacy which now engaged us, and I could not but be conscious that he was looking on with all that attention an apt pupil gives to a respected teacher. My urgency was such that I could not pause to explain to him that under other circumstances our present intimacy would have been prefaced by certain more delicate preparations – nor that his own attentions to her had had the result of readying the lady for a congress for which under other circumstances she must be more carefully prepared. There would perhaps be a time, later, at which I could address him on the subject.

Meanwhile, this was no time for me to rebuke him for paying such careful attention to an act which normally he would not have been invited to observe – placing his head at our sides, then above or below, in order to watch the pestle and mortar at their work. There then came a somewhat disconcerting moment when, aroused beyond his capacity to contain himself, he manoeuvred his body behind and above, so that I felt his instrument against my thighs, and for a moment feared he was about to take a course which would have been as painful to me as embarrassing; but he was of course ignorant of the course which a sophisticated bully might have adopted – and in any event the situation was saved by madam, who catching at him drew him upward and stretching her neck sideways once more approached her lips to his again ready member, and through a combination of the movement of her lips and fingers brought forth in time the thin gruel which only was the result of his third evacuation, and which oozed from him at the moment when my own eruption brought the proceedings to an end satisfactory to all three.

The lady in a short while excused herself; and I taught Kenny the importance of cleansing himself, as soon as possible after the event; not that Mrs Fitzpatrick was in the least likely to be diseased – nor indeed that, if she were, it was certain that the application of soap and water would prevent infection – but that safety, inasmuch as it could be conferred by cleanliness, was worth courting.

The boy was far too excited by the events of the evening to dispose himself to sleep, and we sat for some time, while I attempted to answer those multifarious questions which occur to all young men at such a time – and did so to such effect as will, I trust, enable him not only to satisfy his own desires in carnal matters, but give him an interest in pleasing any young lady to whom he pays attention, rather than merely in satisfying his own needs without relation to those of another.

Next morning we left the rest-house without the opportunity to say farewell to Mrs Fitzpatrick; accompanied by the vulgar young man I had seen the previous day – who after a while enquired whether I had enjoyed a bag with Mrs Walters. On my asking what he could mean, he revealed that 'Mrs Fitzpatrick' was in fact a disgraced widow notorious before her husband's death for her amours, and forced by the threat of withdrawal of his pension to retire from Colombo (where she had been the cause of four duels in three years) to Pusilava, where she led a life of considerable boredom, relieved only by her invariable seduction of any male traveller susceptible enough to accept her advances.

I returned the view that the speaker should keep such gossip for those who were interested in it, and that the lady had made no such advances to me – nor would I, of course, have accepted them should she have done so; and effectively shut the man up for the rest of the journey – being thankful that Kenny was travelling outside the coach, and could not give me away.

After leaving Pusilava, the road entered the forest of that name, which extends for some miles and contains some majestic trees. At Hellbodde, the forest terminates, and the magnificent valley of Cotamalie spreads its gently undulating and varied surface before the fascinated traveller. The winding mountains here form a vast basin in the centre of which the various torrents that descend from them unite into one deep and rapid stream which, after winding a long and tortuous course caused by the peculiar and almost chaotic formation of the country that it traverses, ultimately discharges itself into the Mahavilaganga.

The vicinity of Rambodde is announced by the stunning roar of the falls in its neighbourhood, which greatly contribute to complete the effect of the surrounding scenery. The village is situate at the base of the apparently inaccessible heights that girdle the plains of Newera Ellia. From the rest-house the valley of Cotamalie is seen to great advantage, and while the ceaseless yet soothing sound of the cascades which pour down on every side affords to the ear that indescribable pleasure which the noise of falling waters rarely fails to produce, the eye is gratified by the surpassing grandeur of their appearance.

Some prefer the chilly temperature of Newera Ellia; others the mild climate of Kandy; but the vale of Cotamalie, in whose bosom the bright waters meet, is in the opinion of many the most enchanting spot in Serendib's romantic isle. Its sequestered situation and sublime scenery recommend it to the notice of those who are romantically inclined, and by the margins of the foaming torrents into which the waters, after descending the falls, immediately resolve themselves, we saw during the two days we spent there no less than three couples in a state of nature, enjoying each other's company with every appearance of pleasure – and great was the difficulty I had in restraining Kenny from divesting himself of his clothing to join them, being forced to explain that there were more instances than not in which, while two was company, three would be a crowd.

So we passed on into the pass of Rambodde, which emerges on the plains of Newera Ellia, where we were introduced to the tribe of the Caffres, employed chiefly upon keeping the road in good repair; and took the opportunity of staying for a night in one of their encampments, having learned that there was to be on that evening a Caffre love-dance, which was recommended to us as extraordinary, and which we should take the opportunity of observing – but a description of which must wait until my next chapter.

Chapter Ten

Sophie's Story

The procession of men – presumably, the cooks – which now entered was greeted with a great cry of '*A magiti-i-i!*', or 'Cooked food!' – and the eatables themselves were borne on great oval dishes lined with fresh leaves, each one first being presented to the *Tui Rara* or Master of the Feast, and on his approval then to Tui Nayou, who in courtesy tasted it before it was laid upon the floor upon clean mats generously spread.

As to the food, it was light and plain. There are many different vegetables, and shell and other fish, being highly esteemed, are present in unequalled variety. Fish is served up with a relishing sauce; and sweet sauces are made for the richer sorts of pudding by expressing the juices of the nut, the ti-root, and the sugar-cane.

Almost everything found living on the sea-reef is eaten and enjoyed. Shrimps are used to make an elegant and delicious sandwich, being arranged between two thicknesses of taro leaves. To this is added a dozen varieties of bread, nearly thirty kinds of puddings, and twelve sorts of broths or soups, including turtle-soup. A rich sort of gruel is made from the milk and pulp of the young cocoanut.

The chief dish at our banquet, being a great luxury, was roast pork – three hogs, baked whole, lying on their bellies on top of a positive pedestal of food. These animals, having been killed by breaking the snout across, did not present the quiet appearance of dead pigs, but looked as though they snarled defiance on those assembled to eat them.

Several kinds of infusions are made from aromatic grasses and leaves, the favourite drink being *ava* or *kava*, being drunk as regularly as we take coffee. This is made by young men chewing and then expectorating the flesh of the *piper mythisticum*. Early in the morning the King's herald stands in front of the royal abode, and shouts at the top of his voice, '*Kava!*' Hereupon, all within hearing respond in a sort of scream, '*Mama!*' or 'Chew it!' At this signal the chiefs, priests and leading men gather round the bowl to talk over public affairs while their favourite draught is being prepared.

When the young men, chosen not only for their youth but for their handsome shapes and demeanour, have finished the chewing, each deposits his portion, in the form of a round, dry ball, in the bowl, the inside of which becomes studded over with a large number of these separate little masses. The man who has made the grog takes the bowl by the edge and tilts it towards the King, with the words: 'Sir, with respect, the *kava* is collected.' If the King thinks it enough, he replies in a low voice, '*Loba*,' whereupon water is gradually poured into the bowl and the chewed material mixed, then strained, when the drink is ready.

Both Frances and myself found the ceremonial preparation of this liquor interesting to watch, not least because of the general appearance of the young men engaged in it, who, being as a matter of course unclothed, displayed muscles of the arms and chest necessarily pleasing to the female apprehension; indeed, no combinations of animal action can develop the swell and play of the muscles with more grace or a more pleasant effect than in mixing and lifting the *kava* in the large bowls employed, each of which, when filled, weighs a considerable amount.

The *kava* being ready, two of the most handsome of the young men bore a cup to the high table, when the *Tui Rara* recited the following prayer:

> *'Me loma viuaka na kalou*
> *A lutu mada na tokalau'*

(or, 'Let the gods be of a gracious mind, and send a wind from the east'). Then the young men presented the cup to the King, who poured out a few drops upon the ground, and drank, while the company chanted: '*Ma-nai di-na. La-ba-si-ye: a-ta-mai-yi: ai-na-ce-a-toka: Wo-ya! yi! yi! yi!*' clapping their hands – not to clap, or not to join in the final shout of '*Yi! Yi! Yi!*' would be considered disloyal.

The King drank in the manner of his people, which was by throwing back his head with his mouth open and, holding the cup some inches above the lips, allowing a stream of *kava* to run down the throat. When Frances and I and Dick and St John attempted this feat, it was to shower ourselves with the white and sticky liquid! – however, we were able to swallow a sufficient amount to discover that, while an acquired taste, it results certainly in a lifting of the emotions.

The ceremonial meal over, the King clapped his hands three times, whereupon to the sound of an orchestra which had played during the eating – composed of players of nose-flutes, conch-shells, Pandean pipes, a Jew's harp made of a strip of bamboo, and large and small drums made of hollowed logs – two maidens were led before us clad only in loin-clothes – but also to some extent in their long and beautiful hair, which fell in all directions from the crowns of their heads in twisted locks of a brown and red colour. Their limbs, slender and brown, glistened with oil.

Reaching the King, they bent low in obeisance, when he rose and, taking two *liku* or necklaces of carved ivory points, handed them to the *Tui Rara*, who in turn gave them to St John and Dick. The girls then kneeling before them, it was made clear by mime that they were to place the necklaces about their necks. Upon their doing this, there was a great shout from all present, of '*Veidomoni*!' and it was explained that our friends were betrothed to the two beauties.

Their feelings were clearly mixed; but upon consultation with the *Tui Rara* (through our interpreter, Thakombau) it was explained that this was a purely honorary betrothal, not something for lifetime; but that it would be expected of them that – as is the case when the ceremony takes place between Fijian couples – the two gentlemen should show their affection; whereat our friends cheered up, and on the *Tui Rara* offering to lead them away, were happy to follow him, each with a girl upon his arm, in the direction of a hut where they were left to themselves to pursue what pleasantries they wished.

Evening now drawing on, and the feast showing signs of ending (several of the notabilities beginning to snore, under the effect no doubt of considerable quantities of *kava*), we wondered what was expected of us – though we had a shrewd idea, His Majesty having throughout the meal paid us the most particular attention, picking out rich morsels of food to offer us (which he placed between our lips with his own fingers), and at times touching our shoulders with appreciative hands. We were of the opinion that our dress, which of course covered our persons to such an extent as would be acceptable in an English drawing-room, inflamed his interest even more – it being common with the Fijians that only the single most notable part of a lady's person should be covered by the little clothing they commonly wore.

So, more or less expecting the King to show a more particular interest, we were surprised when at a signal from his chief Minister, four young ladies came forward and reaching out their hands drew us to our feet and began to lead us away – on our enquiring, Thakombau mentioning that in politeness we should accede if possible to any suggestion made to us, assuring us in a quiet tone that nothing but good was intended towards us.

We were now led in the direction in which St John and Dick had been taken, though not to the same hut. Instead, we entered a plain house with only mats and rugs upon the floor, and what appeared to be a selection of pots. Here, with such delicacy and care that no-one could have objected, the four girls lifted our clothing from us, and invited us to lie upon the rugs. Then, fetching cloths wetted with cool water, they wiped our bodies, the cooling effect being delightful after the warmth engendered not only by the crowd of diners but also by the food and *kava*.

They then carried two or three pots to our sides, and, persuading us to turn upon our faces, began to wipe us all over with some other liquid, which had a sweet smell, and felt very slightly sticky to the touch. Their touch was so caressing and gentle that I almost began to fall asleep, when I felt at my wrists and ankles the most peculiar tickling – and opening my eyes found that each of my four attendants was now applying her tongue to those parts, assiduously lapping at every exposed surface. A few feet away, Frances was experiencing the same felicity.

It is difficult to explain to anyone who has not undergone such an experience the ecstasy with which a slow feeling of transport was communicated by those four gentle, yet pointed and inspiriting tongues, as feeding off the liquid (comprising, as I later found, a concoction of honey and the juices of certain fruits) they inserted themselves between fingers and toes, followed the curving of the spine, travelled the hills of the buttocks . . and then, upon our turning upon our backs, and having made a new application of the liquid, touched each surface of the front of our bodies – but seeming to linger with a meaningful insinuation upon our nipples, beneath our arms, about our waists, and finally – our thighs parted by the gentlest persuasion – about our more private parts, ceasing only at that point when it was impossible for us not to express our emotions in a groan or cry . . .

Whereupon, a curtain was drawn, and who should appear but His Majesty, who strode forward still clad only in his skin, now bearing a sceptre of such dimensions that (whether for comfortable or ceremonial purposes) it was supported by two of the youths who had formerly been bearers of the *kava* cup, each of whom placed a hand beneath the King's instrument of generation, one near the base, the other at the point where a splendid bulb swelled from the brown stalk, like the fine empurpled head of a rare plant.

As the King came towards us, so our attendants melted away, leaving us – our bodies still flushed and throbbing from their ministrations – reclining in a position which would have been regarded in polite society as scandalously improper, for our lower limbs were stretched wide, displaying to His Majesty those parts with which he might only have expected acquaintance after a period of more intimate connection than had so far taken place. However, from surprise – and also from not knowing the etiquette of the situation – we remained as we lay; nor did the King show any displeasure, from which I supposed that he was satisfied by the sight of a second feast, no less rich (if I may be allowed to boast on our behalf) than that of which we had so recently partaken.

Reaching a point just between us, the King lifted his hands in a magisterial gesture, whereupon the youths bowed their heads, withdrew their hands and backed away (I could not but notice and admire the fact that his royal sceptre did not bow by one particle at the withdrawal of its supports, but stood proudly erect; from which I supposed that the attendant's attentions were ceremonial rather than practical).

On our being left alone, the King sank to his knees, and taking my right hand and Frances' left, once more placed them upon his person – as at the beginning of the feast. However, it was clear that he expected more intimate gestures than had then occurred; nor could I personally resist passing my fingers over that handsome helmet, the surface of which was velvety to the touch – the velutinous texture extending, indeed, the length of the column, which I allowed my palm to descend until it came into contact with my friend's, who had clearly been engaged in weighing the pair of well-proportioned stones – only proportionate in size, however, to the remainder of the machinery – which hung at the base.

The question now arose, what was expected of us? But His Majesty answered it by pressing us to the ground in our former positions; when, reaching to a bowl placed within reach, he gathered a handful of another unguent, sweet-smelling ointment, with which he thoroughly basted his weapon.

Seeing this, I made the mistake of assuming that we were expected to perform for His Majesty a ceremony similar to that which had been done upon us – and half-sitting, extended my tongue to take up some of the ointment (which indeed was not unpleasant to the taste). But this was clearly not to be the point, for the King once more pressed me back upon the rugs, and lifting himself upon his toes and fingers so that for a moment he was suspended like a canopy over me, lowered himself so that his sceptre first nuzzled, then insisted, then pierced my not unwilling person.

I considered myself fortunate, at that moment, that he had done the courtesy of so generous an oiling, otherwise I could not have escaped a painful encounter, his tool being of such dimensions as (within my memory – which encompassed Mr Nadge's remarkable accessory) I had never yet experienced, stretching my lower lips to their limit, and at once filling the aperture from wall to wall, and – as he continued to lower his body – seeming to penetrate beyond my womb to my stomach, beyond my stomach to my breast, even to entering (as I felt) the very confines of my heart.

Again unlike any lover I had previously had the pleasure of, he did not sink into my arms, but continued (with what strength I could only imagine, for his body was a muscular and substantial one) to hold himself upon the tips of his toes and fingers, merely lifting and lowering himself so that his sceptre, the only contact between us, moved like a piston within its chamber.

Whether because of the extensive preparation offered by the maidens, I cannot say – but within a few moments my spirits had been raised almost to spilling by this strange wooing; my bosom rose and fell, and I was within a few moments of expressing a final pleasure when with a single, smooth gesture and a lifting of his lordly buttocks, he withdrew his instrument and in a crab-like movement centred himself over the body of my friend, who had been watching in admiration, envy – and a certain surprise.

In a movement so smooth and controlled that it could not have been bettered by the most superb athlete, he now pierced Frances as he had pierced me; and again I could not but admire the control which he exercised, the muscles of his calves and forearms standing out as they took the whole weight of his body, his tool, now glistening in the light of the lamps placed about us, gliding rhythmically, and in no short time (as was signalled by her gasps and the clenching of her fingers into the rug beneath her) bringing Frances, too, close to her apogee – when, in a repeated motion, he returned to me . . .

This continual motion continued for what seemed an age, until, perhaps pitying us for the suspense in which we were held (for I could not but believe that His Majesty was in complete control of himself) he permitted himself to continue beyond the point at which our ecstasy could be contained, and first I, then my friend, made it clear through sound and fury that he had entirely conquered us.

Yet he had not, himself, capitulated. The moment Frances, with a splendid cry, had signalled the completion of her pleasure, he lifted himself from between her thighs, and turning, reclined upon his back – his instrument, shining from its endeavours, no whit diminished. Now, once more, he reached for our hands – and it was with gratitude (his ministrations having been no less pleasurable than they were unusual) that we were pleased by stroking, then by a more energetic motion, to attempt to complete his own satisfaction.

It might have been expected that this were a difficult task – but he now relaxed all control, and in a short time we felt beneath our palms the stirring of a quake which soon shook his entire body, as if, primed by his attentions to us, the cannon was about to explode – which it did, in a fulmination which shook the King's whole body as almost in a fit, the discharge being as strongly jetted as it was voluminous, leaving no doubt of His Majesty's virility.

We learned, afterwards, that while it was regarded as proper and courteous that the King should entertain distinguished female visitors in this way, any child born of such a union would have immediately to be slain (as unable to stand with the other princes and princesses conceived upon the bodies of His Majesty's wives), so that he had been trained from his youth not to expel his vital juices into the bodies of such as Frances and myself – hence the curious (but by no means displeasing) experience we had undergone.

The King having clapped his hands, the maidens returned, and with the soft green leaves of some plant, together with yet another sweet-smelling, somewhat astringent liquor, cleansed and refreshed our bodies; when the King saluted us and left us to slumber until dawn, cooled gently by two of the maidens with huge fans made of the leaves of the cocoa-nut.

In the morning, we were re-united with Dick and St John, who did not enquire how we had spent the night – whether out of delicacy, or because they did not wish to reveal the pleasures they had no doubt experienced at the hands of their sweet companions, I cannot say.

We spent several days after this in pleasant recreation, swimming in clear waters, and lounging upon the beaches; but before the time came for us to leave the islands, I asked our friend Thakombau whether it would be possible for us to visit an ordinary Fijian village – whereupon he replied that he would be happy to take us to his own village, where his family would be proud to receive us.

This lay some miles inland, consisting of perhaps thirty houses of various sizes and shapes – some like square wicker baskets, others like rustic arbours, yet more like oblong hayricks with holes in the sides. The walls and fences of the houses are from four to ten feet high, and in some cases are hidden on the outside by the thatch being extended to the ground. On our admiring these, it was proposed that one should be built especially for us – although we were only staying one or two nights! It sounded an impossibility – yet it was run up in about an hour and a half, with its own hearth and an elevation at one end for a divan and sleeping place!

The thatching of the house was delightful to watch. Boys swarmed over the canes of the roof like so many monkeys, then men took up the grass and lashings, and in one mass of people, all talking and joking at the tops of their voices, mounted ladders and fell to work – the noise being indescribable, the voices being intermixed with the stamping down of the thatch.

It was with pleasure that I saw that these villagers took as much care in the decoration of their heads and bodies as the men and women at the court of the King! – indeed, if one accepts the absence of clothes, the care of painting, hairdressing and tattooing is as substantial as the care any *beau* in Mayfair pays to his appearance. The vines and flowers of the forest are used to make chaplets, necklaces and wreaths – which latter are thrown over one shoulder, falling across the body and onto one hip. The hair is, as I have said, handsomely dressed upon all occasions.

The men have strange and often ugly cuts made in their skins, leaving unsightly scars the possession of which is none the less honourable: sometimes concentric circles are seen around the arms, sometimes rows of wart-like spots along the arms and backs.

Genuine tattooing is only seen on the women: barbed lines run along their hands and fingers, patches of blue at the corners of the mouth, and strange patterns upon their bodies – even on the most tender parts. This decoration is quite obligatory, and its neglect is said to be punished by the spirits after death.

It so happened that a young woman was to be tattooed on the day we arrived in the village – a beautiful creature of perhaps sixteen or seventeen years of age, who in two days was to be married, and must undergo the torture (as we would think it) beforehand.

Divested of all ornament, she was laid upon a mat beneath the shade of a tree, in a small compound from which all men were banished. A middle-aged woman who was to perform the decoration then approached with the tools of her trade: chiefly an instrument called a 'tooth', consisting of four or five bone teeth fixed to a light handle six inches long, which is dipped in a pigment made of charcoal and candle-nut oil.

This woman first dipping a twig in the pigment, traced upon the lower part of the globes of the girl's breasts the pattern to be made permanent: a simple but decorative scroll. This was then followed by placing the 'tooth' upon the marks, and striking it with the inside of the hand, driving the sharpened bones through the skin.

The girl bore this with such equanimity that at first I thought it must be less painful than I had imagined; but before it was complete, her sides were red and slippery with the blood which ran from the wounds, and her lower lip almost severed by her teeth biting into it to avoid her crying out – which would have signalled a diminution in the respect in which she would be held by her husband (for any cries would be heard by the circle of men who sat outside the walls of the compound, and indeed by the groom himself).

The absence of any expression of pain was much a matter for congratulation; and after the blood had been washed away and a soothing compress applied, the girl herself seemed to recover with astonishing rapidity, and was soon laughing and conversing as though the scene had never taken place. It is similarly, I am informed, the case with these women in childbirth – they drop their babies in a crouching position, and the cord being cut immediately place it at the breast, and in a short time resume their work.

We enjoyed our observation of the village, and were persuaded with little difficulty to remain for the betrothal ceremony of the girl whose tattooing we had witnessed and her husband – a young fisherman only a little older than herself.

He was engaged, on the night before the ceremony, at a sort of groom's party into which we could not gain admission, and which Thakombau described in only limited detail, somewhat blushingly explaining that it included the ascertaining that the young man was capable of – and here he made an unmistakable gesture which took the place of the verb for which he either knew no English, or believed to be indecent (as well it might have been).

It seemed that the two persons concerned had been betrothed in infancy, as is often the case with the children of the most important members of a village society. A few days ago, the groom had gone to the parents of his fiancée and, presenting them with a whale's tooth, asked for their daughter – to which they were bound to agree. (I am told, by the way, that through greed the most improper bargains are sometimes struck, an old man of sixty being able to secure, through the disposition of his wealth, two brides of under sixteen years of age.)

The parents' consent having been formally given, the girl's *veimei* or nurse accompanies her to the house of her intended husband's parents with a present of teeth, cloth or mats. We saw this ceremony, the girl weeping in a heartbroken manner – but comforted by the presentation of gifts by the friends of the bridegroom. This is called the *vakamamaca*, or 'drying of tears', and leads to the *vakatakata*, or 'warming up', which takes place on the afternoon of the marriage.

For this ceremony the girl's body is anointed with oil, in order that it should look most attractive – which indeed is the case, the oil making her brown skin shine and glisten, and seeming to give her whole body an expensive sheen. The groom comes to her bearing a gift of food, which she accepts; he then raises her to her feet, and taking her by one hand leads her to a pool near the village, into which she steps accompanied by her husband-to-be, who washes the oil from her body with leaves.

This is not, I must say, a very satisfactory process, water and oil being antipathetic one to the other; it is difficult to say for what reason the ceremony takes place – but it is certainly enjoyed not only by the bride but by the groom, for though he stands waist-deep in water, his movements occasionally cause a certain something to break the surface which seems to express his satisfaction at this contact with the body of his bride – for though their being betrothed from childhood permits any familiarity short of the final one, the date of the marriage must always be preceded by as much as a month during which it is the duty of the couple to keep as remotely apart as may be possible in such a small community.

Next, the girl must go alone to the beach and catch a fish. This is not generally difficult (sometimes a dead or half-dead fish being placed conveniently nearby). It is now cooked by her and placed before her husband – who comes with his friends to eat it, all of them with their bodies splendidly decorated and oiled.

On their sitting down, the bride-to-be removes her *liku*, handing it to her nearest friend (it is the supposition, as with the wedding bouquet in England, that she will be next to find a husband), and sits decorated merely with a wreath of flowers while there is the ceremony of *veitasi*, or 'clipping', in which the best friend of the groom steps forward and with a sharp knife cuts first a plait of hair from the head of the bride, then a small lock of her private hair, both of which are then ceremonially burned in a fire.

It is, as far as I could ascertain, at this moment that the bride and groom become man and wife in form – for matrimony, in Fiji, is a social or civil contract only. No priest is needed; it is only the observance of custom which sanctifies the union.

However, there is one ceremony still to be observed – which seemed to me to be the most important. This is the *vakata kakana*, which took place in the evening, when almost the whole village repaired to a sylvan retreat where embowering trees, with their thick foliage interwoven with various creepers, afforded a thick and secluded shade, lit now by small fires – built for light, indeed, rather than heat, the evenings being delightfully warm.

Here there is a feast called the *vakavotu*, or 'becoming visible', at the apex of which there is a great noise upon their drums, when bride and groom are carried into the clearing – the bride upon the shoulders of her friends, the groom upon his. The two groups stands at opposite ends of the clearing while the wedding guests walk in a great circle, making obeisance to them as they pass.

Then comes the time of the *tatavu*, or 'broiling'. The crowd remains in a circle, but slowly gathers itself in, taking the bride and groom – still shoulder high – with them, until there are only a few yards separating them. I should have said that they are, of course, unclothed – the wearing of clothing being so uncommon here, I have omitted to stress it – but on this occasion both Frances and I were, I believed, particularly conscious of it, as seeming so out of place in the European idea of a great public ceremony. Yet it must be confessed that it made a picturesque sight; the couple's bodies again being oiled so that the firelight struck bright orange and yellow flashes from the dark skin of their flanks and sides.

A rhythmical clapping now began, and Frances suddenly striking me in the ribs with her elbow and directing my glance towards the groom, I saw that his member had very suddenly become erect – which seemed astonishing to me, for the occasion was very public, and entirely lacking in the atmosphere which I would have thought consistent with such a display – at least, I knew no European man who would be capable of the flourish. However, Frances now whispering in my ear directed my eyes to what she had been able to see, but had been until then hidden from me: the groom was now supported not by having his legs about the neck of a friend, as had formerly been the case, but by the hands of four or five men placed beneath his buttocks – while another had in his hand a large feather, with which he was busily tickling the young man's fundament, thus no doubt causing the tumidity so obvious to us all – no doubt including the bride, who (I was bound to conjecture) should not have been disappointed at it.

She was also now supported merely upon the hands of her bridesmaids – if so I may call them; and as the clapping continued, the two groups began a sort of dance, inward and outward, so that the knees of the couple almost met before they were again carried off. The bridesmaids now began, on advancing, to open the girl's thighs like the hinges of a door – when it could be seen that upon her lower chest and belly was a fine decoration in white paint or daubing resembling a bird, his head just below her breasts, his wings outspread so that their tips lay upon her hips, and his tail seeming just to spring from that orifice upon which the groom's attention was no doubt fixed, for it was now quite clear that the feather was no longer necessary in maintaining his stand; indeed the light from time to time caught with its brilliance a sheen upon the tip of his instrument, which seemed to be weeping with frustration! That others than he were equally aroused was now obvious, not only upon looking about us, but upon it being impossible not to feel, almost incessantly, some equally rigid member knocking against our own persons – no doubt by accident. I was extremely conscious that my friend and I were now the only persons present whose dress was not in accordance with custom, and I must confess felt an urge to throw off the muslin which covered my body – yet hesitated, not wishing to revert to what civilisation would call a condition of savagery.

The noise now seemed to reach a climax, and as it did so, surging forward in one last movement, the groom's friends bore him actually between the thighs of his bride – held akimbo by her maids (though they did not, it seemed to me, find it necessary to employ much force); and one of them reaching up to grasp his member (for he himself laid his hands upon the shoulders of his wife, and she hers upon his) guided it into its proper seat, whereupon there was a splendid shout of '*Vakalutu!*'

and the bride and groom leaned their bodies backwards upon a willing platform of hands, revealing in a gesture which might in Europe be considered obscene, but here seemed entirely natural, that they were indeed joined in indissoluble bands.

There now broke out a general party of celebration, some couples finding their way out of the firelight to their own nooks of the forest, some simply slipping to the ground where clasped in each other's arms they emulated the passion of the bride and groom (who I was relieved to see had been allowed to disappear, to enjoy each other in privacy). Soon, Frances and I found ourselves the only ones still standing without partners – even our friend Thakombau having disappeared, no doubt with some friend.

Picking our way through the bodies, we found our hut and entering it laid ourselves on the sleeping platform and after a while fell into a fitful sleep, interrupted from time to time with a giggling and whispering as (no doubt) the people of the village returned from the wedding breakfast to their own beds.

I must confess that even had the *Sulphur* not by now been ready to sail, we would have had enough of this interesting island, and were quite pleased to spend some time lazing once more on board; the weather being enchantingly warm and calm, apart from a time at mid-day when it was best to remain in the cool of the cabin.

We were now bound for the Malayan peninsula, where surveys had to be made of the Malacca strait: but it was proposed that we should go ashore at Singapore, whence we could if we wished make an excursion to some other parts of the peninsula. Our friends on board had now concluded what was the truth – that Frances and myself were perfectly able to deal with any emergencies which might arise during our travels, and that it was perfectly impossible to dissuade us from any course we wished to take – whereupon any plans of ours were received with, at most, a mere shake of the head, and we were left to our own devices!

Chapter Eleven

The Adventures of Andy

The Caffres, I should explain, are used chiefly as labourers in the island of Ceylon, for being to a large extent undisciplined they make better workmen than soldiers – there is something in their character repugnant to the etiquette and strictness of military discipline. They are nevertheless social, cheerful and amiable, possessing chiefly the characteristics of the Negro – the woolly hair, the full lip, the long heel; indeed Kenny, upon first seeing them, felt sure that they must be related to the Hottentot (for which I have not been able to find evidence).

The detachment of Caffres on the Rambodde pass consisted of sixty or seventy men, accompanied by an equal number of females, who I took to be their wives – their encampment presenting an animated spectacle amid the loneliness of the surrounding jungle, and offering the traveller a favourable opportunity of studying another, and to the Anglo-Cingalese, a novel impress of humankind.

Without entering into any dissertation touching the charms of Caffre women, it may perhaps be permitted to me to record that their faces are not entirely charming – at least to the European eye. Their figures, however, are another matter, for even in those who are of a certain age, a life of corporeal activity has maintained a suavity of the muscles and a lack of surplus weight which results in their being for the most part extremely slim and active.

It seems that their 'love-dances' occur upon regular occasions, whenever they feel the desire for such a recreation – which, the daily labour of the men being as a matter of course dull and monotonous, is very often; however, they pretended that this was not the case, in order that I – as a rich traveller (every *griffin* is to them rich beyond their dreams) – should bribe them by paying for copious libations of brandy, for which both men and women showed an inordinate affection.

The dance took place in a clearing at the centre of the encampment, right in front of a large hut in which such legal affairs as were necessary – such as the contracting of labour, or the trials of criminals – took place; and so it might be considered as approximating to the main square of a more civilised location. Here, the entire population assembled, dressed in what passed for its best – which consisted of lengths of brightly-coloured cloth wrapped about the loins both of men and women, the upper parts of their bodies being in both cases left bare.

A couple then entered the space cleared for the dance, and began, to the music of home-made flutes and drums. They approached each other with an air of coquetry with steps that somewhat approached those of the *fandango* in Spain, making indescribable but I suppose, to them, loving grimaces and contortions of their faces.

As the man became more ardent, so the woman retired; whereat he began to chant verses which (from the laughter with which they were received, and other gestures) were probably coarse in nature. On the lady of his love still continuing scornful, he began a mimic thrusting of his hips which could not be misunderstood, and in a moment detached the end of the bulky knot of cloth about his loins, and offered it to her. Still pretending a dislike, she took it, whereat he began to revolve, the cloth slowly unwinding – and proving to be of some length (on examining it afterwards I found it to be of a thinner material than was otherwise available in the place, and enquiry revealed that it was specially acquired for the purpose, and loaned to the male member of any couple performing this ritual).

At last, it appeared that only one fold of cloth was left – which the man kept hold of, protecting his body from complete nakedness. The woman desisted from drawing it in, and now stood silent – the crowd too desisting from the clapping and crying which had been taking place – whereat the man raised both his hands above his head, the cloth remaining supported by the only extension of his body capable of bearing it! At this, there was a new outburst of cheering and shouting, and the woman immediately abated the air of scorn with which she had hitherto regarded her impassioned swain.

He now, with an indescribably lascivious shake of his body, dislodged the cloth, revealing himself as ready for the fray – and began again alternately to advance towards and retreat from the object of his admiration. She, meanwhile, still counterfeited reluctance and shyness, but gradually loosed her own loincloth – careful, however, upon its falling to the ground, to protect the last bastion of her honour from the sight of the onlookers, with her hands. (This, I fear, struck me as more humorous than enticing; but I resisted any temptation to laughter, for that might have been crying out for trouble.)

It was now clear from the lady's demeanour that her adorer's was not a hopeless love, and approaching him she lifted up her hands and threw them around his neck – when there followed sundry embraces of a character more vehement than tender, culminating in the man, by placing his hands beneath the fundament of his mistress, lifting her until, embracing him with her legs, she permitted him the last favour – whereat the clamour, which had been insistent and continual, rose to a climax, and sundry similar embracings began to take place in the crowd.

I looked about, to make some comment to Kenny, who had been at my side, and whose eyes – the last time I observed him – had been popping from his head with interest. He had now, however, vanished – I feared to take his chances with some of the daughters of the tribe, for there were a number of young girls who were unaccompanied by their seniors. I hoped that this would not lead to trouble – but myself was prevented from an immediate enquiry into his whereabouts by two Caffre women taking me, one by each hand, and offering in unequivocal terms to provide me with those services with which their sisters were now pleasuring the other men of the encampment.

For all I knew, it would have been a positive insult to deny them – not merely as a matter of common courtesy in falling in with local custom, but because it would have required positive force, for (perhaps urged on by their interest in the body of a white man – Europeans but rarely coming into intimate contact with the Caffre natives) they were now doing their best to discover how my trousers were fastened, and how the buttons of my shirt could be persuaded from their buttonholes, such conveniences being, it seemed, unfamiliar to them.

When I had demonstrated the intricacies of these fastenings, they were all eagerness to discover whether the body of a white man differed in essential detail from that of their own men. Whether they were disappointed or not, I cannot say, though I feared it, for few white men can match our black brothers in the generous dimensions of the flaccid penis. However, under the interested probing of their curious fingers, my dibble soon achieved more formidable proportions – whereat they showed satisfaction, testing its rigidity with their fingers, and even calling to their friends to inspect – in which, however, they had little luck, for the others were about their own business of a similar nature.

There now broke out something like a quarrel as to who should test my masculinity first; whereat, from my supine position (for they had not allowed me to stir from my back, upon which they had pushed me) I simply seized the first that came to hand, and pulling her across my body, with a simple motion of my hips was able to pierce her – which she accepted with as much pleasure as her friend showed resentment.

The bouncing, bucking, springing, leaping, frisking and prancing to which I was now subjected was almost as intolerable as it was pleasurable – I could not but, in the midst of it, wish that my friend Frank and I could have commanded the services of some of these young ladies when we were running our superior brothel in Brook Street*, for they would have tired some of our more voracious customers more quickly than the most vivacious of our English girls.

Indeed, I fear I was a sad disappointment, for after only five minutes I was forced to lift the lady forcibly from her seat, having reached the point where – beyond the ultimate excitement – her motions had become positively painful. Seeing the froth which decorated my parts, her friend admonished her with a friendly but smart smack upon the rump, and sent her off to fetch some water and leaves, with which she thoroughly cleansed me, her touch being more more gentle than any caress I had yet had from them. She then set about reviving me – at first under the ungracious eye of her

*see *Eros in Town*

friend, whose desires I had clearly not succeeded in abating; but on the latter becoming bored and wandering off, she became rather more tender, applying her lips with some subtlety to my now slowly extending prick, so that they together with the apprehensive touch of her fingers, busying themselves about my pouch and even the aperture beneath, soon achieved a rebuilding of the fallen tower – whereat she fell to her hands and knees, presenting a target which I was not slow to hit.

As is so often the case, the second awakening was more prolonged than the first, and despite a wriggling motion of her tail which in other circumstances would have done my business, I was able to prolong my action until, with a howl almost like that of a dog and a final toss of her plump posterior, she collapsed, giggling.

It was now late, and after a few moments' rest, I gathered my clothing together and dressed myself, and rose to make my way to the hut in which Kenny and I had been given bunks. I was resigned to not seeing him until morning – but on entering the hut heard certain noises emblematic of sensual enjoyment, and on lighting the lamp I saw a pair of plump posteriors at work; my servant was in possession of a young woman who I believed (though to this day I cannot be certain) was the one who I had failed to satisfy, half an hour before.

A week ago, he might I suppose have been horribly embarrassed; after the incident at Pusilava, however, he took for granted the fact that I would not be disconcerted by his activity, and calmly maintained the rhythm of his prodding until, with a sigh, he withdrew – whereat (somewhat to my relief) the girl simply rose and made off, no more satisfied – if it was my former friend – than she had been before. She was clearly a young woman of remarkable appetite.

Kenny now looked at me a little sheepishly, and on my

questioning him revealed that he had possessed no fewer than four women during the two hours or so following the dance. I could not but raise an eyebrow at this, whereupon he asked whether it was unusual? I honestly replied that I thought it was not, for his age – and indeed could not but utter a sigh at the recollection of how few the opportunities had been for me to try for the same record, when I was of his age!

In the following day we set out again along the tedious and apparently interminable pass, whose head is nearly three miles distant from the village of Newera Ellia. Though there is nothing particularly fine in this part of the plains, the scene, from the contrast which it presents to the generality of Oriental landscapes, strikes forcibly on the mind of he who for the first time beholds it, and leaves an impression which is not easily effaced from the tablet of memory.

The thatched cottages – the chimneys with their respective columns of smoke wreathing upwards – and, above all, the keen blast which you encounter as you leave the cover of the woods and emerge on the open plain – all these are so entirely dissimilar from all one is accustomed to view and experience within the tropics that the novelty is delightful and exhilarating. The effect is much increased by the appearance of the flowers and plants proper to the colder climes. On every side may be seen splendid wild rhododendrons, which in this mountainous region seem to rival the best of other lands. The violet, the geranium and the rose all flourish in perfection and around the plains.

Nor are the less showy but more valuable plants of the vegetable kingdom in any degree unappreciated or neglected by the dwellers in these elevated plains, where the fruits and productions of Europe appear commingled with those of Asia. In addition to the vulgar luxuries of potatoes, cabbages and other culinary articles, the strawberries and gooseberries which grow in great abundance in the gardens of the European residents deserve honourable mention.

The plains of Newera Ellia contain about seven square miles. A road circumscribes their entire extent and forms the fashionable drive which, there being no rival, it is likely long to remain. The centre of the valley is occupied by rich grassland through which a little river slowly meanders. Around are the houses of the European residents, few and far between, and looking sufficiently sombre and melancholy in their solitude.

The rest houses offering accommodation here are much superior to those generally found in these parts. There are about a dozen rooms, divided into three suites of apartments for the reception of different parties. The windows look out upon the plains, and command a bird's-eye view of the principal houses, which are occupied by the commandant of the station, the government agent, and the few military stationed at the place. Behind the house are the sources of the rivulet that wanders through the plains. In pursuing its headlong course down the sides of the neighbouring mountains, the constant attrition of the stream has worn several natural baths in its rocky bed, the intense frigidity of which operates like a charm on the relaxed nervous systems of the parboiled Colombites!

We were on our first day in the place recommended to try these, and directed towards one bath set aside for gentlemen (the ladies of the place apparently taking objection to bathing with strangers). On the path thither we passed a young fair-haired man who we had seen the previous night at dinner – and who had not been the least of those whose eyes, to my amusement, were fixed with keen interest on the figure of Kenny as he served me my meal! We saluted this young fellow, who was flushed and red (no doubt from the operation of his bathe), and he nodded somewhat curtly in reply.

I cannot say that I positively recommend bathing in water quite so frigid; yet it was inspiriting, and raised my body to a degree of healthfulness which was delightful (I cannot entirely speak for Kenny, whose body, I am sure, can never have felt water so cold during the course of his life in South Africa!)

That evening, after the air had become sufficiently cool to force me indoors, I sat for a while looking out at the mountains, and was somewhat surprised to see Kenny returning to the rest-house in the company of the blond youth, who as they parted laid his hand upon the boy's sleeve and seemed to be speaking to him very seriously. When attending to me as I retired, Kenny seemed preoccupied, and on my enquiring the reason, paused for some time before admitting, in somewhat muffled tones, that the youth had approached him in the village and talked for some time with him, enquiring as to his origin, and showing some interest in his person; and later had asked whether he might call upon him in his room later that night.

I was immediately suspicious, of course, that the youth was a bugger. I had had no idea of it before, though now that I thought, there was something effeminate about his person – a certain subtle manner of walking and gesturing, though his hair was cut short, and his clothes entirely what one might expect of a young gentleman on his travels.

It was clear that Kenny had no apprehension of the notion that there were male persons whose sensual interest was concentrated not upon the opposite sex, but their own. I did my best to enlighten him, even to explaining that act which sets such men apart from others. I am not sure that he entirely believed me; but asked whether he had been wrong in agreeing that the young gentleman might call upon him, thinking that perhaps he wanted merely to continue to hear about life in his native country.

On my allowing myself to doubt whether that was all, he became concerned, and asked me whether such commerce between young men was improper – which from my experience I could only answer by saying that in my own country it was illegal, but that certainly it took place, and that it was my view that only religious zealots objected to it when it was performed in private, though my own personal preference was otherwise.

'Then perhaps I try?' he asked, somewhat nervously.

It might be difficult to resist, I replied, since he had acceded to the young man's request with a readiness which must have seemed to convey enthusiasm. Yet his room was, as always, adjoining my own; so that in any extremity he could call upon me for help.

It did not seem to me that the boy was any more in command of his emotions after our conversation than before; but he retired, and I determined to remain wakeful in case any emergency should occur requiring my assistance.

It was at about midnight when I heard faint footsteps in the corridor outside, and then a gentle knock upon the door to Kenny's room. I immediately climbed from my couch, and applied my eye to a chink in the door between our rooms (I should explain that the doors of rooms in Ceylon are but rarely equipped with locks and keys, or even bolts, and most are flimsy – a circumstance of the general lack of crime in that country).

The first thing I saw was that Kenny, no doubt persuaded by the lateness of the hour that his new friend would not come, had fallen into a deep sleep. The quiet knock, repeated, still failed to rouse him; and I now saw the other door of the room slowly open, revealing the figure of the young man, clad in a full-length robe wrapped fully about his body. Kenny had left a light burning, which showed now a face peculiarly sensitive, with full lips and a somewhat girlish brow, across which a lock of almost golden hair had fallen. I must confess that it was a handsome face, and one few ladies, surely, would have been able to resist – what a thousand pities that it belonged to a nance!

The visitor quietly shut the door behind him, and creeping to the bed stood for a moment looking down at the sleeping figure before gently reaching out to take the edge of the sheet which covered my boy's recumbent form, and drawing it back, then reaching out a hand for the lantern and lifting it so that he could more clearly see his prize.

Kenny was lying upon his back, one arm thrown behind his head, the other reclining at his side; his breast rose and fell in regular rhythm, the breath coming gently from his half-parted lips. One leg was drawn up, and across its thigh lay that remarkable tool which, though similar to a thousand others in young men of his race, so impressed every alien eye.

I saw, rather than heard, the visitor catch his breath. He replaced the light upon its table, and almost as though in a trance, bent over the sleeping figure, and sitting upon the edge of the bed, his back to me, stretched out his hand and laid it gently upon the boy's member, first simply allowing it to lie under his palm, then beginning to stroke it with an admiring motion.

After a moment, the boy stirred, then opened his eyes. They widened as he realised that it was no dream which had awakened him, and I thought I saw for a moment a panic in his eyes. But his visitor laid a finger across his lips, and in a moment slid the gown from his shoulders, revealing a long back drawn in to a slim, almost girlish waist, and surprisingly broad hips.

I could see, I should remind the reader, only my servant's lower limbs and his face, as it looked first up to his companion's face, and then down to the area where, I have no doubt, there would be an unequivocal sign of the stranger's intentions. To my surprise, a broad grin spread itself over Kenny's face, which, raising himself upon one elbow, he now buried in the young man's lap.

Well! – this, I thought, was quick learning indeed! Nothing loath, the stranger laid himself along the bed, and first trailing his tongue along the boy's belly, took between his lips the extremity of that engine which to my knowledge had only so far known the gentler lips of a female.

I must confess I was almost disgusted at the sight. Though I have known a number of men whose tastes lie upon the slant, and have even at times (through no fault of my own) partaken of certain familiarities in their company, it seemed improper that my servant, so young and relatively innocent of the ways of the world, should be so handled. I was almost ready to burst in upon the couple, when in what seemed a tumult of pleasure, the stranger threw his hands beneath Kenny's arse, and one leg astride his shoulders – the better no doubt to present his own cannon's mouth to the boy's lips.

It may be that the reader is already ahead of me, but I must confess that it was with complete astonishment that I saw, depending from the visitor's chest, a counterfeit of womanly breasts! For a moment I was even more disgusted – what freak had imposed himself upon my servant? But at that moment Kenny laid his head back upon the pillow, panting for breath, and I clearly discerned not the engine of a man, but the less complex and (to me) infinitely more delightful female aperture which proved the importunate intruder most certainly of the feminine gender!

My amazement was such that I was quite unable to withdraw my eye from the door's chink, and so was forced to witness the common pleasure with which the pair soon indulged their natural instincts – the young lady, having laved Kenny's prick with her saliva, lowering herself upon it as though she doubted her body's capacity to accept so splendid a cunny-splitter; while he was no less eager to please her than himself.

Next morning, upon the boy bringing my shaving-water, razors and morning coffee, I enquired whether he had suffered greatly from his visitor's importunities.

Not greatly, he replied, grinning.

So he was still able to sit down in moderate comfort? I enquired.

At this he was no longer able to contain himself, and out came the story – which I accepted as a surprise to me, not wishing him to think that I would always be a spy upon him (despite his having started out by bribing another servant to grant his eye witness to my own endeavours on the couch of love).

I congratulated him, and invited him to take a cup of coffee to the young lady's room and invite her to present herself to me at her convenience. He was some time before returning (when he looked a little flustered, and I noted that the loose white breeches which I provided for him to wear were now tied with a neater knot than it was usually his habit to form); but announced that the lady would be in the smaller of the two lounging rooms of the rest-house at midday, if I cared to meet her there.

She continued her pretence, for when I entered the room she was still habited as a young man – and peculiarly fetching I found her, now that her secret was out; and rather than a manly handshake could not resist pressing my lips to the inside of her wrist, upon which she looked around slyly, to ensure that no-one had seen.

She introduced herself as Miss Jane Knowles – though imploring me to address her as 'James' – the daughter of a former commander of the contingent of guards at Colombo, who had died some time ago, leaving her orphan; she was to return to England shortly, but had determined first to see something of the country, and lacking any friends with whom she could travel, had disguised herself as a young man the better to protect herself from male importunity.

'However,' she said, 'I did not foresee the difficulty of meeting your servant, nor the impossibility, having set eyes upon him, of not tickling his cods . . .'

I must have shown some surprise at this turn of phrase; but she then remarked that there was little about the commerce between men and women that would be new to anyone brought up as one of only half a dozen women in a barracks.

'Why, then . . .' I began . . .

'Why should I feel the need to masquerade? Well, Mr Archer,' (for I had of course introduced myself), 'the truth is that I like to choose my own companions in affairs of the bed, and did not care by travelling alone and in female grab, to offer myself, as it were, to every passing stranger who took a fancy to my pouter.'

I could not but laugh at her admirably forthright vocabulary; nor could I resist – his having left the room – informing her of Kenny's confusion at having his body so valued by a fellow male! – whereat she was much amused, and on his return passed her hand in a pleasant fashion over his buttocks, almost causing him to drop the tray of lemonade which he was bearing.

Her liking for the boy was clearly undiminished, and though by now I must confess to a distinct curiosity to

sample her wares, it was not my business to interfere.
Upon each of the following four nights, then, it was my
melancholy fate to hear, from the neighbouring room, the
sounds of excessive enjoyment – Miss Knowles insisting
that she should attend her lover there, rather than per-
mitting him to come to her room, which was next to one
occupied by two extremely curious maiden ladies, to
whom she (or rather, he) had become something of a
hero, whose reputation would be irreparably damaged
were an unmistakably male servant seen to attend on him
in circumstances advertised by such noises as the pair
seemed incapable of disguising.

I will admit (for surely the reader will sympathise) that
upon the occasions when these sounds reached a certain
height, the impertinence of glimpsing the proceedings
which gave rise to them was irresistible; and must admit
that among those many ladies whose skill in making love
it has been my happy experience to encounter, Miss
Knowles was one of the most adept. Kenny was acquiring
knowledge and skills which few young men of his age
could be master of; it was an education for which many
would have paid much – rather than, in his case, gaining
them by spending only those juices which naturally
renewed themselves at no expense!

The time came when it was necessary to leave; and to
Kenny's great pleasure Miss (or Mr) Knowles agreed to
accompany us back to Colombo – on our acquiescence
to her scheme of making, on our way, a brief excursion
to Badulla, where coffee is grown – and where elephants
might be seen, it being her ambition to set eyes upon a
herd before leaving the country. I was equally eager to
have a sight of these majestic creatures, and at Alipoot,
the most advanced post in that direction, entered into a
negotiation which allowed us a place in a carriage placed
upon the back of a large captive elephant, which would

then be taken in the direction where a herd of his com-
patriots might be found.

Early one morning, we mounted our beast – about
twelve feet in height – climbing into a sort of box set
upon his back; immediately before and below us, a
driver sat upon his neck – and we set off at a sort of
lumbering walk, leaving a rather downcast Kenny behind
(for whom there was no room).

The box was a small one, and it was only possible for
us both to occupy it by my kneeling at the back, while
Miss Knowles placed herself immediately in front of me.
The motion of the elephant was such that it was impossible for her rear parts not to be brought, at every stride,
into contact with my belly and thighs – which very naturally resulted in the erection of my vital organ, of which
she could not possibly be unconscious.

After a while, the motion and the friction was such
that I become acutely uncomfortable, and was forced by
inserting my hand into my trousers, to attempt to protect
myself from serious injury. In a moment Miss Knowles
turned her head and whispered that it was a sore waste of
so sturdy an instrument not to employ it for its proper
purpose – which would also result inevitably in my eventually becoming rather more comfortable – and without
further comment undid the belt of the trousers she wore
(in her capacity as a young gentleman), and lowering
them to her knees, by placing her arms upon the front of
our box-carriage, lifted her rump, easily enabling
me – having in similar fashion uncovered myself – to
slip my wand into an orifice more than ready to receive
it.

The only inconvenience we experienced was that,
being accompanied by several Cingalese on horseback, it
was impossible for me to employ those movements
which would normally accompany such an attitude; for

the observation of one English gentleman busily buggering another on top of an elephant would in no time, in anecdote, run round the country, and might result in the restriction of our freedom of movement in more ways than one.

However, the continued lumbering of the elephant gave us considerable pleasure, while our attitude was a more mutually pleasant one than our previous uncomfortable posture.

What we did not anticipate, however, was the sudden appearance – with a crashing sound of breaking underwood and jungle growth – of ten or twenty wild elephants, surrounded by their young; upon sight of which, ignoring the blandishments of our driver, our beast broke into a charge which resulted in his immediately falling off, and our having to hang on for dear life to the sides of our box.

The sensations of those engaged in copulation have often been remarked upon as exclusive of any other emotion – and upon our later conferring, Miss Knowles and I both agreed that our chief feeling was one of intense pleasure as our elephant's increasingly violent motion threw us about like peas in a pod, resulting in the most acutely delightful exacerbation of our animal parts!

Happily, at the very moment when my companion experienced her keenest throe of pleasure – with a squeal so highpitched that any observer might suspect her of being female! – and I observed more quietly my own paroxysm, the herd threw itself into a river which suddenly presented itself, and our beast, not ready to follow them, came to an abrupt halt. Almost immediately, we were surrounded by the horses of our accompanying party, and it was only with difficulty that we managed to adjust our dress before leaving the elephant.

It was, we agreed, the last we wished to see of

elephants for some time; though we were also forced to conclude that the experience had been one unusual enough to stick in our memories for some time – and no doubt to offer amusement to any of our grandchildren with whom we became sufficiently familiar to tell the story.

Rejoining Kenny, we next day made for the coast – a journey of some length, which she enlivened for my young friend (when it was safe to do so without coming near to betraying herself) by passages of love. On the last day we were accompanied by an apoplectic coffee-planter who took me aside on our reaching Colombo, and advised me to get rid of 'that nigger boy', who had been a great deal too complaisant in allowing the young puppy accompanying us to fondle his privates in the privacy of the coach – to which I enquired how, if the action was so private, it had been that the planter had observed it, which resulted in his complexion deepening by several shades of purple, and his taking himself off.

Miss Knowles also took herself off – but in a manner I had not expected: that is, accompanied by none other than my young friend Kenny. His departure, I think, was partly the product of his being infatuated by the lady, whose enthusiasm for his person resulted in his being for the first time able to gratify at almost any moment of the day or night those masculine urges which were still relatively new to him; but partly also that she had announced her intention of stopping, on her way back to our country, in South Africa, and offering him a large sum to be her guide in that country – which would ensure not only his return there, but his being in command of a sum of money with which he would be able to set himself up in some small but secure way of business.

I made it my business to ensure that he understood the situation, and that more than simple guide-work would be asked of him (he was far from distressed at the prospect); I assured myself also – as far as it was possible for me – that Miss Knowles intended to do the proper thing by him; which, both cases being satisfactory, left me with no other course than to approve the situation with what grace I might, and to present Kenny with a small sum in gold with which to remember me – I needing no such encouragement to remember so lively and interesting a companion, to whose education I flattered myself I had contributed more than a little.

I now found, to my concern, that the *Proper Pride* had sailed a week ago for Siam – but not before Robert had brought my relatively few belongings on shore and left them at the shipping office, with a message hoping that we might meet again one day.

At that same office I was able to ascertain that the *John Adam* was to sail the following day for Siam – and more particularly for Bangkok – and was without difficulty able to acquire a berth for the journey.

Chapter Twelve

Sophie's Story

The town of Singapore was only established by Sir Stamford Raffles in 1819, and so when we stepped ashore was very much an unknown quantity – though because of its favourable position it had within a few years become a thriving and populous community of various peoples: most of them Chinese – some six thousand in all – with about three thousand Malays, a thousand or so imigrants from the Coast of Coromandel, and a sprinkling of Armenians and Jews, Arabs and Malays, Javanese, Caffres, Parsees, Hindustanis, Bugis, Balinese et cetera – and perhaps fifty Britons only.

The town lies in the most romantic setting of a deep bay in which the lover of the picturesque will find ample material to gratify his taste as he passes through the cluster of islands which here gem the bosom of the deep. Barn Island, Alligator Island, the Rabbit and Cony – two small islands which bear a strong similarity in figure to the animals whose names they bear – besides several others present to the inexperienced and bewildered eye a labyrinth through which the mariner must thread his way. The unexpected manner in which the town and shipping burst upon the view as the vessel sweeps round the island of St John's, which forms the left point of the bay of Singapore, is striking in the extreme.

The harbour itself presents a bustling and a pleasant scene. Outside of the merchantmen are the king's ships, easily to be distinguished by their low, long hulls, while their light and airy masts and spars rest in faint and delicate relief against the deep blue sky. Next to them, the huge Indiamen are to be seen, like Leviathans half emerging from the deep, and as it were frowning disdainfully on the smaller country craft lying closer in shore. And the group is completed by the clumsy appearance of a Cochin-China frigate or two, and the grotesque Chinese junks, which, varying in size and vying with each other in the gaudiness and fancifulness of their colours and decorations, lie to the eastward of the bay.

As the eye traverses this scene, the most conspicuous object is the Court House, whose snow-white structure is finely contrasted with the green herbage and foliage of Government Hill behind it, on the top of which the British colours are seen flying in the breeze which propels your vessel in foam to the anchorage. The eye next rests upon the neat and elegant private garden houses which fringe the sandy beach on which the clear ripples break in sparkling light.

It was one of these that we were able to take for as long as we might require it, upon the advice of a British gentleman in charge of the customs payment required of imported goods from Europe which are landed here, these being most valuable – whether bales of cloth or bottles of liquor. The cost of renting a house here is so small as to be negligible, and we were delighted with our little kingdom, consisting of two bedrooms, a handsome chief room whose verandah looked out upon the beach and harbour, and a room for the two male servants who came with the house as a part of its furnishings.

Our villa lay on the outskirts of the town, and upon the left side of the mouth of the river of Singapore, which is about twenty yards wide here, though broadening later to a positive haven. On the point or tongue of land opposite us on the right bank were the artillery barracks and house of the artillery officers, with a few pieces of ordnance. The town had some very good European shops at which almost everything requisite could be bought, and where we were able to replenish some necessary articles of female attire.

One portion of the town which interested us is inhabited by Chinese shopkeepers and artisans, the former dealing principally in glass and crockeryware; the artisans are mostly tin-men, carpenters et cetera, the latter of which make very good furniture. The houses are in general good, and the streets regular and clean, those that run parallel to the river having a curve similar to the Regent's Quadrant in London, from their having followed the sweep of the river.

The whole town has an appearance of great bustle and activity, which inspires the spectator with an idea that he is gazing upon a settlement which is rapidly rising into importance under the united influences of English capital and industry and an advantageous locality.

We had been ashore for less than twenty-four hours when an invitation was delivered to dine with the Governor – or rather with his wife, His Excellency being unavoidably absent. So, dressed in our best, we set out in the early evening for Government House, which is a neat bungalow with venetians and an *attaped* roof; the centre consists of two parallel halls with front and back verandahs, terminated by two square wings which comprise the sleeping apartments.

The drive up to this spot is exceedingly romantic. A spiral carriage road winds up the hill, and at each progressive step fresh beauties attract the eye. Eminences undulating above each other display broad patches either cleared for cultivation or shining in the bright green livery of clove plantations, or yield a prospect of inviting coolness by the forest clumps with which they are chequered. The only *desideratum* to render the scene such as a painter would love to study, or a poet to retreat to, is a sparkling stream whose waters should glitter through the foliage and break in murmurs on the ear as it rippled through the bosky dell beneath the traveller's feet.

We were received by the Governor's lady, who was pleasant enough but somewhat distant – giving the immediate impression that she wished no more picturesque ladies than herself to be seen in the environs of Government House (which would have been a difficult ambition to fulfil, she being fully fifty and plump as a pouter pigeon). More enthusiasm was shown by a young officer of artillery, who proved to be the Governor's nephew, and clearly the apple of his aunt's eye; which accounted no doubt for the dubious glances he received from time to time as he attended upon us, pressing us with food from a generous table, and with wine from a loaded side-board.

Captain George Retallack was a well set-up young man of perhaps the middle twenties, who had obviously had some experience of life, for his addresses were neither the obvious blandishments of a bore nor the green advances of a puppy, but were shown in the pleasant easiness of his conversation and the politeness of his intention that we should enjoy the evening. I must confess that it seemed obvious to me that I was preferred by him to my friend, and indeed at one time he remarked that he was sorry his friend Captain Wendsley Dale was not with us – his being in command of the artillery barracks until eleven that evening – for Lady Frances would enchant him, he being more attached to . . and here he stumbled, his meaning however clearly being that his friend preferred the slightly more robust figure possessed by my friend, her bosom being fuller than mine, and her hips broader. But this was the nearest approach to a *gaffe* shown by my new friend, and that remarkably well disguised, so that it was inoffensive, and even caused Frances to smile, and to hope that an interview with Captain Dale could perhaps be afforded at a later date.

I had some hopes of the evening, in short; which were raised upon the Captain suggesting, after an inspiriting dance (for a small orchestra of somewhat odd instruments, some western, some eastern, played in the main room) that we should take some air upon the rear verandah; where after only a brief period, he placed his hands upon my shoulders (in the first instance, to discover whether the delightfully warm breeze which played in the open air was not chilling my skin). I raised my lips to his, which I was convinced were about to descend, when footsteps announced the approach of his aunt, the Governor's lady, whereat it was necessary that we should part, the lady pointedly requiring my presence in the library where she wished to show me and Lady Frances (whose attention she had had less difficulty in commanding) the most recent maps of the Malay peninsula, which would perhaps help us to plan some pleasant excursions.

These proved, in fact, of interest – though I must admit to being scarcely in the mood for them; but upon the party ending, at about ten o'clock, Captain Retallack, bowing over my hand, whispered that if it was acceptable he and his friend would wait upon us later; whereat I smiled compliance.

Frances was no less pleased than I to hear of the coming visitation, and on returning to our villa, we took cooling drinks out upon the verandah overlooking the beach and the narrow mouth of the river. Across its waters we could see the walls of the barracks, and a few low glittering lights, and in a moment heard the sound of a bell sounding the hour of eleven o'clock, at which time it will be remembered Captain Dale was released from his duty.

We were therefore prepared for the two young men's arrival, but scarcely for its mode; for as we sat, perhaps ten minutes later, we became aware of a disturbance upon the smooth waters of the river where they met those of the bay itself: at first this was a mere shimmering in the moonlight, a small uproar among the little waves. But then two dark spots became clear, and by the time they approached the beach upon which our verandah looked, we had recognised them as two men's heads – and guessed (as will the reader) to whom they belonged. By the time the captains were within their depth, we had left the verandah and walked down the sands to meet them as they strode dripping from the waters.

Nothing could have been more invigorating than their appearance, the moonlight silvering their bodies, quite bright enough to allow us to differentiate between them: for they were very different – Captain Dale being fair-headed, tall and slim, with a body almost appearing to be that of an undeveloped boy; Captain Retallack, as I had inferred from the manner in which his uniform had been filled out, altogether more sturdy, his shoulders broader, the dark hair of his head also evident upon his breast and belly – for the two gentlemen were clad for their swim in the same manner as Leander upon crossing the Hellespont – and indeed as they had swum towards us, I recalled the words of Marlowe upon the subject, wishing myself Neptune, to have embraced him as did that god:

He clapped his plump cheeks, with his tresses played.
And smiling wantonly, his love bewrayed.
He watched his arms, and as they opened wide

At every stroke betwixt them would he slide
And steal a kiss, and then run out and dance.
And as he turned, cast many a lustful glance.
And throw him gaudy toys to please his eye.
And dive into the water, and there pry
Upon his breast, his thighs, and every limb.
And up again, and close beside him swim,
And talk of love. Leander made reply.
'You are deceived. I am no woman, I.'

Of that latter statement there could be no question in the case of Captain Retallack, I was glad to see, for the moonlight was quite sufficiently strong to show that amid the dark forest which decorated his thighs there crouched an instrument descriptive of full manhood – and still impressive in dimensions despite his having walked that instant from the waters of the bay!

Perhaps seeing my glance, the Captain remarked upon the warmness of those waters, and spoke of the pleasures of swimming, in the moonlight, with two such nymphs as we; whereupon it was a moot contest which of us, Frances or myself, was the soonest out of her dress and, a proffered male arm happily accepted, walking into the sea.

It was true that the waters were fully as warm as our friends had described – I have often taken baths in waters more chill; and that they were perfectly incapable of chilling the emotions of the officers was made clear by the approaches they were not slow in making, in passing their hands over our breasts and sides, and, catching us by the upper arms, drawing us upon our backs while they insinuated their bodies beneath ours, the better to pull us along behind them like larger and more robust boats assisting weaker vessels – whereupon the nestling of a strongly fashioned spar, as it were, rigged with a fine growth of wiry rigging, showed their eagerness to reach a secure harbour.

Though Captain Dale in a moment lifted Frances in his arms and carried her to the shore, where they sank to the sand so closely embraced as to seem one body, Captain Retallack was not so patient – and while we were yet to our waists in the shallow waters, lifted me, his hands beneath my rump, so that he was able to reach that desired harbour and come to rest in it with the confidence of a practised oarsman. This was not, I confess, a position I had hitherto much relished, few lovers being in my experience sufficiently strong entirely to convince me that they would not let me fall during the course of the congress. However, the waters now helped to support us both – so much so, indeed, that I was able to lie back upon them, while my friend remained standing, gripping me now only by my hips; and there to move me so gently that our congress seemed part of the scarcely rippling water, our passions mounting, however, so that a storm soon arose which sent out strong waves about us, and only blew itself out with our achieving mutual happiness.

Carried ashore, then, in the arms of my gratified lover, I was laid upon the sands at the side of my friend, who was still in the arms of her swain, lying upon her side, one of his slim but powerful thighs thrown over her waist.

We all four rested for a space, but soon Frances – Captain Dale perhaps having proved – I know not – less thorough in his ministrations than his friend – raised her head, and sliding down the length of her lover's body, began toying with his person, whereat an instrument so small that at first I had pitied my companion began rapidly to swell to something more considerable; indeed, I would have been puzzled to say which of the officers had been more generously endowed by nature, and in order (I confess it!) to satisfy my curiosity, myself paid Captain Retallack the same compliment. Catching my eye, Frances immediately guessed what I was at, and with her fingers began secretly to measure off the length of her lover's prick, while I did the same – the result being, as far as we could see in the dim light, that they were much of the same dimensions, though my captain's having (I will insist) a thicker core than the other's, perhaps by as much as a quarter of an inch!

Captain Retallack was not one for long to lie supine under such attentions as I was paying him, and throwing me off somewhat violently (perhaps fearing a premature detonation of his weapon) buried his head in my lap, where presently I felt the tip of an energetic tongue seeking for my most apprehensive part; and Captain Dale, clearly influenced by his friend, was soon following his example, which resulted in the deserted beach soon echoing to cries which roused the sleeping sea-birds from their nests!

Were I to detail the various pleasures that ensued, I would seem to boast, for I cannot but admit that Frances and I rose to the renewed lusts of our visitors as often as they offered tangible proof of them; so that when, as a hint of dawn began to show itself, they rose from the sand and made their way reluctantly into the water, we could not but fear that even a swim of so little as twenty yards might prove too much for them. However, the rosy light of the sun was now just sufficient to show us their two bodies as they appeared upon the opposite beach, pausing to salute us as they staggered towards the barracks, where doubtless they found entrance at the same point as they had made egress – while my friend and I, after one more dip into the waters to wash the sands from our backs, made our way to our villa, where we slept until past three in the afternoon.

We spent a pleasant week or ten days in Singapore, attended whenever possible by our two captains, who by the end of that period must have been running a risk of prosecution for neglecting their duty to their battery on at least two points – that of being often absent, and that of being, when in attendance, too exhausted to do anything more energetic than sit half-asleep upon whatever bench presented itself.

Frances and I wished, however, to see a little of the Malayan peninsula, and happily Captain Retallack had the opportunity of accompanying us to Malacca, a town some distance up the eastern coast of the country, whence he must bear a message to the commander of its military base. Captain Dale was a great deal less enthusiastic about losing the company of Frances, who, however, wished to accompany us; and indeed we set out, the captain on horseback and Frances and myself in a military wagon which he had insisted was necessary to bear supplies (though what form those supplies took was, I am convinced, entirely unknown to his superior officers).

The road to Malacca was not alongside the coast, but through quite thick jungle; but the first view of the settlement was none the less impressive, with remains of the old fort (blown up by the English in 1807) standing around the foot of St Paul's Hill, accompanied by a number of modern houses almost exclusively occupied by the officers of the British force, and by their appearance affording a pleasing contrast to the fine old ruin of the church, dedicated by Albuquerque to the Visitation of our Lady, which crowns the summit, whilst a noble and magnificent grove of *ansanna* trees edges the brow, leading from the Church to the Government House.

We arrived at the settlement late one night, and went immediately to one of the officers' houses set aside for visiting military men, but presumably also open to their guests (though I did not question Captain Retallack as to whether he had obtained permission for Frances and myself to be present). Once there, he gave an order to a servant, who after a while returned and said something in his native language, upon which the captain rose, and offering us his arm said that that refreshment which he was determined we needed after so trying a journey was now at hand, and taking us from the room escorted us out of doors and to the bottom of a small garden, where under an awning woven of some bark, a large pool had been excavated, which was filled now with fresh water from a conduit nearby.

Upon Captain Retallack asking whether we would object to his sharing this cool retreat, we were bound of course to give our permission, and in a very little time the three of us, relieved of any covering but our skins, were immersed in the pleasantly cool liquid, only recently admitted to the pool from the conduit (for it was drained, we were told, until evening, so that the sun never had the opportunity of warming it). The servant who had accompanied us also stripped off his loincloth, and devoted himself to lathering Captain Retallack's body with soap; and, desisting at a signal, was clearly uncertain whether he should turn his attention to us – for this was, I imagine, the first time such a circumstance had arisen; however, stepping forward I presented my back to him, whereupon he began to go at it with some form of soft bark tissue, which was most inspiriting as to texture, but also presumably efficacious in removing the grime of the day. On my turning about, the man (who was of indeterminate age, but of a not unpleasant robustness) continued his attentions, from which it was clear (the water still being relatively uncloudy) that he obtained some pleasure – while

Captain Retallack, with a second piece of cloth (or whatever it was) was busily scrubbing Frances's person.

We permitted no amorous dalliance to delay us at that time, but after dinner, when the time came to retire, the captain revealed that only two bedrooms were available, and asked – with a twinkling eye which rejected before it was spoken any idea that he should remain in the sitting room – whether one of us would offer him a night's accommodation: that term being taken, as I believe, by all three of us as including amorous embraces.

With a sideways wink, I as it were offered the captain to Frances, suspecting that she was perhaps a little envious of my capture of him – for though her lover had been sufficiently enthusiastic, I knew that she preferred gentlemen of a more muscular build than young Captain Dale. At all events, she was not slow to rise to her feet with the suggestion that Retallack might care to share her couch, since she believed that I was rather more exhausted by the exigencies of the journey than she.

This was not, in fact, true; but I countenanced it for the sake of friendship and variety, and bidding them goodnight took myself off to my room – under the eye of the servant, who was lounging in the passageway, perhaps hoping (who knows?) that I might need him. However, I required no assistance to sleep well, waking only once to a cry from the neighbouring room which seemed to denote that Captain Retallack was offering my friend every satisfaction as a companion.

The next day, in the cool of the early morning, the three of us walked up to the Church, whose roof has long been off, and whose interior is nearly covered with flat and ancient tombstones having several quaint devices carved on them. The inscriptions are much obliterated in consequence of their exposure to the weather, and are nearly illegible. Some of the old Dutch families have vaults here in which the remains of their relatives are to this day deposited in preference to being taken to the English burial ground at the back of the hill.

The town of Malacca, which we then explored, is inhabited chiefly by the Dutch, Portuguese, Malays, Chinese, Chuliahs, and so on. The houses of the Dutch are very substantial in their structure, the walls being unusually massive. The inhabitants do not appear to trust, however, entirely to their solidity, as the beams of each flat are strongly riveted to the walls by iron clamps. The ground floors are generally bricked, and mats are seldom spread over them, under the idea that thus the houses are cleaner and less dust accumulates.

The Dutch houses are for the most part neatly furnished, but those of the wealthy Chinese very splendidly fitted up, the term being taken with reference to their national taste. They generally consist of two parallel houses connected by porticoes and balconies, the one furthest from the street constituting the private apartments. In addition to ornaments peculiarly Chinese, the walls are covered with European pictures, mirrors and pier glasses, handsomely framed, and chandeliers, wall shades et cetera are to be seen in profusion.

Captain Retallack accompanied us after luncheon to one such house, which was let for a period to the British commander of the garrison. On our arrival, the commander was elsewhere, but his servants admitted us, and on our appearing somewhat overcome by the heat – which was very considerable – Captain Retallack suggested that we should lie down for a while in the commander's bedroom. This proved to be a fine room, and though principally furnished in the Chinese mode, handsomely fitted up, with a large four post bed adorned with passive open work and gilt cornices (for which, when tastefully executed, the Chinese give a prodigal price), and upon the side wall placed a smaller or single couch, without curtains, for repose in the day time.

Allowing me the bed, Frances took her place upon the couch, and removing our clothing the better to experience what cool air was admitted by the open windows, we soon fell into a doze – from which I awoke to realise that a third person had entered the room. Opening my eyes, they fell upon the extraordinary sight of a Scottish kilt, which adorned the lower part of a gentleman who was hanging a ceremonial sword upon the back of a chair by the bed, and then in a moment had removed his shirt and, his hands at the buckle of his belt, turned to the bed – to see, with surprise an unclothed woman lying upon it! Yes, it was the commander, who entering the house without seeing his servant had been entirely unaware of our presence.

From beneath my eyelids I saw his surprise, and saw it turn to pleasure. He took a step towards the bed, and his eyes travelled the length of my body with interest scarcely discriminated from pleasure. I had, I regret to say, fallen in sleep into a somewhat inelegant posture, for one leg was drawn up, the thigh thus falling open and disclosing to plain view those portals which discretion, modesty or simple caution would normally conceal.

I could not but be acquainted with his interest, for the front of his kilt almost immediately betrayed it in a manner the nature of which the apprehensive reader will guess; and which soon became plainer to me even than inference had suggested, for he now released the buckle of his belt, and the kilt fell about his ankles, revealing that even if in northern climes the Scots occasionally disregard the rule which claims that nothing should be worn beneath that sacred garment, in the warmth of Malaysia it was a positive pleasure to conform to the law.

I had always heard that the Scots were a vigorous race,

and the splendid weapon which now confronted me supported the claim, rising as it did from a grove of red hair which matched that of his head and beard. Such was the manner in which, though severely at attention, it betrayed its eagerness by a regular jerking which (as I guessed) matched the beating of the commander's heart, that I feared an immediate rape – and thought it best to open my eyes wide: at which he took a half step backwards, and opened his mouth to utter – who knows? – perhaps an apology. But conscious of the claims of a host – after all, I was occupying the man's bed – matched, I must say, by the emotions engendered by my knowledge that Frances had during the previous night enjoyed the sweets which normally might have fallen to me, I parted my lips and smiled, at the same time holding out my arms; whereupon, without pausing to ask whether I was a traveller, the wife perhaps of a fellow officer, or had been issued by the Army with supplies, the gentleman climbed upon the bed and in no short time we were embraced, and I had locked heels behind an energetically pumping pair of Scots cheeks.

The gentleman had, I suppose, been so long deprived of female company that he could not but express himself in muffled cries of pleasure, which – his lips being drowned in my hair, and his accent being extremely thick – I was incapable of translating, but which had the effect of waking Frances, who until that moment had been asleep upon the couch across the room, entirely unapprehended by the visitor. She now, being unable to see from her reclined position who I was entertaining, rose from her couch and approached. The arse of my new friend being dusted with a down of red hair, it was clear that it was not the property of Captain Retallack; and she gave me a smiling wink, as if to ask how I had come by my lover – without the least reprehension.

At that moment he gave a final leap which resulted in our two bodies bouncing some inches in the air, and I felt a scalding torrent within which seemed to continue for some two or three minutes; after which he withdrew his person, planted a kiss upon my lips, raised himself, and flopped to the bed at my side, upon his back – whereat Frances gave a loud cry and sank to the floor insensible!

Were this a book of fiction rather than an entirely honest and factual account, there would be an ideal place at which to end a chapter! But since my narrative is of plain and simple fact, I must now reveal that I was dumbfounded at my friend's sudden collapse, and immediately raised myself to go to her side and cradle her head in my arms. In a moment, the head of my lover appeared over the end of the bed, all red hair and bewilderment. My friend's eyes opened – met those of the Scot – and in a single gasp he uttered the name 'Frances!' while she breathed – 'Jamie!'

'Twould be superfluous to spend long in explaining the circumstances of this remarkable coincidence: which were that Lieutenant-Col. Jamie Ferguson, the commander of the garrison at Malacca, had as a child been a neighbour of Frances's family at their home in Northumbria, and – as she blushingly confessed – their friendship had ripened from the exchanging of birds' eggs to the learning of Scottish dances; and shortly after their sixteenth birthdays – for they were of an age – to the exchanging of such compliments as young people of spirit will often venture at such an age, if left to themselves.

Unfortunately, Frances's father, a Presbyterian of singularly joyless persuasion, had come upon them making the beast with two backs in her bedroom (whither Jamie had climbed up a drainage-pipe earlier in the evening), and had banished Frances to her aunt's in

England, where after some few years' captivity she had been introduced to Sir Douglas Sperries – and the rest of the story the attentive reader will remember from the second chapter of the present volume.

It appeared that Jamie had spent most of his army service – amounting only to some seven years – in the East, and as the result of outstanding attention to his duties (his progress being unencumbered by a wife) had had early promotion. That he was as delighted as he was amazed to recognise his childhood friend goes without saying – and that they were reunited immediately need not be questioned – I, of course, making an excuse to leave the room in order that they might renew their acquaintance in whatever fashion most satisfied them, without the embarrassment of an interloper's presence.

Captain Retallack was most intrigued at the story, as I told it to him; and in the evening the four of us dined together, when there were many recapitulated stories from the past history of all four of us – with which I will not weary the reader; any more than I need detail the pleasant night which followed, when Jamie's bed proved more than capable of bearing the four of us, and when his gratitude to me – for he seemed to believe that Fate had used me as the instrument of bringing himself and Frances together – was expressed in terms which would have made any persons more jealous than Frances and Retallack uneasy.

As it was, however, the four of us were as cosy as a nest of birds, and enjoyed as much innocent diversion as can ever have delighted young persons in full health and freedom from the unnecessary restraints of polite society.

I realised, of course, that the circumstances must part me from my friend, taking it for granted that Frances would wish to stay with her lover. Indeed, with a salutary speed, they were married within the week! – and after a wedding supper notable for a splendid indulgence in a malt liquor with which Jamie had been used to comforting his lonely state, Captain Retallack and I set off to return to Singapore, myself making a farewell to Frances which was the strangest mixture of sorrow and joy that my life has so far afforded!

Chapter Thirteen

The Adventures of Andy

Our captain having to make deliveries there, we made good time to the new settlement of Singapore, for which I foresee an excellent future, it being from its situation calculated to become the centre of the trade carried on in the China Seas and the neighbouring countries, and its harbour affording a safe and convenient anchorage at all seasons of the year.

We were only at anchor here for two days, but during the evening were taken ashore and entertained at Government House by the Governor's lady – himself being absent on some business elsewhere – and an attaché, a Captain Wendsley Dale, a well-set up young gentleman who is stationed at the artillery base which commands the harbour (but which seems to be more for decoration than for use). The Captain seems entirely contented with his station here, and on my suggesting that there must be some shortage of amiable females, remarked that while that was so, the life was easy, and that among the businesses set up by the industrious immigrant population was an excellent and well-managed brothel which was perfectly adequate to satisfy the corporeal urgings of nature – while from time to time there passed through ladies from Europe, travelling to or from foreign stations, either to join their husbands (and therefore in a fever of expectation which it was any man's duty to relieve) or having left them, and therefore in a passion of regret which it was surely proper to console.

Apart from this, ladies occasionally appeared who were travelling for pleasure; two such had recently called at the colony, with whom he and a friend had become extremely friendly (and though the good captain declined, quite properly, to elaborate, I imagine that the relationship established with them was enjoyed on both sides).

From Singapore we sailed to the extreme point of the Malay peninsula, and despite the wind blowing strong against us, gained the mouth of the straits within three days, and after the remainder of a voyage unmarked by incident, dropped anchor at the mouth of the river upon the shore of which, some distance from the sea, lies the town of Bangkok. Here a small boat came alongside bearing a young Siamese who introduced himself as an interpreter, and was for hire as such. Our captain denied him employment, being only in harbour for a few days; but I was delighted, on discovering that his charge was negligible, consisting only of a few English shillings and his keep, to engage Loi as my personal servant, in place of the lamented Kenny.

Loi bore the characteristic national features of the Siamese, being small and lithe, with a face the features of which were somewhat flat and the jawbone prominent, but engagingly bright and humorous. He spoke English with ease and fluency, and Portuguese somewhat imperfectly.

I here said farewell to the captain, and transferred my luggage to a small junk which Loi had hired, and which took me upriver. The banks of the river are very low and thickly planted with the *attap*, which gives them a picturesque appearance; the betel palm grows in great abundance, too, so that the whole view is one sea of green. Further upriver extensive plains open out, which presented a rather sterile aspect, the harvest having lately been gathered in. These plains occupied the left bank of the river, over which they are elevated about eight or ten feet – but I was given to understand that in the rainy season they are covered with water to the depth of two or three feet, and are therefore well adapted for the cultivation of rice.

The river itself is about a quarter of a mile in breadth, and almost entirely covered not only with canoes and junks, but with houses! – for the most singular feature of the scene is the appearance of houses floating on water in rows of about eight, ten or more in depth from the bank. This novel appearance is peculiarly neat and striking. The houses are built of boards, of a neat oblong form, and provided with a floating platform facing the river on which are displayed numerous articles of merchandise – fruit, meat, rice et cetera. This is in fact a floating bazaar, in which all the various products of the country are exposed for sale. At either end the houses are bound to long bamboos driven into the river, and are thus enabled to move from place to place according as convenience may demand. Every house is furnished with a small canoe, in which they visit, and go from place to place to transact business.

In place of those wagons and coaches which crowd the roads of Europe, here were boats passing and re-passing – so light and sharp in their form that they mount rapidly against the stream. They are rowed with paddles, of which the long canoes often have eight or ten on each side.

Loi directed our own larger vessel, propelled by six sweating Siamese, to one of the more prominent houses in view at what seemed the centre of Bangkok: it was perhaps forty feet in length and about half that space in breadth, and consisted of a single stage, the floor raised above the water about a foot, and the roof thatched with palm leaves. As we approached, he caused a little bell to be rung, when four servants appeared upon the landing-stage before the house – two male and two female. These, like the other people in view, were unclothed above the waist, and wore only a twist of blue cloth below. Their upper bodies were slightly rubbed over with a yellowish colour, either turmeric or powdered sandal wood. The two women had long necklaces of moonstones thrown over their shoulders, it seems in my honour. All four bowed with great grace as I stepped onto my house!

It being little after mid-day, it was necessary – Loi explained – that I should visit the Minister responsible for the conduct of all visitors to Bangkok. Changing into a decent set of clothes, I therefore set out accompanied by my interpreter. The Minister lived, or did his business, in one of the few houses of Bangkok which are built of stone. He was a man of about forty-five years of age, tall, active and rather thin, wearing upon his shaved head a small white cap.

He received me in a large and lofty hall, open on one side, spread with carpets and hung with glass lights and Chinese lanterns. Through Loi, he greeted me courteously – but any pleasure I took in his regarding me with respect was diminished by the servility which the attendants of this man observed towards him – for during the whole visit they lay prostrate on the earth before him, and at a distance. When addressed, they dare not cast their eyes towards him, but raising the head a little and touching the forehead with both hands united in the manner by which we would express the most earnest supplication, their looks still directed to the ground, they whispered an answer in the most humiliating tone.

His lower servants, bringing us refreshment, crawled on all fours, supported on the elbow and toes, the body being dragged on the ground. In this manner they pushed the dishes before them from time to time in the best manner that their constrained and beast-like attitude would admit until they had put them in their place, when they retreated backwards in the same grovelling manner, but without turning round.

How abominable! How revolting this assumption of despotic power! Yet this minister was only a relatively lowly servant of the established court – for every man in this place is doomed to crawl on the earth before his superior; the nation must be considered as entirely the slaves of the king, of whose lives as well as property he can dispose at will.

I was pleased to return to my house – followed by three small boats containing all the food and sweetmeats which had not been consumed during my audience, it being the custom to send these after the guest, for consumption at his leisure. On my telling Loi to distribute these among the four servants of the house, of course taking for himself whatever he wished, he expressed amazement and they a degree of gratitude which in England would have been overweening had the gift been that of a thousand guineas!

I was happy to spend most of the next day sitting on my floating terrace and watching the coming and going of the traders upon the river; in the evening, Loi enquired whether it was my wish to make an excursion for pleasure. Not entirely understanding him, I questioned whether there was some theatrical entertainment which could be seen, or some place where the best food of the country could be tasted? But his reply was that the entertainment most prized by visitors to Bangkok was that provided by the courtesans of the place, who are, it seems, notable for their skill.

Accordingly, we set off in the early evening in the

small canoe which was one of the conveniences of the house, and after about fifteen minutes' paddling Loi and I were landed upon the terrace of a house, one of a row of similar buildings which formed a sort of floating street somewhat separated from the town. Upon Loi ringing his bell, a row of young ladies appeared to hand me onto the landing-stage. They were all of the small size which characterises the Siamese, the lower parts of their bodies wrapped in the usual blue cloth, and the upper parts decorated with ornaments of gold and precious stones, none of them of great value – suspended from their necks, for instance, were large, broad golden ornaments studded with diamonds, sapphires and rubies, all of inferior quality and of trifling value, but pleasantly decorative. Placing their hands together, they bowed their heads, all smiling, and formed themselves into a double rank in the midst of which I walked into the house.

There we were shown – for Loi must accompany me always, the language being entirely foreign to me – into a room upon the floor of which was a soft red carpet, with several large cushions lying about, and a mattress covered with chintz, upon which I was invited to sit. Food and drink were then brought – the food consisting of small fragments of meat which had been cooked in a delicious series of sauces, together with rice and cooked vegetables some of which I recognised and others which were unfamiliar. The drink was pleasant and seemed harmless, not being at all strong.

A girl who seemed to be somewhat in charge of the others then addressed me, and Loi explained that she asked if I would be pleased to be introduced to those young ladies who would be happy to entertain me. On my agreeing, a young man appeared in the corner of the room and began softly playing a stringed instrument, the music of which was quiet and insinuating; and after a while, five young ladies appeared and took up their station along the wall, sitting upon their heels, then one by one rising to present themselves to me.

This they did by coming forward and making their bow, their hands pressed together before their foreheads. They then each performed a little dance – or rather a sort of swaying walk – before me, showing themselves off with modesty but at the same time without concealing the ease and elegance with which their limbs moved, their bare arms seeming to float in the air in gestures which were at once graceful and inviting.

After each had come forward in this manner, they retired and, standing in a row, lifted their hands to their necks and released the ornaments which hung there, dropping them to the ground at their feet. Turning to each other, from side to side in turn, they appeared to be complimenting each other upon their youth and beauty – lifting each other's breasts upon the backs of their hands, trailing a finger down the side of each other's necks, or by placing a hand upon each side of their friends' heads, lifting them to show the shapeliness of the line which fell from ear to shoulder.

The musician then striking a series of chords which they recognised as a signal, the girls in one motion released a knot of material at one side of their hips, and dropped to the ground the cloth which had until then concealed the lower portion of their bodies, standing entirely naked before me, their eyes cast down, certainly – but I was happy to remark, clearly from natural modesty rather than servility.

It has always been difficult for me to choose between beauty and beauty, but at least in most parts of the world, there is a variety which makes it easier – one girl will be plump, another thin; one will have generously proportioned breasts, the other less so. Here, I might have

been faced by five identical sisters – for they all had
bodies of similar proportions, with narrow hips and nar-
rower waists, breasts which were certainly individual,
but of much the same size – being small and firm, without that generosity typical of the great proportion of
European ladies; and a characteristic which seemed to
make them even less dissimilar was that there was not a
single hair upon their bodies (this, Loi later told me, was
for reasons of hygiene, all houses of entertainment in the
place being regularly inspected in order that disease
should not originate there – a custom which might profitably be copied in European cities).

Somewhat to my embarrassment, I was forced to
enquire of Loi whether in his view any one or other of the
young ladies was for any reason preferable to another; to
which his reply was that he did not know, for he could
not afford to attend so expensive a house – but that it
was usually the case that in an establishment of this
order, one lady was a skilful as another. On seeing that
this reply was of no assistance, he suggested that I should
employ them all! – and on my remarking that I was not
made of money, revealed that the price of the favours of
each was only what in English money would amount to
perhaps two shillings – yet this in Bangkok is equal to
two or three of our *pounds*, if paid in English currency,
which is valuable here. Since I always make a point of
carrying English change with me, for that very reason, I
found no reason not to comply with his suggestion – on
the understanding that (since it would be unlikely I could
require the continual application of all five) he should be
my guest.

This clearly pleased him as much as my engagement of
them all pleased the young ladies, who in a moment were
transformed from somewhat distant exhibits to a picture
of enthusiastic young humanity, now gathered around

me and helping with such eagerness to divest me of my clothing that I was soon reduced to helpless laughter, in which they joined!

Having concluded their operation of denuding me, they laid me upon the centre of the carpet, and stood around me, apparently in silent admiration. Though I had been somewhat aroused by their attentions, I was by no means at full stand – yet it seemed that the sight even of my half-awakened weapon was of more than usual interest to them. It may be of course that they were simply complimenting a patron, yet the intent manner with which, now kneeling around me, they all examined my person seemed to indicate a greater than usual degree of pleased surprise – which increased as, under the gentle touch of their hands, my tool expanded to its usual dimension in such circumstances.

One of them now clapped her hands, when a young man appeared bearing a vessel of sweet-smelling oil, and dipping their hands in it, four young ladies took my hands and feet under their care, and beginning with the fingers and toes, gently applied the oil to my skin. This was in itself pleasant enough, but what added to the sensation was that for a platform to support those limbs they used their own bodies, two of them fitting my heel into the recess between their thighs, as they knelt at my feet; the two others resting my hands upon their bosoms.

Meanwhile, what of the fifth? Her attentions became most agreeable of all, for first stroking my face, she then oiled my neck and breast, circling my paps with an attentive and rhythmical motion, then my sides and belly.

All this occupied a much longer time than it takes to tell – but by the time two of the girls were reaching with insinuating fingers into the cave beneath my arms – my sensations being now too intense for laughter! – and the two others were admiringly stroking the muscles at the inside of my thighs – the fifth was beginning to stroke the length of my tool with a touch so light that it was scarcely more than a breath.

My feelings were now in such a tumult, my desires so mixed, that all I could do was to lie still – for while I longed to clasp one of the girls in my arms and to sheath my sword in the approved manner, yet to do that would be to force the others to cease their attentions, none of which I wished to put a stop to!

The reader will apprehend the solution: for my body, so racked with pleasure that it could not longer endure the pleasurable plain, revolted – and whether I would or no, with an involuntary spasm concluded the proceedings – the girls lifting their hands and then beating them together in delighted and admiring applause at the height of the jet which the culmination of my joy forced from my body! The relief and pleasure was such that while I could not but regret the cessation of my enjoyment, I was forced myself to laugh with delight, at which they also broke into expressive smiles and giggles.

Another clapping of hands brought the boy with warmed towels, with which they cleansed my body – at the end of which operation, I suddenly caught sight of poor Loi, still fully clothed, sitting in the corner of the room. While on meeting my eyes he smiled, I could imagine that he was somewhat depressed at the sight of a pleasure in which he had no part; and called out to him to remember that I intended to make a present to him of similar entertainment, should he desire it.

He brightened considerably at this, and addressed to the girls some sentences in his own language – at which they looked very surprised, and turned to me with a questioning glance. On my smiling and nodding (for I guessed that they were uncertain whether he was telling the truth) they still looked somewhat surprised, but by no means revolted; and one of them, perhaps the leader, said something to me in what seemed a questioning tone. Loi, perhaps a little embarrassed, translated her query – which was, whether I intended that they should all give their attention to him, or but one. I asked him to invite the chief maiden to remain with me, but that he could proceed at whatever rate he wished, among the others.

On hearing this, he conveyed my meaning in a very few words, and without more ado leaped to his feet and in a moment threw off the single piece of cloth wrapped about his loins, revealing that indeed he had had more than a passing interest in the scene which had just been played before him, but suggesting also a possible reason for the girls' admiration of my own virility – for his amatory aparatus was distinctly diminutive, while perfect in form being not much bigger, even in extension, than the average European thumb.

I was amused to see that the girls had no intention of proceeding with him on those somewhat ceremonial terms with which they had pleasured me. There was to be no careful massaging with sweet-smelling oils; they merely threw themselves upon the boy like puppies at play, snatching at his prick and fumbling it as though it were part of some ball-game, wrestling with him – and with each other – with a sort of enthusiastic clumsiness which seemed to me to denote more enjoyment on their part than the more attentive motions with which they had raised me to my rapture!

It was in fact a scene as delightful for its play as for its amorous proclivities; yet it was clear to me that the girls were enjoying themselves much more than they had while pleasuring me – which I could not but regret, being one whose enjoyment of the act is much enhanced by the knowledge that I am giving as well as receiving pleasure – an ambition perhaps doomed to disappointment where the lady concerned is a professional person.

It was soon clear that no one of the group was to be disappointed as to enjoyment, for after what seemed a very few minutes, it had disposed itself into a montage in which no-one was deprived of delight: one young lady was crouching over Loi's thighs and receiving his short and stubby, but no doubt firm, instrument within her – it proving, while small, evidently strong as horn and perfectly capable of both expressing and conveying passion. At each side crouched two more beauties, his fingers playing about their persons; while the last bestrode his chest, and her friend, enjoying the benefit of Loi's manhood, caressing her breasts, offered herself to the boy's tongue, which busily sought out the centre of pleasure between her lower lips.

This interesting sight naturally engaged my attention, and as naturally roused my spirits as I lay at the side of the remaining girl, upon whose breasts I now pressed my kisses, inferring from the protruberent nipples of her charming breasts that she too found the *tableau* of interest; and wishing this time to complete my pleasure in the more conventional manner, I persuaded her upon her back and insinuating myself between her thighs presented my soldier – more than ready for battle – at the fort's entrance. This I at first feared was too narrow to accommodate me, being proportionate to the slender figure of the young lady; however, upon the head of my instrument nudging at the door, she raised her hips and with a wriggle contrived that an entrance should be begun – after which the slippery unguents of desire enabled her to receive me completely, though so narrow was the corridor that it was as though the limb was embraced by a glove.

In a moment, as I began those natural movements concomitant with my situation, I felt as it were a hand squeeze my person – and even, raising myself, glanced down to see whether some mysterious force was exerting itself; but no – my prick was clearly embraced only by its natural sheath. Yet in some manner I have yet to experience in any other part of the world, the young ladies of Siam have so educated themselves that they have produced muscles where other ladies have none, and by contraction can tighten or loosen the embrace with which their cunnies receive the masculine form – something which is as effective as it is surprising, for it enables them almost to milk one of desire; and the result, in the first instance, was that once more my exercise was completed rather earlier than I would have wished!

Rather than wishing us out of the way, as would more often than not have been the case had we been in a house of entertainment in Paris or London, these young ladies continued their hospitality not only by causing more hot towels to be fetched, but having made our bodies more comfortable, by sending for more food, and all of us having wrapped ourselves for the sake of decency in clean robes of the material commonly worn here, we sat for some time eating and drinking and making what conversation we could within the restriction of my having to have all my remarks translated by Loi.

The next day, I was flattered to receive a communication from the court, inviting me to present myself there in the afternoon for an audience with the King – this being common, as I understood, with distinguished private visitors to Siam, His Majesty being eager that a more energetic correspondence should be established between his people and those of western nations.

At noon, a special boat came for the purpose of conveying me to the palace. It was without ornament of any kind, but neat, with a boarded space in the centre over which was erected a matting roof. A piece of old carpet and a small but old velvet cushion were placed upon this boarded space, where I sat with Loi standing at my side while we were rowed by thirteen paddles, the rowers being dressed in caps and loose jackets made of coarse red cloth.

We proceeded to the palace at a moderate rate. Our presence seemed to excite but little attention on the part of the inhabitants of the floating houses which line the banks of the river, on the part of those on board the junks, or those passing or re-passing on the river. A few minutes brought us to the landing-place, within a few paces of the outermost wall of the palace. The place where we landed was dirty, inconvenient and lumbered with wood and small canoes. It might have been taken for the entrance into a wood-merchant's yard, than many of which this was much less clean and convenient.

There, below the gate and wall of the palace (which was lofty, but mean-looking and in bad taste) I stepped into a *palanquin* – merely a netting in the exact shape of a hammock suspended from a pole – and was carried, Loi walking at my side, to an inner gate, where I was detained for a few minutes before it was thrown open. Here I left the vehicle and walked into a spacious and open court of great extent, with various ranges of large tiled buildings disposed in tolerable order, and traversed by roads paved with coarse-grained granite.

I was now led into a room in which was placed a small platform, raised about a foot from the ground, covered with a coarse white cloth, and close by a large old carpet was spread on which I was desired to seat myself. The place was crowded with a multitude of low people, some of whom were resting on their knees and others standing, and all of them very noisy. After a few minutes two men, dressed in an upper garment of white cloth in the fashion of a wide shirt with a narrow strip of coarse lace about the middle of the arm and another at its extremity, notified us that I was called for.

I now left this room, and once more traversed the granite path, upon each side of which a line of men armed with muskets was drawn up. Nothing could be more ridiculous or more unsoldierlike than the appearance of this guard, composed of puny boys scarce able to stand under a musket! In their caps only was there anything like uniformity observed: these were all painted red, and I cannot give a better idea of them than by saying that they exactly resembled the slouched helmets once worn by the workers of fire-engines at home!

I now entered another large hall, at the entrance to which a band of musicians played; they were furnished with horns, trumpets, chanks and other instruments, and the music, though rude, was not inharmonious, and even agreeable. We rounded the end of a Chinese screen, covered with landscapes and small plates of looking glass, and suddenly found ourselves in the presence of majesty.

The hall was lofty, wide and well aired, the ceilings and walls painted with various colours, chiefly in the form of wreaths and festoons; the roof was supported by wooden pillars, ten on each side, painted red and dark green. Some small and rather paltry mirrors were disposed on the walls, and to the middle of each pillar was attached a lantern, not much better than our stable lanterns. The floor was covered with carpets of different colours.

At the further extremity of the hall, a large handsome curtain made of cloth covered with tinsel or gold leaf and suspended by a cord divided the space occupied by the throne from the rest of the apartment. On each side of this curtain there were placed five or six singular but handsome ornaments called *chatt*, consisting of a series of small circular tables suspended over each other, diminishing gradually so as to form a cone, and having a fringe of rich cloth of gold, or tissue, suspended from each.

With the exception of a space about twenty feet square, in front of the throne, which was kept clear, the hall was crowded with people to excess. Those of every rank from the highest to the lowest, from the heir apparent to the throne to the meanest slave present, had his proper place assigned to him, by which alone he was to be distinguished.

The curtain placed before the throne was drawn aside as we entered. The whole multitude present lay prostrate on the earth, their mouths almost touching the ground; not a body or limb was observed to move, not an eye was directed towards me, not a whisper agitated the solemn and still air.

Raised about twelve feet above the floor and about two yards behind the curtain alluded to, there was an arched niche on which an obscure light was cast, of sufficient brilliance to display the human body to effect, in the sitting posture. In this niche was placed the throne, projecting from the wall a few feet. Here, on our entrance, the king sat immovable as a statue, his eyes directed forwards. He resembled in every respect an image of Buddha placed upon his throne; while the solemnity of the scene and the attitude of devotion observed by the multitude left little room to doubt that the temple had been the source from which the monarch of Siam had borrowed the display of regal pomp.

He was dressed in a close jacket of gold tissue, and on his left was placed what appeared to be a sceptre, but he wore neither crown nor other covering on the head. There were neither jewels nor costly workmanship nor precious stones nor pearls nor gold observable about the person of the king, his throne or his ministers.

I pulled off my hat and bowed in the European manner, Loi at the same time falling prostrate and crawling before me on the ground towards the throne, in a whisper informing me that I should advance in a stooping posture. Not being given, as an Englishman, to stoop to any foreign monarch, I merely stepped forward in a normal gait – hearing immediately a sullen murmur from the crowd.

The king was clearly not pleased. He was remarkably stout, but apparently not bloated or unwieldy; he appeared to be about sixty-five years of age. He addressed a remark to a vizier standing at his side, who stepped forward and handed me a paltry Chinese umbrella, which might be purchased in the bazaar for a rupee. I enquired the purpose of this, and raising his head in order to be heard by me, Loi informed me that it was meant as a present from the king.

I could not suppress a smile at this, at which again there was a murmur from the crowd. I asked Loi to convey to His Majesty my thanks for so munificent a present. In order to do this, my interpreter was so unwise as to lift his head rather further from the ground than was considered proper, and to raise his eyes towards His Majesty in what was construed as too familiar a gesture – at which a guard stepped forward and applying his foot to the side of Loi's head, sent him sprawling to the ground.

I was not the man to have my servants misused before my eyes, and stepping forward lifted Loi to his feet. He struggled to release himself, no doubt in the knowledge of what so extreme a contradiction of etiquette would result in; but it was too late. The king drew himself up in insulted silence, two men stepped forward from the guard, seized Loi by the arms and dragged him immediately from the audience-chamber, his legs trailing on the ground behind him – and without his as much as raising his voice in protest (knowing, no doubt, that this would be fruitless).

A scarcely subdued hubbub of noise was heard, undoubtedly directed at me, who only remained untouched because I was known to be British, and therefore under the strong protection of His Britannic Majesty's forces, which would be quick to avenge any discourtesy shown to me. But the King merely stared stonily at me, and though I asked whether I could not be heard in my servant's defence, the fault being entirely mine rather than his, there was merely a silence – either because no-one present understood the English language or, more likely, because they did not wish to hear.

After a moment, an officer of some kind stepped forward and by unequivocal signs signified that my audience was at an end. Nodding my head in the King's direction, as curtly as I could without giving more positive offence, I turned my back and made to the door – I was certainly not going to back away from so unpleasant a monarch. Outside, I found that my small retinue had vanished, and was left to myself to make my way out of the palace and to the river bank, where after great trouble I found a boatman who permitted me to board his canoe, and who then thrust off into the crowded channel without being able, I was sure, to comprehend the instructions I gave him – which were to take me immediately to my floating home.

As we jostled our way between the throng of large and small boats, we passed behind the high stern of one junk which seemed very differently built to the rest – and as we did so, a large parcel flew from its deck, landing only a few feet from us, and threatening to overturn us. I shouted a reprimand to the crewmen responsible (at which my boatman showed every sign of distress and fear, attempting by every gesture to quieten me).

On looking into the water, I saw to my horror that the package, which for a moment had returned to the surface of the filthy water, was moving about – so that there appeared to be something alive within the sacking of which it was composed. The villains on board the junk had clearly chosen thus to dispose of some dog or cat or other animal! In a moment, driven by that natural sympathy with the lower orders of creation with which every Englishman is naturally endowed, and without thinking of the consequences, I leaped overboard, and with difficulty supported the struggling parcel while I undid the rope which roughly secured it.

It was only as the rope came loose that I was struck with the fear that the animal, freeing itself and no doubt crazed with fear, might reply to my kindness by attacking me – but nevertheless opened the mouth of the sack (for that is what it was) before beginning to back away.

The reader will be as astonished as I to hear that what first emerged from the sack was a naked arm; that it was followed by another, then by the head and neck of a human female. But that astonishment will no doubt be as great as mine when I reveal that the face, distorted by want of air and by relief at being able once more to breathe it, belonged to none other than – my friend and adopted sister Mrs Sophia Nelham!

Chapter Fourteen

Sophie's Story

After a few days in Singapore, Captains Retallack and Dale suggested that it would be enlivening were I to accompany them upon a mission of duty to Bintan Island, held by the Dutch, and placed some few miles from the port.

This island has the very great advantage of being intersected by several broad and navigable streams – among them the Rotjo, the Ayer Jawar, the Gindi, the Iant Jookang and the Pho Touwo – by means of which its produce is principally conveyed to the ships which carry it away. Having been sailed to the island by a small sloop, we disembarked and in a canoe or *sampang pookat* were rowed for about an hour up-river to Singkang, where live some thousand or more people in about forty houses; these comprised the whole city – apart from one arrack distillery, one opium den and one opium farm.

It might be questioned that there was such a disproportion between accommodation and population, but many of the people derived from huts scattered in the vicinity, and were attracted to Singkang by the concomitant and pernicious excitements of the arrack and the gambling.

My two friends having delivered a message to the head man of the place, their time was for a couple of days their own, and hiring three horses they set off to show me a place upon the coast, to the east of the town, where it was their wont from time to time to make holiday. This was known as Little Sebong, and comprised two or three small houses upon a handsome beach – one of which (one of the houses, I mean) was immediately vacated by the family who occupied it, bribed to do so by some insignificant piece of money. This, Captain Retallack explained, happened upon each visit, and the result of it was that they always had a decent house in which to live whenever they should decide to break some time there.

The house was a simple hut built of wood: one room only, with a sleeping platform at one end and a hearth at the other upon which a fire burned sufficiently high to cook eggs or meat.

The first thing we did upon arrival was to bathe ourselves in the sea, thus relieving the perspiration and dust of the journey. Here we were immediately joined by a group of young women of all ages between fifteen and thirty, whose familiarity towards my companions was such that I could not but believe they had been previously acquainted – which on my asking, was admitted.

'You would not ask us to live as eunuchs? said Captain Dale – and indeed I was forced to laugh at the suggestion, the gentlemen's previous behaviour not being such as to allow me to credit it. Nor did it seem likely that it would be the case during our stay, for there being only one space for sleeping, unless I took myself off onto the open beach – or insisted upon my friends doing so – there was no other recourse than our sharing a bed.

Since I had upon occasion seen not only Captain Retallack (who was my particular friend) but Captain Dale in a state of nature, I had no special reason to expect them to be modest; nor did they, I dare say, have that expectation of myself. Still, the freedom with which they both at night threw off their clothes and reposed upon the bank of rushes on the sleeping platform seemed to me to be somewhat over-confident, and led me to place myself near to them, but still entirely clothed – though as had been the case since my arrival in the tropics, the word 'entirely' should not be taken to mean much, a single shift-like garment being my only covering – and I had often wished that tradition did not deny me the pleasure of clothing myself as the native girls did, solely with a strip of cloth about the loins; for the exposure of as much flesh as possible to the few winds that stirred was the only means of remaining relatively cool, while the only disadvantage was that such flesh was more freely opened to the depredations of the mosquito – which, however, as time passed, had increasingly come to regard me as a native, and had largely ceased from troubling me.

I was somewhat pleased to see that the gentlemen were disconcerted at my remaining clothed; and after a while, there having been a certain nudging and whispering between them – each being reluctant to begin – Captain Retallack, as being best qualified, delivered himself:

'Mrs Nelham,' he said, 'Captain Dale and I are . . that is, I hope that you may be disposed to . . uh . . do you not find the heat oppressive?'

'You mean,' I replied, 'that a walk in the cool of the evening would be pleasant?' – and rising, took a step towards the exit.

'That was not entirely . . . .' said the captain . . .

I was forced to laugh.

'My dear Captain Retallack,' I said, 'I am aware of your meaning. However, if I may utter a word of advice, your separation from western society has perhaps contributed to your forgetting that under no circumstances should a friend of the opposite sex be taken for granted. It is well to continue to woo after you have won, if you wish to retain favours already granted.'

The men had the grace to blush; and getting to their feet gave a bow – which, their being entirely bereft of clothing, and their private parts shrunken and utterly deprived of the habiliments of desire, was so irresistibly comic an effect that I could not repress my laughter – at which they also laughed, and coming forward took me by the hands and led me back to the sleeping platform, where with another bow, they laid me down and with great tenderness took the straps of my gown from my shoulders and gently drew it from me (my own contribution to the effect being, I must admit, willingly to lift my body to enable them to do so).

Caresses, of course, followed; so that in no short time their bodies' reticence was overcome, and any lady would have been flattered that the effect of her presence should be so signally shown by the engorgement of those natural parts synonymous with corporeal pleasure.

The problem now arose of how best to satisfy them both – for one must be allowed the compliment of entering my person, while the other must be satisfied by other means – a hard business, for the latter would certainly believe himself to be somewhat slighted, even if he knew that needs must. And in this case not only did Captain Retallack clearly believe he had the prior claim, but his friend showed no signs of retiring, or of – for instance – placing himself in such a posture that my lips could pay him the compliment denied (at least for the moment) by that other aperture towards which the first officer was showing so proprietorial an attitude.

However, the answer in a moment occurred to me – suggested by the fact that (as I believe I may have already reported to the attentive reader) Captain Dale's sugar-stick was smaller in circumference than his friend's, and would for that reason make the course I now suggested possible without too much discomfort.

Lifting my hands and for a moment persuading the two men to discontinue their toying, I persuaded Captain Retallack to lie on the sleeping platform, but with his legs over the edge, so that his feet being on the ground (perhaps two feet below) the cheeks of his arse almost overhung it. Now, throwing a leg over his body, I sank upon his strongly perpendicular prick – the emotions thus raised being so keen that for a moment I almost forgot the purpose of the arrangement, beginning those motions which, once put in train, it is so difficult to stop!

However, the sight of the disappointment upon Captain Dale's face speedily reminded me that I was being selfish; and spitting upon my hand, I caught him by his own prick, and having so lubricated it, directed him to stand behind me, and, bending myself so as to reveal to him the unexpected target, invited him to enter me by the rear entrance – which, rarely used for that purpose, was one of which few men are entirely unaware, and yet fewer will not be disposed to accept rather than to be deprived altogether of their prize.

This form of congress is not, I must confess, normally prized by me; yet on the few occasions when (in general, as my readers will recall, as the result of unusual circumstances) I have thus been penetrated, I have been unable not to recognise a certain pleasure – which upon this occasion was keen, for Captain Dale, appreciative of my kindness, not only entered with that trepidation and care which altogether avoided discomfort, but in his movements was so gentle and courteous that what I felt was merely a delightful friction entirely complementary to that made when, suiting the rhythm to his movements, I rose and fell upon the body of Captain Retallack, for whom the spectacle of his friend enjoying a simultaneous congress was keenly inspiriting.

Our mutual pleasure was soon mutually expressed, and the two gentleman vied for words and gestures with which to thank me for my hospitality – which resulted in time in their showing me the full repertoire of their amorous tricks; and while none of these were new to me, there could certainly be no question of boredom in renewing acquaintance with them where such handsome and energetic practitioners were concerned.

In an hour or two, all replete, we had sunk into healthful and undisturbed slumber – undisturbed, that is, until we all three awoke to overhear a series of blood-curdling shrieks – and having awakened, had scarcely time to move a muscle when the hut seemed full of people, and we were all three seized by the arms and hustled onto the beach. The few huts about us were already ablaze, and apart from a few supine and unnaturally still bodies, the place was deserted of those natives we knew – their place being occupied by a group of smaller men with yellower skins, many rummaging about in the wreckage for whatever they could find there.

We were held hand and foot – Captain Retallack having merely the opportunity to whisper to me that these were Chinese pirates, before he was struck heavily across the mouth and silenced. I subsequently learned that he was indeed correct, and that we had been captured by one of the many bands of Chinese robbers who infest the shores of this part of the world, and who, crafty and ferocious, prey upon any civilised people they can find. Many is the unfortunate Englishman that has met with an untimely end, either through his own temerity or through over-anxiety to make money, entering into schemes with nefarious natives to over-reach the revenue officers, and falling a victim at the hands of the very fellows whom he had instigated to assist his own purposes.

Blackmail, apart from the smuggling of opium, is one

of their chief occupations. The week before we were attacked, the Lung-moon-heep, a mandarin in charge of revenue on a nearby island, had been taken, his ears cut off, and 60,000 dollars demanded for his return. Even large vessels are not defensible, so powerful are the piratical forces. The English lighter *Enterprise*, under Captain James Sharpe, was recently taken while on the way from Macao, being run aboard by pirates and the vessel plundered of a very valuable cargo of about £25,000 worth, and then set on fire. Captain Sharpe's throat was cut as he lay in his bed, and most of the crew murdered – the only persons to survive being the steward and a Chinese female, who contrived to secrete themselves in the pantry – where they were discovered and badly wounded, being left for dead. On the pirates setting the boat on fire and leaving her, the steward and female contrived to get into a small boat which had been overlooked, and at the mercy of wind and tide drifted to the island of Potoy, where they were kindly received by the fishermen, who hospitably gave them food and dressed their wounds; the poor steward expired from his severe hurts, only the Chinese female surviving to give an account of the affair.

I must say that had I known all this at the time I would have been considerably depressed. However, I believed then that the presence of two naval officers would be sufficient to protect me – the only problem being that since they were entirely unclothed, they were not likely to be recognised; and indeed in a very few moments a man who was clearly the leader of the band beckoned to his men to bring them forward and spread-eagle them upon the beach before him, whereupon he took a sharp knife, and bending over Captain Dale, seized his genitals in his left hand and seemed about to apply the knife when one of his men came shouting from the hut bearing part of a naval uniform – at which the chief pirate paused, laid down the knife, and after a brief talk contented himself with having my two friends gagged and bound hand and foot – then uttering a command which had the effect of all his crew returning to the spot, whereupon they made for a boat drawn up upon the sand, carrying me with them; I was thrown upon the bottom of the boat, and the men, thrusting it into the sea, began to row – one of them, sitting directly above me, taking the liberty of inserting his bare foot between my thighs in an attempt to persuade me to disclose to him what lay between; in which action he persisted until the chief, noticing it, caught him such a blow across the side of the head that he fell unconscious upon my body, almost stifling me until with a bump we landed against the side of a larger vessel, and, kicking the still supine oarsman aside, the leader slung me across his shoulder and with a strength considerably greater than his size suggested, mounted a net falling from the ship and carried me up it, throwing me unceremoniously upon the deck, where I remained as the crew made hasty preparations to get under way – hampered by movement only by a cord which bound my hands behind my back, and tethered me to a mast.

I may for a moment digress to say that my two friends lay bound for some hours until some of the villagers nervously returned to free them, whereupon they were forced to return without me to Singapore, when the Governor was not pleased to hear either that they had repaired to so lonely a place with an English female of considerable wealth and impeccable respectability, nor that they had then allowed her to be captured by pirates. Within a month, not having received any demand for ransom, they considered me dead, and Captains Dale and Retallack were posted to Pangkallang Nattang, an extremely uncomfortable stockade under constant attack by rebel forces of the Malays – where, as far as I knew, they might well still be serving.

However, to return to my predicament: this was clearly considerable, and I had plenty of time to consider it as the boat sailed on through the dawn and the sun rose, after a while becoming unpleasantly hot, so that I had to move about to find what shade I could.

After a while, I found myself surrounded by a number of the crew who, the vessel now being on course, had the leisure to examine – I suppose for the first time – an unclothed white woman, themselves all being Chinese. None of them, however, dared touch me, being terribly afraid of their master, the pirate captain, who was called Lamqua (as I later discovered, and so might as well refer to him by that name). He was not of great stature (I mean in the ranks of pirate captains), commanding only this one junk – as opposed to some others, who commanded whole fleets; but he was unregenerate in his discipline – as witness the fact that the poor man who had been inquisitive enough to attempt to examine me while I was upon the floor of the small boat, had been pitched into the sea and left to drown; a lesson which resulted in his shipmates leaving me severely alone, apart from feasting their eyes upon me (something which, my hands being tied behind my back, I was unable to prevent).

In a while, they fell back, and their chief appeared. Lamqua was if anything somewhat under the common stature even of the Chinese; but had clearly attempted to overcome this debility by the cultivation of his natural strength – or even unnatural strength, for he had in some way fed his muscles until they had become almost disproportionate to his build. This, he showed off by wearing a minimum of clothing – a uniform being unnecessary as a mark of his rank, for he carried a short cutlass stuck into the belt about his waist, with which he was given to striking out at the least sign of insubordination, such blows being always damaging and frequently fatal.

From his belt – a thin leather one – a pouch depended into which his manhood was thrust, and which was supported behind only by a simple string laid in the crevice of his arse and attached, behind, to the same belt. The very cheeks of that arse and the thighs which supported it seemed to consist entirely of muscles – and that that was true could be seen on the occasions when, mistrusting the look-out stationed at the top of the mast of the pirate vessel – he leaped to the shrouds and mounted with a speed and dexterity which I have never seen equalled.

His shoulders and arms, too, were ribbed with muscle – and enabled him to descend from the mast-head simply by seizing upon a rope, and letting himself down hand over fist, sometimes pausing in mid-descent to hang supported only by one hand, while with the other he shaded his eyes to view the horizon or made some gesture to the crew below him upon the deck.

That he was a commanding figure is obvious; but knowing nothing of the danger in which I stood, I failed to fear him, regarding him with disdain – though not with insolence, for I had learned from various situations in which I had found myself during the course of several years (and recalled in no less than four volumes of narrative, if I do not include the present one) that discretion is often the better part of valour.

I suppose that my being thrown about the beach, then about the deck, had resulted in my appearing somewhat dishevelled (even though this could not apply to my dress, for I had none); for Lamqua turned and bellowed a name – at which, to my surprise, a female Chinese came forth from a hatch nearby, like a Jack- or Jill-in-the-Box, and on his giving instructions stepped forward and began to fumble with the rope that bound me. Seeing her clumsiness, Lamqua thrust her impatiently aside, drew his cutlass and with what seemed a dreadfully careless thrust, cut my bonds within an inch of my wrists. The female then helped me to my feet, and taking me by the arm drew me towards the rear of the vessel, where stood two or three pails of sea-water and one of fresh, from which I was glad to drink, having bathed my limbs.

Looking around, I saw that none of the men had had the temerity to follow us, and so whispered a question to the female – whom I now saw to be a girl of perhaps a little under my own age, dressed merely with a rag about her loins. But on my asking whether she could provide me with some clothing, I received no answer, from which I gathered that either she understood no English or was not permitted to answer me. On my gesturing to the cloth which covered her, and then to my own nakedness, she drew back as though terrified. No doubt she would do nothing for me unless ordered by my captor.

She now took me once more by the arm and led me back towards the centre of the vessel, and seeing that Lamqua was no longer there, looked about her and after some hesitation took me further aft, and knocking at a door and receiving some answer, into a cabin which was clearly that of the captain or chief. On seeing us, Lamqua burst into a rage, which seemed to have something to do with my lack of clothing, for coming forward he seized the unfortunate female by the hair, and with his other hand deprived her of her loincloth, which he handed to me!

Reluctant though I was, I wound the still warm garment about me, while the girl was sent reeling from the cabin. Lamqua now looked at me with insolent but perhaps not entirely unappreciative eyes, and pointed to a couch which stood under the cabin window. This, I sat upon, expecting an approach to which no doubt I had better acquiesce. However, Lamqua remained where he was, merely leaning against a table; then from a bowl at his side seized some bread and tossed it to me. Catching at it, I was pleased to eat some, being amazingly hungry.

He stood watching until I had finished, when turning what was (I had to admit) a not unshapely back upon me, he left the cabin, locking it behind him, and I saw no more of him for the rest of the day, which I passed as best I might: some in sleep, I must confess; some in staring from the window at an empty sea; some in wondering about the prospects of my escaping; and some in wondering what fate awaited me.

In the evening, the door was unlocked, and the Chinese girl – clad with a new, or rather a different, piece of cloth – brought me a dish of food which was not at all unpleasant, consisting of a sort of fishy stew; and as I had finished it, Lamqua appeared bearing a jug of liquor which I later recognised as cocoa-nut brandy, a harmless-tasting drink of which I took rather too large a gulp before realising its strength – this causing a coughing fit which gave Lamqua considerable amusement.

Going to a cupboard, he opened it, taking from it a lamp – which he lit – a pipe, and a substance which I recognised as opium. Forming a piece of this into a ball, he heated it over the flame upon the end of a piece of metal, until it was roasted; then placing it in the bowl of the pipe, heated this in turn over the flame, and lying upon his bunk inhaled the smoke. After a while, his whole demeanour changed, all evidence of cruelty or violence vanishing, so that even when I rejected his offer of the pipe he made no objection, but simply continued himself to smoke.

When he had finished one pipe, he placed it aside, and by gesture summoned me to the bunk at his side, where

stretching out his hand he began to toy with my breast –
this being perhaps unusually generous in his experience,
Chinese ladies not being over-lavishly equipped with
mammary glands. I must confess that I was incapable of
not testing the muscles of his shoulders and chest, so
improbable was their remarkable size and strength; but
that they were entirely genuine was never in question, the
effect being almost of iron springs beneath a velvet
covering.

It was soon clear from a change in the shape of the
pouch between his thighs that his reaction to my presence
was very much that which might be expected of any man,
and experiencing perhaps some discomfort on that
account, he rose to his feet and fumbled at his
waist – but either from haste or from the effects of the
opiate, without effect; whereupon I thought it as well to
assist him, and reaching about, in a moment unloosed
the knot at the centre of his belt, whereupon the cord
sprung from my hand as though upon a spring – which
in effect was the truth, for his phallus appeared to be as
remarkably cultivated as any other muscle in his body,
and, tossing the pouch aside, sprung not merely to a
horizontal, but almost to a vertical position, slapping
against his belly with a cracking sound – at which I was
forced to laugh. I feared that this would anger him, but
though for a moment he glared at me, he barked a sort of
oriental giggle, and taking my hand placed it immediately upon the vigorous jutting limb.

This was shorter than any similar appendage in my
experience, being perhaps no more than five inches in
length – but at the same time being both remarkably
thick, with a helmet of perhaps three or even four inches
in diameter, and quite astonishingly hard; the pressure
of my fingers could scarcely feel any resilience, and without thinking of the consequence, I even applied my nails

to it with such force that any European would have flinched. In this case, however, 'twas like testing the renitency of wood; and rather than causing pain, had the effect of pleasing – for a positive roar of appreciation came from Lamqua, who seizing my loincloth with one movement rent it entirely in twain, then seizing me by the waist lifted me into the air so that my head struck the ceiling of the cabin, making me cry out with pain – which perhaps he mistook for pleasure, for placing my legs over his shoulders, he let me fall backwards so that the back of my head was almost at the floor (so short was he), while he buried his face between my thighs, and in a moment I felt another of those extraordinary muscles of which he had command – this time an extensive and voracious tongue – examining my quim.

He soon discovered, perhaps, that in that department there was not much to choose between an European and a Chinese lady, for he dropped me to the floor (I was finding his methods of making love somewhat of the earthquake or typhoon variety) and in one movement situated himself in such a position that he could penetrate me, which he did, without delay.

I had committed the silly error of regarding his prick with something of disdain, so short was it; but of course was misled, for its girth was such that it positively stretched the aperture to which it now addressed itself, thus bearing upon the most tender portion – and, his spirited movements at once beginning, I was in no time – aided by the unusual situation, by the roughness of his treatment (which, not being designedly unkind, had been if anything somewhat arousing) and, I must confess, by his person – as enthusiastically engaged in battle as he.

Will I be believed when I say that this single engagement lasted for over an hour? This, I am told, was the result of the pipe of opium. A normal person, under such an effect, would be reduced to satiety within a minute or two. One of Lamqua's exceptional virility and spirit, however, needed some quietening of the spirits if he were not to be equally quickly satisfied without the effect of the opiate – but under its influence was sufficiently calmed to take control of his senses, and to be able to retain perfect control of his limbs for a remarkable period.

In ten minutes, I had cried out in satisfaction; whereupon without breaking the rhythm of the dance, he rose, lifting me with him by the simple pressure of a hand beneath my back, and placed me with my arse upon the edge of the bunk, when he was able to caress my back and other limbs, now pinching my breasts between his teeth – his lack of height aiding him in this – and in a while raising me again to a cry of pleasure. Now once more he stood, and holding me impaled upon his entirely unflagging cock, leaned backwards until he could place both hands behind him upon the floor, so that his body resembled a table or bench, which, bestriding, I was happy to continue to mount until I was again satisfied.

I would by now have been happy to rest; but no. His vigour still undiminished, he lifted one of my legs and turned it so that I now sat facing his feet – whereupon he raised himself until we both stood, and he was able to continue the motions of connubial pleasure behind my back, curiosity leading him at the same time to reach around and make a manual exploration of the manner in which I was receiving his limb.

It was clear to me that if the exercise was not soon finished, I would die (though no doubt pleasantly) of exhaustion; and reaching between our legs, caught at his cods and with all my strength twisted or wrung them in a manner which would have disabled any normal man.

The effect was immediate: there was a bellow so loud that it almost deafened me, and I felt every muscle in

Lamqua's body tense and relax as he was forced to the climax of his pleasure.

If I hoped for some gesture of affection, I hoped in vain. Thrusting me from him, he simply turned, opened the door of the cabin, and thrust me outside – not even troubling to throw my torn loincloth after me. I stood for a moment in the darkness; then felt a hand upon my arm gently pulling me, and saw, or thought I saw, the figure of the Chinese girl – which indeed proved to be the fact, for she escorted me to a nook or corner behind the chief's cabin, where she had made a sort of nest for herself of unsavoury mats and pieces of cloth; there she found another cloth with which I could conceal my sore but (I must concede) satisfied secret parts, and though she looked on me entirely without affection – as, I suppose, a rival and a successful rival – I almost immediately fell into a deep sleep.

There now expired a number of days; in honesty, I did not record how many, for I was in a state of almost continual exhaustion. To any woman who longs for an inexhaustible lover, may I now express the view that this has disadvantages as well as advantages, especially when that lover is as insatiable, as vigorous, as strong, as unremitting as Lamqua. Sometimes at dawn, sometimes at dusk, sometimes in the afternoon – sometimes at all three – he would suddenly appear and seize me. Congress might be joined in his cabin, but often he would not bother to seek privacy, but would simply take me wherever I happened to be standing, sitting or lying – I might be merely leaning upon the side of the vessel looking aimlessly at the featureless ocean, when I would be attacked from behind with a violence that would set my belly knocking against the wooden hull; or I might awake from a morning slumber to find that small body, adamant as gnarled timber, already upon me.

The Chinese girl, whose name I never knew, regarded all this with growing anger. I made every attempt to ingratiate myself with her – but without success; she regarded me as her inveterate rival, and the fact that my treacherous body could not but respond to the chief's attentions no doubt helped to convince her that if she was ever to retain her own position – which I presumed was that of Lamqua's wife or courtesan – I must in some way be disposed of.

I woke one day, after a rare night during which I had been left undisturbed, to hear a babble of voices, the splashing of oars, and noises which seemed those of some sort of civilisation. Raising my head above the bulwarks, I saw that indeed the junk was moored among a great number of others in a river upon whose waters floated some vessels larger than ours, but most smaller, between them scurrying a myriad little canoes or rowing boats – and incongrously, behind them, what appeared to be a veritable township of houses which were in essence also boats, being as far as I could see entirely independent of the land!

Where we were, I had no idea. Seeing the Chinese girl approaching, I was about to attempt to ask her, in sign language – though without much hope of a response – when I noticed with some surprise that she was accompanied by two members of the crew, one carrying a large sack over his arm. That she had bribed these men, no doubt with attentions of a personal nature, I cannot doubt; for one now caught at me and spun me around, the other held me, a hand was placed over my mouth, and in a moment the sack thrust over my head and tied there. Now, I felt myself hoisted into the air – was falling through it – and with a splash landed in the water.

My dangerous state I need hardly describe. My hands, certainly, were not bound – but I was incapable of undoing the tie at the sack's mouth; nor could I swim. Kicking out with my legs, I hoped to bring myself to the surface, while I closed my mouth and eyes against the encroaching water – but, stifling, was about to give myself up to despair, when I felt myself partially lifted from the flood, then felt the air upon my face as the sack was torn from it – and opening my eyes, saw . . whom? The reader will already know; and will scarcely doubt that my surprise at setting my eyes upon Mr Archer was quite as extensive as that with which he recognised me!

Chapter Fifteen

The Adventures of Andy

I will not waste time in rehearsing how it was that my sister Sophie had arrived at the unusual means of egress from what I now discovered was a Chinese pirate junk. The reader will already have been apprised of the facts in the previous chapter of these memoirs. But it will not be doubted that our reunion was as surprising as it was unexpected.

It was clearly best to get away as quickly as possible from the vessel from which she had been pitched, though on looking back, it was clear that we were not being followed – and upon the deck appeared only the disappointed figure of the chief's concubine (who had hoped permanently to dispose of her rival) and her two male accomplices, from which it was clear that Lamqua and his crew were about their nefarious business upon land – no doubt selling to willing merchants material stolen by them from other vessels.

We made swiftly away from the craft, and shortly afterwards I recognised – from my shirt hanging from a line upon its balcony – my floating house, and tied up there, where I provided some rice brandy for my friend – and indeed for myself.

Sophie was remarkably soon recovered from her ordeal, and was ready to recount her adventures since I saw her last on board the *Flower of Kent* in Margate Roads – but I interrupted her, and told her of the predicament of my servant Loi. It has always been the case that our servants have been regarded also as our friends, and indeed sometimes more (my regular readers will know the truth of that statement), and Sophie was at one with me in wishing to rescue the boy – who from the attitude of the King's servants who had borne him off, and from what I had heard of that despotic monarch, was not likely to be in the happiest of circumstances.

The first thing was to find someone who could translate for me, and the only place I could think of where English was likely to be spoken was at the whore-house where I had been so kindly received. I had no shame in informing Sophie of those circumstances, she being neither unaware of the needs of a high-spirited youth of my years, nor at all inexperienced in the manner in which they were slaked.

I seemed to remember that one or two of the girls there had exchanged a word or two in our language, though I had no means of knowing how experienced they were in it, but could think of no other solution to the problem. It was now early evening, and after the brief refreshment of a dish of rice (in which the food of the Siamese chiefly consists, eaten with a substance called *Balachang*, a strange compound of fish) we set out, my boatman being the very one who had rowed Loi and myself there on the previous night – so I was easily able to direct him by the universal gesture made by a crooked forefinger and thumb together with the forefinger of the other hand, which he instantly understood (though he seemed a little bemused by the fact that I was already accompanied by a young woman!).

We were greeted with much the same ceremony as before, though only by three young ladies – who also seemed somewhat surprised at Sophie's presence. On my enquiring whether they spoke English, they looked uncomprehending, but beckoned us to follow them – which we did, into a room where one of their companions, in a state of nature, was holding a dish of drink for an elderly gentleman similarly clad (or, rather, unclad). No embarrassment was shown upon either side, though the gentleman gave an impression of wishing to be introduced to Sophie, from which we had, as politely as possible, to dissuade him.

His companion proved indeed to have a very reasonable command of our language, and upon our beginning to explain no sooner heard the name of the King than she led us to another smaller room, where there was no company (so complete is the fear His Majesty's name commands). She confirmed my view that Loi was indeed in a bad way, for the court is severe on the slightest departure from a strictly imposed ceremony. This made me feel even more guilty, for it was of course I who had forced him to disobey the common manner of the court.

Tiu-Hon, the young lady with whom we were closeted, had no idea how he could be rescued – indeed, seemed to think it entirely out of question. It would not be possible for me to visit the unfortunate boy; the only people who might be allowed to do so, taking food, would be the female members of his family – and she did not know even that he had a family, much less where its members might be found.

An idea then occurred to me, and I put it to Sophie. Though I spoke only tentatively, for the risk involved was very considerable, she immediately concurred – and I then explained my notion, speaking more deliberately, to Tiu-Hon. She at first showed great fear, but both Sophie and I were as persuasive as we could be – both as to conscience and as to cash – and it was soon clear that Tiu-Hon was unwilling that a foreigner should risk her life to save a Siamese, when one of his own race demurred.

(It also seemed to me that she was rather fond of Loi, as indeed turned out to be the case.)

She therefore agreed; we spent some time discussing the plan; then on payment of a sum of money to the controller of the house – a sum equal to that which would be paid by a male visitor who wished to purchase Tiu-Hon's services for the entire night (which was not infrequently done) – we returned to my house, and there slept as soundly as we could.

I must now leave the narrative to Sophie, for my plan depended entirely upon her and Tiu-Hon.

At half-past ten, the Siamese girl and I dressed ourselves in the usual clothing of the country – which in her case consisted only of a cloth about the waist. I could not do the same, for the whiteness of my skin could not be denied, especially were the entire upper portion of my body revealed; so I took the part of an older and bereaved person – as it might be the widowed mother of the imprisoned boy; my body was entirely covered except for a small portion of my arms and hands, and my face – which was so treated with dirt that it was impossible to tell whether it was old or young, or whether my skin was white, orange or brown!

We then went ashore in the boat, accompanied by friend Andy, still dressed as himself, and made our way to the gateway of the palace, where he strode up to the guard and in English ordered him peremptorily to fetch his commanding officer. The lad understood not a word of this, but the officer in the case soon appeared, and on his not understanding, either, Andy gestured to Tiu-Hon, who introduced herself as Loi's sister, and me as his elderly mother, asking as a favour that we should be permitted to take him the food which we had in a basket.

The basket having been thoroughly searched, we were

allowed to enter the palace – though the gate was firmly shut, as we had imagined it would be, against Andy. A young soldier, dressed in a white loincloth with the red fringe which denoted his being of the king's guard, and with a turban similarly coloured, now led us across a courtyard and through a door, along a narrow corridor, and then through a doorless entrance down narrow and well-trodden steps (the platforms of which were deeply pitted, even the bare feet of prisoners having worn away the stone, which suggested how many forlorn men had trodden that way).

At the bottom was a locked door at which the accompanying soldier knocked. It was opened from within and we stepped onto a sort of balcony, lit only by a single torch, with a grill through which only the most shadowy light fell, looking down into the sunken cell where we imagined Loi must be lying. Our guide said a few words to the man, armed with a scimitar, who stood on guard upon the balcony, and then withdrew.

The guard who remained seemed not to be a soldier so much as a common gaoler, dressed merely in a loincloth – but clearly ready to use his weapon in an emergency, and of a physiognomy as unattractive and brutal as it was dirty. Tiu-Hon was, it must be admitted, an extremely handsome young woman (hence her great success at the brothel), and now stood as near to the torch as possible, the light of which fell across her body, making even more golden the skin which clad her delightful shape. The guard, a rough and unprepossessing fellow, looked far from uninterested by so attractive a sight. He approached, with the ostensible view of again searching the basket (which contained only a little rice); and as he bent to do so, Tiu-Hon leaned to open the whicker top of it, so that her breasts brushed for a moment against the fellow's cheek. He licked his lips, involuntarily, and as though by accident allowed his hand to lie against her thigh.

Rather than moving or showing offence, she smiled, and even ran the finger of a hand up his dirty and hairy arm to his shoulder, then addressed him in a low voice. He grinned, then looked for a moment at me; but Tiu-Hon said a few more words, and as I had been instructed, I drew a fold of my clothing over my face.

The guard could clearly not believe his luck. Quickly striding to a little door at the side of the balcony, he unlocked it with a key which hung some way from it, and threw the basket into the dark – where no sound of movement was heard to suggest that the prisoner received it. Locking the door again, the man merely dropped the key to the floor – and returning to Tiu-Hon, seized her in his arms and fixed his mouth to one of her breasts.

She could not refrain from a momentary look of repugnance (though in her profession she must have suffered as ill-looking fellows even as this), but now slid her hands beneath the man's loincloth, and clutched an arse as large as it was hairy (both facts being clear to me even in the restricted light, for the loincloth fell away to confirm them).

No subtlety of lovemaking was either expected or required. The guard stepped back, tore the single garment from my companion's body, and revealing a dibble of not gargantuan but sufficiently impressive proportions, lifted her thighs in his hands, crammed her into the corner of the cell and in a moment was lunging in a paroxysm of pleasure which was clearly – so violent was it – not to be long sustained. Over his shoulder, Tiu-Hon gave a signal which I did not need. From the folds of my cloak I produced a thin, sharp knife with which Andy had provided me, and took a step towards them.

Some seventh sense warned him, for he not only

turned his head, but remarkable though it might seem, actually withdrew his weapon and faced me (as I speedily hid the knife again). I believe he may have thought that I was jealous, for stretching out his hands he seized my shoulders and though neglecting to attempt to uncover my body (which presumably he believed to be too old and unattractive for him) forced me to my knees and approached so that his reamer was within inches of my face.

I was just preparing for the unattractive task of caressing it, when Tiu-Hon, stepping close to him, pressed her body against his from behind, and reaching around caught at his cock with one hand, and with the other made herself acquainted with his cods – whereat a lascivious grin spread across his face, and with a some-what pitiful look, as though he apologised for denying me a treat which I had been keenly anticipating, he turned again and once more impaled my companion, who this time locked her calves about his waist, and throwing her arms about his neck so tightly embraced him that he could not have escaped even if he would.

This time I waited until his thrustings and pantings became so excited that nothing would surely distract him – then again took out the knife, and with a sharp jab hit at his back.

Despite the instructions which Andy had given me on the previous night, I misdirected the blow, which was turned aside by some bone; he can scarcely have felt any pain, for he continued his work for the two seconds which it took me to withdraw the weapon and strike again – this time without mistake – and at the very moment when his body celebrated the conclusion of his fucking: for he let out a great bellow of pleasure, which turned to surprise, then to pain, then to a gasping bubble, and then to silence, as his body broke from Tiu-Hon's grasp and fell to the floor.

I was not delighted at having for the first time killed a man; though the reputation of the King's gaolers was such that I would not have regretted it had I paused to do so. As it was, I stood for only a second over the body when Tiu-Hon stepped over it, picked up the key, and unlocked the cell door. There was silence from within, but when she spoke Loi's name, an answering cry – yet still no movement. Grasping the torch, Tiu-Hon stepped through the cell door, I following, and there in the small room revealed below, water streaming from the walls to fall within a channel in the floor which was the only means of drainage, was – no-one to be seen.

We stood for a moment aghast – then heard another faint cry – from the far corner, and what seemed a gap in the wall, close to the floor. Approaching this, we saw that there indeed was a gap – of about two feet square, at the bottom of the wall; lowering the torch, we saw that it opened into a short chute of perhaps eighteen inches, which in turn led to a coffin-like space just large enough to take a body – and within it one lay indeed: as we discovered, the body of Loi.

Only the fact that he had lain there, bound hand and foot in a living grave, for twenty-four hours rather than several days, allowed him when released (and after a painful period) to stand and to embrace Tiu-Hon, her naked body now smeared with the dirt of the cell and her arms still covered with the slowly drying blood of the guard.

She explained our presence to him, as we made ready for the next stage of the plan, which was the most dangerous – especially since it relied on Loi commanding at least some of his strength after so unpleasant an imprisonment. Tiu-Hon now replaced her clothing, such as it was, and by rubbing her arms against the streaming walls of the cell, managed to remove most of the blood. We then pulled the guard's body into the cell, and locked the door before passing through the second door and climbing the stone steps, leaving Loi behind us at the bottom.

Tiu-Hon peeped around the corner of the stairs, to see, a few yards away, the youth who had accompanied us there. She immediately gave a cry – alarmed enough to attract his attention, but insufficiently strong to be heard by anyone else. He turned and came swiftly towards us – when she gabbled some words, pointing down the stairs (she was in fact informing him that the guard appeared to have had some kind of a seizure).

He ran lightly down the stairs, to be caught about the neck by Loi, who swiftly rendered him senseless (I later learned, by means of a special trick of fighting which they learn in those parts, and practise for pleasure as well as for self-defence). Then taking off his own clothing and tearing it, he tied the boy's limbs and gagged him; then himself donned the King's turban and loin-cloth, and joined us at the top of the stairs.

We marched across the courtyard to the door – and as we reached it, I gave a cry and sank to the ground. The guard at the door immediately came towards me, leaving his post – whereupon Andy, who had been waiting outside, stepped in and came up to me, helping me to my feet and comforting me. By the time we had turned and Andy had assisted me to an ass which was waiting to bear me, Loi had vanished into the crowd – his going unnoticed by the doorman, who at all events would not be responsible for the comings and goings of a colleague. He ill-temperedly slammed the palace gate, and we made our way to the river.

*　　　*　　　*

To continue the narrative where Sophie left off, we arrived at the house to find it empty (except for the servants) – and were concerned that perhaps Loi had been recaptured; but in a moment heard a splashing, and the exhausted youth pulled himself onto the balcony of the floating house, having slipped into the river after jumping from boat to boat in a route employed, he later told us, by smugglers.

We were happy at the success of our scheme – but must immediately make ourselves free of the place, for it was the first that the King's guards would approach on discovery of the escape – and now murder had been added to impertinence in the scale of Loi's crimes (though truth to tell, the King's autocracy is such that there seems little distinction between mere breaches of etiquette, petty thieving, grand larceny or mass murder!).

The question how to do this was a difficult one. I had a limited amount of cash with me – certainly insufficient to hire a substantial vessel – and it would be unsafe for us to remain in Bangkok until a British ship happened to enter the port, upon which we could take refuge.

Tiu-Hon came temporarily to our rescue by insisting that we should go to her house of business, where, after a conversation with the Madame we were taken to a small back room normally reserved for confidential visitors whose reputations might suffer from a more public visit; and there spent the night. Loi by this time was suffering from the recollection of how near he had been to an unpleasant death, and began to shiver; whereupon Tiu-Hon took him in her arms and comforted him. Sophie and I, too, spent much of the night embraced – though as purely as brother and sister (not that that, in our experience, was always as pure a relationship as custom would relate), for the situation was not such as was conducive to erotic pleasure.

Early next morning, Tiu-Hon spoke for some time to
Loi, who now had somewhat recovered himself; and he
translated to us her fear that with the day would come a
house-to-house search for him and for those who had
helped him to escape, and tried at first to persuade us to
go back to my house – for, he asserted, though the King
would suspect us, he would do nothing to one of His
Britannic Majesty's servants. We naturally declined to
be parted from our friends in their time of danger, and
Sophie having no money (having taken little to the island
from which she had been removed by the pirates, and
their having confiscated that little) I counted mine, and
while 'twas not a fortune, it was certainly enough for the
purpose I now held out – which was that we should bribe
the pirate junk to take us down-river and to whichever
nearby port would be most likely to be visited by a British
vessel.

This was objected to by all except myself; yet seemed
to me to be the best possibility of an escape – for the
pirates would certainly be left alone as unlikely to interest themselves in an escaped prisoner. Amid protests,
therefore, on my insistence – who held the cash – we
were rowed to the vessel in question, and there greeted
upon deck by Lamqua, a villain quite as unregenerate as
Sophie had described; but in his way I believe quite
pleased to see her again – and certainly pleased to see the
colour of my money, and for a purse (myself being careful to keep some coin hidden about my person) agreed to
my suggestion, so that within half an hour, after some
bullying and kicking of his crew – who were mostly dozy
and ill-tempered after an evening spent testing the
Siamese rice brandy – we got under way, he proposing
that we should make for the port of Saigon.

We left Bangkok and the river with no difficulty; but
upon our reaching the open sea I began to believe that I

should have listened to the warnings of my friends, for Lamqua became troublesome immediately upon my demanding something to eat, attempting to get extra money for the mean bowls of rice he set before us. However, I insisted that what I had paid (half of the fee for the journey) should command food and drink, the remainder comprising an ample total sum for such a journey. At this he went grumbling away.

Our having eaten, we took ourselves upon the deck for some air, where I was forced to strike a fellow who laid hands upon Tiu-Hon in the way of familiarity – Loi turning upon him fiercely but being restrained by me on the grounds that an Englishman would be more likely to command respect than a native Siamese. (I must confess that what I later learned of the piratical brotherhood, would, if I had known it, have made me less free with the hand which I laid about the side of the fellow's face.)

The next thing was that Lamqua appeared, and without so much as a by-your-leave placed himself square in front of Sophie and lifting his loincloth disclosed a tool of formidable proportions, and prepared for work. I was for a moment too astonished to move, but my sister was entirely in command of herself, and merely looking coolly at the thing, turned her back. It looked for a moment as though this would not in the least be a deterrent – but on myself and Loi moving to Sophie's side, the man desisted. (I am convinced that it was not so much we who were the cause of his hesitation, as his crew – who from a distance had been admiring not only Sophie but Tiu-Hon; so that had any fracas occurred, they might despite Lamqua's command of them have rebelled upon the promise of the prize of more desirable female company than the single miserable Chinese female who we had seen in the distance, looking extremely dissatisfied with her lot.)

At night, we closed ourselves into our cabin (which was in fact Lamqua's, so Sophie told me) as best we might, by pushing a heavy chest against it. Next day, we kept ourselves together upon the deck; and at one o'clock came in sight of a small island which lay alone upon the broad sea, a little group of palms at its centre. Just off this place, the ship was halted; and in a moment Lamqua and most of his crew approached us and stood around us with an air of menace. Lamqua then spoke at length to Loi, who explained to me that he demanded ten times what I had offered to take us on – but that he (Loi) was convinced that they meant to murder us at all events, the captain merely playing with us.

I explained, through Loi, that I had no more money; whereupon Lamqua gave an order, and we were immediately restrained by the crew and unceremoniously stripped of our clothing, my little extra store of money immediately being discovered hidden in the lining of my coat. He then stepped up to Sophie, who – as I would have expected of her – showed neither fear nor shame at having to stand naked before such a gang of cut-throats. She looked him directly in the face, and on his stretching out his hand to touch her upon the breast, with an accurately aimed foot kicked him with the utmost violence in the cods – at which while he buckled in pain, his crew (or some of them) laughed, which provoked him to a paroxysm of rage, so that he seized his cutlass from his waist – and fearing our entire slaughter, I turned to Sophie and at my word she dived from the deck into the sea below.

I was prepared to remain with my two friends rather than leave them to be killed or worse – but happily they too were excellent swimmers (a concomitant, I presumed, of living always upon the river) and followed Sophie – as I did. We all struck out for the island, and in a while pantingly drew ourselves up upon the beach – I feared, out of the frying-pan and into the fire, for there was some business upon the pirate ship as a small boat was prepared to be lowered. At my command, we withdrew to the small grove of palms at the centre of the island, where we all searched for what fallen wood we could find which was not rotten, and might be tool of defence in our nakedness.

However, to our indescribable relief, as the small-boat was half lowered into the water, there were shouts and confusion, pointing and hasty movement to recover it – for into sight sailed a vessel which must have come hastily from the horizon while we were all preoccupied and no watch was kept. It flew the British flag.

Lamqua made a very quick getaway indeed – so much so that we were in danger of the vessel missing us entirely in the desire to pursue it; but happily the look-out, being more attentive to his duty than he of the pirate vessel, did not miss the sight of four unclothed persons, two white and two native, dancing and calling upon the shore; and we soon saw a commanding figure upon deck issuing orders, and then climbing into the lowered long-boat.

I now come to a fact that the reader will own as improbable: I can only say that I was as staggered at the coincidence as any of my hearers, upon my telling the story when we reached port. I had from the start thought that the vessel seemed familiar: and as the long-boat made contact with the sand and came to a halt there, and I saw who commanded it – I realised that the parent ship was indeed my old friend the *Proper Pride* – and the officer who now leapt ashore and came towards us was none other than Robert Hooke!

Our mutual amazement barely restrained, I was happy to introduce Sophie, whose figure he could scarce refrain from admiring, despite his attempts to conceal the fact in the terms of common politeness. He greeted Tiu-Hon and Loi with all that kindness I would have expected of him, and in no time we were on board the parent vessel, which I was delighted to hear was returning to Singapore from Saigon – for there I could recover funds, and we could decide upon our future course.

There were, of course, no female clothes upon the ship, but Loi and myself were supplied from the chests of the officers, while Tiu-Hon, with some pieces of cloth that one man had bought to take back to England as a gift, taught Sophie how to tie a secure loincloth about her person – which in fact my sister rearranged to conceal her breasts, at least while in sight of the ship's crew, though I was amused to see that she was not quite sufficiently careful in Robert's company to spare him an occasional glimpse of a delightful curve or an entrancing titty.

Indeed, it was soon quite apparent that my friend, deprived for too long of the elegant company of an English female, hoped for more than mere verbal conversation; and on my encouragement, I was not unhappy that she excused herself from the common cabin which we four refugees shared, in order to make her way (as I gathered) to his quarters, where I trust she gave him adequate reward for his kindness to us.

Meanwhile, I contented myself with the pleasure once more of lying in a comfortable hammock (for I had had enough of the hard sleeping platforms of this part of the world), where I dozed, only half awakened by the incursion of Tiu-Hon and Loi, who now came down from the cool of the deck to take their places upon the floor of the cabin, where they preferred to sleep.

It was impossible for me not to be aware that they were however not disposed to sleep, for it soon became clear that having recovered from their privations – or perhaps as an aid to such recovery – they were enjoying each other; nor could I fail to see in what manner, the cabin being so small; nor could I deny that it was a delightful sight, both being young and handsome, and enjoying to the utmost the pleasure on which they were bent.

It is the case in the east that by far the most common form of congress is that which takes place when the man approaches the woman from behind, in a coupling much like that of quadruped animals – for which resemblance our missionaries continually argue against it, claiming that the similarity must lower men and women to the condition of rude beasts. I have never personally believed that; nor can it be denied that the position has great advantages – in that the stimulating limb of the man bears more insistently upon that portion of his mistress's privates most delighted to apprehend it – while it is easier for her lover's hands to caress not only that area, but the more delicate parts of her body; which, when we lie face to face, are impossible to reach without inconvenience.

At all events, Tiu-Hon now showed no dislike for Loi's attentions, nor was he lacking in enthusiasm – except that on looking up and meeting my eyes, he immediately withdrew himself, and with a gesture invited me to take his place. It would clearly have been an insult to them both had I declined – to Loi in that I would have refused a polite and kindly gesture; to Tiu-Hon in that she might have thought me unadmiring of her beauty – which was far from the case.

At all events, it was without reluctance on any grounds that slipping from my hammock I took my servant's and friend's place, and from her appreciative wriggling and mewing cries was no less successful than he in rousing her emotions. Having been deprived of female company for some days, I must confess that I was not long about the business – and on Loi's placing his hand upon my rump (unable, he later explained, to avoid the temptation to stroke the hair there, eastern men being bald upon the body except for some tufts about the privates) reached a conclusion; whereat Loi replaced me, and completed the task he had begun – both on his own account, and by her reaction upon Tiu-Hon's.

Indisposed to move, we lay in a tangle of limbs upon the cabin floor – which is how Sophie found us a while later, her happiness in Mr Hooke's company having been less complete than his (who, more deprived even than I of the pleasures of love, had come to a too speedy culmination). On her kneeling at my side and greeting me with a kiss, I was not long in wishing to show her that affection which we had shared since children – and Loi and Tiu-Hon being by could not but imitate our actions.

But the reader will not be interested in further description of such personal conversation, and I will confine myself to saying that, while there was certain mild confusion in the disposition of Sophie's time as between Mr Hooke and myself (not to say Loi, whose handsome figure and intelligent quick ways persuaded her that she must enjoy him) – so that her life was even more *mouvementé* than upon the pirate vessel – the rest of the voyage to Singapore was pleasantness and convenience themselves.

There, I was happy to find that the officer whom I had formerly encountered, Captain Dale, was known to Sophie and delighted to see her again – though not as delighted as Captain Retallack; with their aid and that of a local man of business I was easily able to raise funds which permitted us to stay in the town until letters of credit arrived from England, allowing me to purchase our passage once more to that land.

An account of our return journey to Portsmouth, being devoid of untoward or unusual incident, need not be appended; while, as to the remarkable occurrance which followed closely upon it, and which led to my intervention in matters of state close to the very government and Crown of England – the history of the consequent incidents must wait until I, and Mrs Nelham, are sufficiently at leisure to prepare for the public the sixth volume of these our memoirs; which remark, with our grateful thanks to those faithful readers whose kind attention and applause is a continual support to us, must conclude the present narrative.

EROS
IN THE
NEW
WORLD
Anonymous

Provoked once more by their unquenchable
appetites for delight, the exquisite Sophia and her
beloved Andy set sail for pastures new and
naughty: the Americas. With open minds and open
arms they resolve to experience the land of the
free, from the most salacious Southern gentleman
to the sauciest slave girl.

And for Sophia another challenge beckons: the
carnal sampling of a dozen young studs, each of a
different astrological aspect – and of intriguingly
diverse erotic inclinations. From New York to New
Orleans, from Montreal to the Mississippi our
enthusiastic duo reveal a lusty land, bursting with
an amorous ingenuity and enterprise to inspire
the most sated of Old World sensualists . . .

FICTION/EROTICA   0 7472 3310 1   £3.50

MAID'S NIGHT IN

A novel of smouldering eroticism

ANONYMOUS

The darkly arousing story of Beatrice, a
nubile Victorian newly-wed, lately
estranged from her husband and left to
the charge of her mysterious aunt and
uncle. Ushered into a shadowy Gothic
world of champagne and sensuality,
the young ingenue finds herself
transformed into the prime player in
exotic games of lust and power. *Maid's
Night In* is a disturbingly erotic
revelation of Victorian sexual desire.

FICTION/EROTICA   0 7472 3333 0   £2.99

A selection of bestsellers
from Headline

FICTION

THE EIGHT	Katherine Neville	£4.50 ☐
THE POTTER'S FIELD	Ellis Peters	£5.99 ☐
MIDNIGHT	Dean R Koontz	£4.50 ☐
LAMPLIGHT ON THE THAMES	Pamela Evans	£3.99 ☐
THE HOUSE OF SECRETS	Unity Hall	£4.50 ☐

NON-FICTION

TOSCANINI'S FUMBLE	Harold L Klawans	£3.50 ☐
GOOD HOUSEKEEPING EATING FOR A HEALTHY SKIN	Alix Kirsta	£4.99 ☐

SCIENCE FICTION AND FANTASY

THE RAINBOW SWORD	Adrienne Martine-Barnes	£2.99 ☐
THE DRACULA CAPER Time Wars VIII	Simon Hawke	£2.99 ☐
MORNING OF CREATION The Destiny Makers 2	Mike Shupp	£3.99 ☐
SWORD AND SORCERESS 5	Marion Zimmer Bradley	£3.99 ☐

All Headline books are available at your local bookshop or newsagent, or can be ordered direct from the publisher. Just tick the titles you want and fill in the form below. Prices and availability subject to change without notice.

Headline Book Publishing PLC, Cash Sales Department, PO Box 11, Falmouth, Cornwall, TR10 9EN, England.

Please enclose a cheque or postal order to the value of the cover price and allow the following for postage and packing:
UK: 60p for the first book, 25p for the second book and 15p for each additional book ordered up to a maximum charge of £1.90
BFPO: 60p for the first book, 25p for the second book and 15p per copy for the next seven books, thereafter 9p per book
OVERSEAS & EIRE: £1.25 for the first book, 75p for the second book and 28p for each subsequent book.

Name ....

Address ....

....

....